Meet Cute

STORIES BY:
JENNIFER L. ARMENTROUT · DHONIELLE CLAYTON
KATIE COTUGNO · JOCELYN DAVIES
HUNTLEY FITZPATRICK · NINA LaCOUR
EMERY LORD · KATHARINE McGEE · KASS MORGAN
JULIE MURPHY · MEREDITH RUSSO
SARA SHEPARD · NICOLA YOON · IBI ZOBOI

Houghton Mifflin Harcourt

BOSTON   NEW YORK

Produced by Alloy Entertainment
1325 Avenue of the Americas
New York, NY 10019
alloyentertainment.com

The text was set in Adobe Garamond Pro.

Typography by Liz Dresner

The Library of Congress has cataloged the hardcover edition as follows:
Names: Armentrout, Jennifer L., author.
Title: Meet cute / stories by Jennifer L. Armentrout and thirteen others.
Description: Boston ; New York : Houghton Mifflin Harcourt, 2018. | Summary: A collection of short stories exploring the moment when a couple meets for the first time—from an African American girl in upstate New York who simultaneously finds a prom dress and a date to a transgender girl who confronts the student blocking her right to use the school restroom.
Identifiers: LCCN 2017039396 Subjects: LCSH: Interpersonal relations—Juvenile fiction. | Dating (Social customs)—Juvenile fiction. | Short stories, American. | CYAC: Interpersonal relations—Fiction. | Dating (Social customs)—Fiction. | Short stories.
Classification: LCC PZ5 .M5437 2018 | DDC [Fic]—dc23
LC record available at https://lccn.loc.gov/2017039396

ISBN: 978-1-328-75987-0 hardcover
ISBN: 978-1-328-60428-6 paperback

Manufactured in the United States of America
DOC 10 9 8 7 6 5 4 3 2 1
4500761050

TABLE OF CONTENTS

SIEGE ETIQUETTE

— – — – — – —

KATIE COTUGNO

YOU'RE GETTING ANOTHER beer in the kitchen and watching two badly dressed sophomores try not to be too obvious about the fact that they're staring at you, when the cops show up outside Madison Campbell's house.

"Uh-oh," Jay says when he spies them. You follow his gaze through the living room window where, sure enough, two cruisers are gliding to the curb with their lights flashing, silent as sharks. "Friends are here." Right away he heads down the stairs to the basement, motioning for you to follow without actually waiting to see if you do. Boyfriend or not, you guess you can't really blame him. After all, it's not like you get in trouble anymore.

"Everybody down," Nicole calls from the hallway, flicking the kitchen lights off so you're plunged into darkness, save the glow of the water dispenser on the front of the stainless-steel fridge. Nicole's parents are both law professors an hour away from here at Cornell, and firm believers in the importance of exercising one's constitutional rights: *Never, never open up the door to the police unless they have a warrant,* you've heard them say over a number of bagel breakfasts at Nicole's kitchen table, same as other parents would remind you to make sure to be home by curfew. "Somebody get the rest of the lights!"

"Are you serious?" a panicky-looking freshman asks as everyone dashes for cover—into bedrooms and under coffee tables, inside the immaculately organized pantry. "You're not going to let them *in?*"

"Do you want to go to jail?" Nicole snaps, which seems a little dramatic. "Turn off the music. They'll be gone in a minute."

You're not entirely sure about that, actually, but before you can register your concerns, the bell is ringing; the police are knocking hard and insistent on the front door, glowing flashlights visible through the frosted glass. The combination of noise and sound sets something off in you, a cold animal panic. Suddenly it feels very important to hide. You scurry up the short flight of stairs off the foyer and through the closest door, shutting it firmly behind you before turning around and realizing that a) it's the bathroom, and b) Wolf Goshen is sitting on the edge of the tub in the dark.

"Hi," he says.

"Um," you say. Fuck. "Hi."

"Sorry," Wolf says, standing up and wiping his hands on his jeans. "I can get out of here, if you have to—I mean, everybody was just yelling to hide and stuff. I kind of panicked."

"No, I don't need to—" You exhale, heart pounding with a savage ferocity wholly disproportionate to the seriousness of this situation. That happens to you sometimes, now. The cops are still ringing the doorbell. "I mean, that's why I'm in here, too."

"Oh." Wolf nods, shoving his hands into his pockets. "Okay."

You look at each other for a moment. You breathe. Wolf has been in your class since kindergarten, but you've never actually talked to him before. He only ever comes for half the year because of some arcane agricultural law that lets him be homeschooled for the fall semester so he can help his parents at their farm, thirty miles outside Ithaca, one of the last working family-owned operations in the entire state of New York. Every autumn you forget about him and every January he shows up at school again, blinking and dazed, like he's spent the last six months wandering dumbly through a cornfield. You've never seen him at a party before in your life.

"I came with my cousin," he explains, like he can see you wondering, as if he thinks you're going to ask to see his pass. You think he might be afraid of you. You'd probably be afraid of you, if you were Wolf. "You know Jared? He dates Madison now. So I came with him."

You nod, not particularly caring. God, this whole night sucks. You're about to make an excuse and get the hell out of here, but before you can come up with something plausible the beam of a flashlight shines directly through the bathroom window, and like an instinct you're grabbing Wolf's arm and jerking roughly, pulling him back into the shadows beside the tub.

"Sorry," you say once the light has moved away again. "Close call."

"It's okay." Wolf sits back down on the edge of the bathtub.

— 3 —

When you were little kids he was notorious for falling asleep at his desk every day during free read. His fingernails were always too long. You remember not wanting to get stuck next to him in line or at lunchtime or in the Starlab, a traveling planetarium that came to school every year, all of you crawling into a big inflatable tent in the middle of the gym to look up at the constellations. "Don't be giving that boy a hard time, Hailey," your mom scolded when you came home and complained about it. You were already popular back in elementary school, and she was worried it was going to turn you mean. "He's got enough trouble without you piling on." It occurs to you, all of a sudden, that you never actually asked her what that meant.

The police are still banging on the front door, insistent: "Madison Campbell!" a man's voice calls, authoritative. "I know your parents, Madison, and they're gonna want you to open the door now." Madison's parents are in Harrisburg dealing with some kind of disciplinary clusterfuck at her brother's boarding school. For a second you feel kind of bad for them.

"This happen a lot?" Wolf asks.

You sit down on the lid of the toilet seat. "Sometimes," you allow. "They'll be gone in a minute." In fact you're not at all as confident as you sound. You've waited out the police in this very house before, plus once at Amber Dooley's and another time, memorably, while fooling around in a coat closet with Jay at Nicole's: normally the partiers lay low, the police get bored or tired or hungry, and eventually they go away. But this feels different. The last week of summer, two juniors drank a twelve-pack of Budweiser and killed almost a whole fucking family at the intersection down by the Walmart, and now it's like the whole town thinks everybody else is breathtakingly stupid enough to do what they did. It occurs to you, as you listen to the incessant banging on the front door of the house, that the McCormack County Sheriff's Department might be looking to make a point.

Well, you think, pulling your legs up on the toilet seat and wrapping your arms around your knees, *let them make it, if that helps them.*

Wolf is glancing at you across the bathroom, seemingly unconcerned about the scrum of law enforcement out on the front lawn. It's his first party, after all. You guess it's not like he's got anything to compare it to. "Should have brought snacks," he says, sliding off the lip of the bathtub and making himself comfortable on the tile floor, crossing his legs at the ankles, and before you can respond either way he grins. "You remember how Mrs. Hollander used to give out Atomic FireBalls during tests?"

That surprises you. Mrs. Hollander taught fourth grade. "Uh-huh."

"I was obsessed with those things," Wolf says. "Every day I used to ask her if we could have them. Like, I used to get so excited for tests, just so I could cram a bunch of FireBalls into my mouth and chow down. And finally one day she kept me after the last bell, and I thought I was in trouble, but it turned out she'd been at the dollar store and gotten this giant tub of FireBalls just for me. She told me I was going to make myself sick, but of course I walked outside and ate like a hundred of them all at once. Burned all my taste buds off, and that wasn't even the worst of it. Anyway, that was the end of me and FireBalls." He shuts up abruptly then, shrugging his shoulders. "I'm rambling."

"It's okay," you say. You kind of liked listening to him, actually. Nobody has talked to you about something as stupid as Atomic FireBalls in months. "I don't mind."

Just then your phone buzzes with a text from Nicole: *Where are you???* she wants to know, the question followed by a long row of screaming emojis.

Upstairs bathroom, you text back.

Wtf are you doing up there? We're all in the basement. Come down now.

You look at the screen for a moment, then back at Wolf. You don't know if you've ever actually bothered to look at him before, like in your head he was a walking, sentient wheat stalk. That's not the impression you get now at all. His clothes are clean, if a little bit trashy: light-wash jeans and a faded T-shirt with the Ghost-busters logo on it, plus a pair of knockoff Timberland boots. His eyes are bright and intelligent and sharp. He could do okay, you think, in a place like New York City or California, where the past doesn't cling like the smell of dirty laundry. Unfortunately for him, this is a suburb of a suburb of Syracuse. People have long memories here.

You turn your phone over so the screen is facing down, tucking it underneath you on the toilet seat. "How's your senior year going so far?" you ask him, then immediately feel like an idiot, remembering that he hasn't even set foot in school yet this year. "I mean, such as it is."

Wolf's mouth twists at that, not quite a smile. "Can't complain, I guess." He tilts his head to the side, looking up at you. "How's yours?"

"Good," you chirp like a reflex, which is of course a giant lie, and not even a good one, and you're thinking that of course Wolf knows that, until the moment that it suddenly occurs to you that he might not. After all, who can say what the hell news makes its way out to the Goshen Family Farm during harvest season? It might as well be medieval times over there. The idea of him not knowing makes him oddly compelling to you, like here is the one person in all of New York State to whom you're exactly the same as you used to be. You want to keep up the facade. "I'm applying to schools, mostly. Are you—?" you start, then break off, but there's nowhere to go but forward. "Applying to schools?"

Wolf smirks at that. "No, Hailey," he says quietly. "I am not applying to schools."

Something about the way he says your name makes your stomach do a strange flip. You've never heard him say it before. You look down at your hands in your lap, at your manicure. You and Nicole went to the nail place this afternoon. She's been your best friend since ninth grade, which doesn't mean she probably doesn't talk about you when you get up and leave the room, just like everyone else does. It's entirely possible she's talking about you right now.

Wolf reaches up and picks a fat candle off the side of the bathtub, probably pumpkin or cinnamon bun or something equally disgusting, and roots around in his pocket until he comes up with a book of matches. "There," he says, lighting it and setting it back on the side of the tub.

"Is that a good idea?" you ask, motioning to the window.

"They can't see it," Wolf says, and for some reason you believe him. He looks oddly handsome in the flicker of the candlelight, all sharp cheekbones and serious expression. Nicole will die if you tell her that. You might not tell Nicole anything about this at all.

"This is a really ugly bathroom," you observe instead of thinking about it, looking around at the faux-Mexican tile and brightly painted sink, the sunken bathtub that looks like its sole purpose was orgies in the 1970s. Above the toilet is a framed stock photo of a baby wearing a shower cap and holding a rubber duck. "I never really stopped to notice it before."

"Oh, I don't know," Wolf says, peering around. "I could sit in here all day, personally. Have a bubble bath. Read a romance novel."

You laugh at that, surprisingly. You didn't expect Wolf Goshen to be funny, like maybe he's from someplace where laughter is verboten, and then you realize what a stupid thing that is to think. "Use a bath bomb," you add.

Wolf shakes his head. "What's a bath bomb?" he asks.

"It's like a fizzy soap thing," you try to explain. "You put it in the tub and it kind of explodes and bubble bath and sometimes glitter comes out."

Wolf considers it. "That sounds like a gigantic mess," he says.

"Sometimes," you agree.

You look at each other for a moment. Neither one of you says anything. You remember, suddenly, a morning in the spring of third grade when he came into school with a hole in the collar of his T-shirt and a bruise the size of a new potato on his cheek. You remember how afraid it made you—not for Wolf but of him, like

— 8 —

maybe black eyes were catching somehow. The memory makes you feel about two inches tall.

The police are still shouting Madison's name, doorbell chiming. It reminds you, stupidly, of the Siege of Bastogne, which was part of the Battle of the Bulge in World War II. Lately when you can't sleep, which is often, you've been reading all the old history books from the shelves in your dad's office, poring over maps and committing battle plans to memory. You still have circles under your eyes the color of overripe eggplants, but you think chances are good you'll pass the AP U.S. History test at the end of the year.

Wolf tilts his head toward the window, listening. "Doesn't really sound like they're giving up, huh?"

You smile, though it isn't actually funny. The Siege of Bastogne lasted for seven days. "Nope," you agree. For an instant you wonder what might happen if you strolled out onto Madison's lawn right now, waved to the police in the porch light. *Hey, guys. It's me, your good buddy Hailey. Let's all call this off and go home.*

Your butt is starting to fall asleep on the toilet seat, so you slide to the floor and stick your legs out in front of you, your knees a few inches from Wolf's. He's got his hands folded in his lap, like he's praying; he's got long fingers and round, knobby knuckles, the nails bitten way far down. You imagine them tending an animal or fixing some kind of complicated machinery, which immediately makes you feel like an idiot. God, you must be further gone than you thought.

Your phone chimes again then, insistent: *Are you ok???????* Nicole demands. You can picture them all down in the basement, draped over armchairs and sitting cross-legged on the carpet, stifling giggles in the arms of their hoodies. You used to wonder if Nicole might have a crush on Jay, back when you used to care about things like that. You think she might resent you a little, especially lately, although you know she would never admit it. You think you might resent you, if you were her.

You switch the phone over to silent and tuck it back under your butt, but when you look up again, Wolf is watching you. "What are you doing up here?" he asks suddenly, in a voice like the thought has just occurred to him that possibly this might be a trick.

"What?" You don't understand the question. "Same thing as you're doing," you say.

"Yeah, but, like, why are you up here with me and not downstairs?" His face has changed, gotten sharper somehow. "I mean, what are you after?"

"What?" you say again, stalling for time. You can't tell him the truth, which is that you're up here with him in this bathroom because you cannot bear to be down in the basement with people who know you; because you cannot bear to be anywhere at all. Telling him will break the spell, which is the whole point of being up here to begin with. "I'm not *after* anything."

He shakes his head. "People like you are always after something."

"Seriously?" Your spine straightens up against the bathroom door. "People like me?"

Wolf shakes his head. "You know what I mean."

"I don't, actually." Suddenly you're spoiling for a fight—craving it, even. Lately everyone is so fucking nice to you; there's a certain dark pleasure in this sudden nastiness. It feels good. It feels *normal*. "And you don't know anything about me."

"I'm not stupid," Wolf insists, as if you've called him stupid, which you have not. "If you're up here with me instead of with them, there's a reason why."

"Oh, I'm sorry," you snap, drawing yourself up against the door and thrusting your shoulders back, your anger like a fire burning deep inside your chest. In one of your dad's books about the Civil War you read that the only real advantage the North had was industry: that the round-the-clock shoveling of coal into giant roaring furnaces was the only reason the Union didn't fall. You think of that sometimes now, when the alarm goes off in the morning and you feel like you can't get out from under the covers: You imagine that you are a munitions factory. You imagine that you are a train. "What's wrong with my friends, exactly?"

"What?" Wolf looks stricken, like he thinks you're about to go completely insane on him here in Madison Campbell's mother's ugly bathroom. It's possible he knows the truth about you after all. "No, I'm not saying anything's wrong with your friends, I just—"

"You didn't seem to have a problem with them when you were tracking your dirty boots all over their houses and drinking their beer," you say snottily—and that's good, you think with some nasty satisfaction. That's exactly the kind of thing the old you would have said. "Back when you were doing that, they were all just fine."

Wolf's eyes go hot and injured. "I didn't drink anything of theirs," he snaps. His whole body is suddenly made of angles, all shoulders and knees. "Me and Jared, we stopped and got beers on the way over here. We aren't freeloading."

He sounds so upset that you feel yourself soften. "No, I know," you say. "I didn't mean—" But you *did* mean, a little bit, and both of you know it. You were picking a fight, using him as some kind of messed-up scratching post. Your mother would be appalled. "Sorry," you say finally, leaning your head back against the door. All the energy has drained out of you at once. "That was bitchy."

Wolf doesn't contradict you. "You don't know anything about me, either," he points out. "Do you think this is, like, my dream? Like I've spent my whole life just dying to be stuck in a bathroom at some lame party with you? Princess Hailey Adkins?"

That stings. Not the nickname—God knows you've been called worse—but the idea that he's doing you some kind of favor. You don't want anybody's pity. You never have. "A lot of people at school would die for exactly that chance, actually," you retort. "Which is more than I can say for you."

Wolf blows a breath out, shakes his head a little. "Wow," he says, disbelieving. "You're kind of exactly as horrible as everybody says you are, huh?"

"So then what the hell are *you* still doing in here with *me*?"

Wolf shrugs. "That's a good question, actually," he says, and gets up. "See you, Hailey."

You remember something else then, pulled from the depths of your brain like a slimy scrum of seaweed: seventh grade, piss in Wolf's gym sneakers in the locker room, all the boys hooting gleefully about it down the hall. You didn't piss in them yourself, certainly. But you didn't help him, either. You've been thinking that a lot lately, all the teeny tiny choices that can change your entire life. *That boy's got enough problems without you adding to them.*

"Wolf, stop," you say, reaching out and grabbing his ankle before you can think better of it. It's warm and surprisingly solid through his jeans. "Can you just wait for a second?"

"What are you—?" Wolf shakes you free, but gently. *"Why?"*

You sigh loudly, and then you just say it. "Because I don't want you to leave."

Wolf makes a face at that, openly skeptical, but he does what you tell him—sitting back down beside you, closer than he was before. He smells like soap and grass and leaves, nothing like you remember from when you were a kid. "What," he says, his voice low and flat.

You think for a moment. "What's your favorite thing?" you ask him. "About working on the farm?"

Wolf rolls his eyes. "Riding the tractor," he deadpans immediately. "Picking my teeth with hay, ma'am."

"Can you stop?" you say, knowing you sound cranky. "I'm asking you a sincere question. You're right, I don't know jack all about you. But I'm asking."

Wolf exhales loudly. "All right," he says, leaning his head back against the door, the skin of his throat pale and exposed. "I like sleeping outside in the summer, I guess. My cousin Jared, who I came here with? We camp out most nights, instead of staying indoors, and that's what I like." He shrugs. "Sorry if it's not farm-specific enough for you."

"That sounds nice," you lie. Actually it sound terrifying, but to be fair, these days you're not exactly a good gauge of what's scary and what's not. You imagine it, staring up at the sky with nobody else around, like if you weren't careful you could fly right off the face of the earth and never be heard from again.

"So what about you?" Wolf asks. He's not mad at you anymore, or at least he's decided not to act like he is. You feel disproportionately relieved. "What's your favorite thing about being the queen bee?"

"I'm not the queen bee," you say automatically, which is also a lie, and both of you know it. But part of the power is in never having to admit it out loud. You're the most popular girl in your grade—or at least, you were before everything happened. Now you kind of don't know what you are. A curiosity, maybe.

Wolf snorts. "Okay."

You shrug. The truth is that your favorite thing about being popular is being able to control when and how people look at you and what they see when they do, like you're the curator of a fancy museum and your only exhibit is yourself. The problem is that lately you haven't been able to do it. You've lost control of your own story, somehow, since everything happened. You can't figure out how to get it back.

"I like having a lot of friends," you tell him finally.

It's a bullshit answer, but Wolf doesn't push. "Yeah," he says, putting his hand down besides yours on the cool bathroom tile. "That sounds nice, too."

You look at each other for a minute. You remind yourself that Jay is right downstairs. You and Jay have been dating on and off since last fall, and by all high school metrics he's a decent-to-good boyfriend: Lord knows he got more than he bargained for when he asked you out that day by the fountain at the Clearview Mall. Still, every once in a while while you're talking you can see that he might as well be on planet Mars for everything he's actually hearing. There

— 14 —

is something about Wolf Goshen that makes you think he'd listen for real.

Then again, you think, even as your pinky inches closer to Wolf's on the tile, *maybe he wouldn't.* You're dimly aware that you're making him up in your mind even as he's sitting here, like you're writing yourself into a story. You're dimly aware that Wolf is making you up, too.

Maybe it doesn't matter. Maybe, for as long as you're in here, you can both be whoever you want.

You pull your legs up underneath you, look at him through your eyelashes in the dark. "It was your dream a little bit, though, right?" you ask him, smiling a little. "To be in here with me?"

Wolf laughs at that. "Are you serious right now?" he asks, but he's *blushing*, and you know you've won. "You are something else, truly."

You're about to tell him he's right—that you *are* something else, and that something can be his for one night only—when you hear a familiar voice trilling out across the driveway. "Jay!" she's yelling. "Jay Montalto, are you in there?"

"Oh, Jesus." You scramble across the bathroom and peek out the window like a prairie dog, but you already know what you're going to see: It's Jay's mother, a big-haired Italian woman who has hated your guts from the time you started dating her son and continues to hate them now, which gives you a grudging kind of respect for her. It takes a set of brass balls to be mean to someone like you. Squinting through the screen you can see a handful of faces you recognize: Jillian's parents, and Harper's; even Nicole's parents' Volvo is parked down the street. "Shit," you say, turning back to look at Wolf. "Okay, this part has never happened before."

"They called people's parents?"

You shrug. "Some people's."

Wolf looks at you sharply. "*Fuck*," he says, and you think you've alarmed him in the moment before you realize he's talking about his own. Maybe you really are as selfish as he thinks you are. For the first time all night he looks sincerely afraid. "You don't think—"

"No," you tell him honestly. "I don't think anybody would have thought to call yours."

Wolf looks reassured by that, though not entirely. "No," he echoes. "I guess not."

You're quiet for another minute. You can't stop staring out the window, even though you know somebody's going to see you. You guess it doesn't matter at this point. You guess none of it really does.

Here is what will happen next: You'll go home with Nicole's parents and sleep on the spare bed in Nicole's bedroom, just like you have been for the last two months. Because your parents aren't out there waiting for you in the silver SUV you learned to drive on, angry at you for drinking and disrespecting authority but relieved, at the end of the night, that you're safe. Your parents are in freshly dug graves at Woodlawn Cemetery six miles away from here, where they've been since two drunk juniors from your high school T-boned them on their way home from a dinner at TGI Fridays at the end of the summer. If they were still alive you like to think they would want you to go out and live your fucking life.

"Come here," you say, holding your hand out for Wolf in the darkness.

"Why?" he asks, getting uncertainly to his feet.

"Because," you say, letting the nonanswer hang there. You have never been the aggressor in a situation like this in your entire life, and you find you do not hate it.

Wolf comes closer, cautious. He's taller than you are by nearly a foot. You reach up, put your hand on the back of his warm, shorn head, and kiss him. You don't hate that, either, it turns out.

He pulls back after a moment, blinking at you. "What was that for?"

"Keeping me company," you say, which is sort of the truth.

"Okay," Wolf says, and smiles, kisses you again. He's not a great kisser, unpracticed and a little spitty, but you actually don't care about that at all: there are tiny explosions going off all over your body, like sparks flying up out of a campfire. Wolf puts both hands on your face. You want to stay like this forever even though you know it's impossible, that it's just a weird stopover, like how during the Revolutionary War the two armies took breaks and had Christmas together, then went back to shooting each other with muskets after the roasts were gone. You aren't sure where you got that fact, actually—you didn't read it in any of your dad's old books—and you don't know if it's true or just something someone made up to make the world seem less brutal. Here in this bathroom with Wolf Goshen, it feels like maybe it could possibly be real.

"I'm not breaking up with Jay," you blurt finally, your face on fire, your whole body buzzing like a burned-out neon sign. It's hot in this bathroom, even with the window open. "I can't—I mean. I'm not breaking up with Jay."

Wolf laughs at that, a quiet baffled sound. "Jesus, Hailey, did you hear me asking you to?" he says, but he bends down and kisses you *again* then, his hands finding yours by your sides, and you're opening your mouth to tell him maybe he *should* ask you to, you're actually about to say that, when you hear the cops coming through the front door downstairs.

"Everybody out," a man's voice is yelling; through the crack under the bathroom door you can see that the lights have been flipped on in the hallway. Your heart is a siren wailing deep inside your chest.

"Somebody must have let them in," Wolf says. He's still holding your hands, your fingers twisting absently together, and it's like you both realize it at the same time, letting go too fast.

"I bet it was that fucking freshman," you say, clearing your throat and pushing your hair behind your ears. You're already thinking about how you're going to make her life a living hell come Monday. There are some benefits to being the queen bee.

"Hailey—" Wolf begins, but you hold both your hands up. Suddenly you know just what he's going to say.

"Don't," you interrupt, and you're surprised by how steady your voice sounds. You need to remember him as not knowing, even if that's not how he actually is. "I mean it. Whatever you're about to say to me, I just . . . really want you to not say it."

Wolf looks at you. "Okay," he says quietly. "Yeah. Of course." He wipes his hands on his jeans and blows out the pumpkin candle, motions toward the door. On the other side of it you can hear people shouting like the goddamn end of the world. "You ready?" he asks.

You won't even see him in school, you realize. By the time he turns up again in January you'll probably both have forgotten all about this. You swallow down a sour taste like panic in your mouth.

"Yup," you say, because there's nothing to be done about it. There's nothing to do about any of it but to keep going. "I'm ready."

Wolf moves aside to let you past him, your shoulders barely brushing. You've got your hand on the doorknob when he changes his mind. "Wait," he says then, and, "*Hailey*." When you turn around to look at him, his eyes are dark and wide.

You rest your forehead against his chest for a moment, breathing. Wolf holds very, very still. You can hear the sound of his heartbeat, steady, drowning out the sound of the mayhem raging on the other side of the door.

PRINT SHOP

— — — — —

NINA LACOUR

A HIGH SCHOOL parking lot at eleven p.m. My car under the
bright light of a single streetlamp, a lit-up classroom in the distance,
and you next to me, asking how all of this started. You are so new
to me. Minutes new. And you're probably wondering why I'm trembling, and I might be reading too much into the way you faltered
before you said hello, the blush that washed over your face.

But I don't think so.

It's early, I know. We've only just met. But this might be a love
story, so I want to tell it the right way.

— — — —

I should start with Print Shop. The romance of it: the dark wood
and the ink smell, the papers everywhere, sheets of it cascading off

every surface. The old lights on the desks and the framed mono-types and screen prints. The mugs of steaming tea and Eduardo with his accent and Neve with her pregnant belly and especially Alexander—the shop owner, the artist—holed up in his office at all hours while his husband, Terry, calls and sighs and eventually shows up with a frown and dinner on a tray.

And me, the bell jangling as I walk through the door in the beginning of the summer for my interview. I chose this shop because it was the only one I could find that didn't work digitally. They didn't even have a website. Everyone is always telling my generation that we aren't going to know how to engage with people. We're all going to end up with computer chips implanted in our brains and screens stuck in our eyes like contact lenses. But no one gives us any solutions, so I decided to find my own. Plus, I wanted to learn how to make that kind of magic. Ink and metal and screens and paper. I wanted to do something with my hands.

Neve introduced herself and led me to two stools. Somehow, I had expected to be meeting Alexander, the owner, but I didn't. I heard his footsteps in the lofted studio above us, though, and I sat in the glow of one of the skylights that lit his space, prepared to give my best answers.

"We need someone to help out and cover for me while I'm off," Neve told me, hands resting on her belly, explaining that the shop had a staff of only three. Alexander did all the printing, while Neve handled customers and Eduardo managed the finances and the "back end." My dad had told me it's good to ask questions. It shows you're interested, he said, and that you'll be a quick learner.

"What does the 'back end' consist of?" I asked.

"Behind-the-scenes stuff. Ordering the ink and paper. Basically he deals with supplies and keeps the roof over our heads. I get sales. Alexander makes magic. So when the baby comes, it's going to be tough. Even the appointments have strained things a little. Every time the doctor calls we're down two-thirds of our staff. The phones just ring and ring because Alexander refuses to talk to anyone."

I glanced across the room to Eduardo, who was busy with a catalog. So he was the father? This was a question about which I was sincerely curious, but I didn't want to get too personal. But then Neve leaned forward and said, "We've been basking in a seemingly eternal youth, and now, *shit*, I'm thirty-seven. I told Eduardo now or never and threw the condoms away." She leaned back and laughed. "Okay, thanks for tolerating my overshare. I like you. You're hired."

"Oh," I said. "Thanks!" I shook my head to rid it of the image of the two of them having sex, and stood up to shake her hand. That's another lesson my dad taught me: the importance of a firm handshake.

And thus began my eleven-week wait.

I spent my mornings researching print techniques so I could talk knowledgeably when customers called. And I'll be honest: I wanted to impress Alexander. I thought that maybe—after so many years of doing this all on his own—he would want an assistant. An apprentice. I wanted to impress him so that maybe he would let me watch him work. In between learning printing terms—bleed (when the ink prints beyond the edge of the page), debossing (when an image is pressed into the paper instead of printed onto it)—I tried not to check Instagram for posts from my ex-girlfriend. We'd been broken up for three months. She was headed to another state for college and I was stuck here in my hometown for another year. So we were trying to be "friends," which, since school got out, seemed to mean very little to her. As soon as the days got hot enough, a group of us would gather at Becky's or Kirby's house, the two of our group with pools in their backyards, and nibble away at their seemingly endless snacks. I always kept my phone near me, not for news or gossip, but in case the shop called me. At the end of July, I broke down and called to check in, fearing they'd changed their minds. But Neve assured me they were just behind, so swamped that it would still be a few more weeks.

"I just want to remind you that once school starts I'll only have later afternoons and evenings and weekends," I told her.

"Oh, that's fine. Alexander rarely arrives before two."

And then, two nights before the beginning of the fall semester of my senior year, she called and said they were ready.

Which brings me to this morning. Picture it: I am standing in the doorway. Everything I'm feeling—nervousness and determination and excitement, the weeks I've spent researching printing techniques and the years I've spent pinning Alexander's work to my Pinterest page—it's all on my face. And so is a carefully blotted coat of red lipstick, a pair of chunky black glasses, and a little mascara. My hair is in a neat bun instead of the usual messy one, and I'm wearing a sleeveless shirt buttoned up to the collar and a pair of nice jeans. It took me ages to get it right. I wanted to feel like I belonged, even though I was two decades younger than the youngest of them.

So I was standing in the doorway. I was ready to travel back in time, to when people looked into each other's faces instead of at their phones, and used landlines to place calls, and worked with wood frames and cans of ink and brushes. The bell jangled and the door shut behind me and I heard Neve's voice, saying, "*Ohhhh . . . Principal not principle.* Shit. Okay. We thought it was, like, the principle of hope. We were actually a bit perplexed by the phrasing but there was something sort of poetic about it. *Welcome Principle Hope.*" She spun in her chair, listening to the person on the other side of her call, and waved at me.

I lifted my hand to wave back, and as my eyes adjusted from the bright summer morning to the dim, dusty clutter of the front office, I saw something. It was like one of those pictures in kids' activity books: *Find the object that doesn't belong.* But instead of blending into the scenery, it leapt out at me. Too silver and too new, too deliberately placed on a newly cleared off patch of desk with a chair right in front of it. A chair that might as well have had my name on it.

A laptop. My heart sank.

"I sincerely apologize. We'll get a new one printed right away. When do you need it? . . . Ah. Hmm. No, no, we can do it. I understand. I'll call you when I have an ETA."

She hung up. "What a shit show. But welcome! *Eduardo! She's here!*"

Eduardo appeared from the supply closet. "Happy first day," he said.

But it was not quite the happy day I had imagined because, at their request, I was soon seated in front of the sole computer in the shop I had chosen for its lack of computers.

"This is a really exciting day for us," Neve said. "We've been trying to convince Alexander for *years* that we need to have an online presence. Business is okay, but we rely almost exclusively on repeat customers, and some of our equipment could use updating—"

"Replacement," Eduardo said. "More replacement than updating, unfortunately."

"So we need to reach a new pool of customers. We've been thinking about it, and then you walked in. A real live Millennial. And we knew you could be the one to make it happen for us."

"We need to hold on to our image," Eduardo said. "Analog. Classic. A little . . . *quirky.*"

"But also serious. Radical, even," Neve said, gesturing to the upper wall with a row of framed prints from various resistance efforts. A cluster of them caught my eye. Audre Lorde and James Baldwin and Harvey Milk and Oscar Wilde. "Alexander should be central, but not too prominent. More photos of the shop than the man. He likes to stay behind the scenes. So we need Twitter, Facebook, Instagram . . . What else? Snapchat? Pinterest? Flickr?"

"Wow," I said. "*I* don't even have all those."

"We can start small," Eduardo said. "Just a couple. What would make the most impact?"

"Twitter, maybe?"

They were eager, ready to believe me no matter what I said. Neve was wide-eyed and nodding; Eduardo's head tilted like a giant bird's, watching me for guidance. It was not at all what I expected. I thought they would be teaching me. I thought I'd be watching *them* this way. It was my first day of my first-ever job, and I came ready to take notes and try and make mistakes and learn from them. I was ready to absorb, but instead they were asking me to impart. I was trying not to let the disappointment engulf me. Trying not to think so much of the colors of ink and the techniques I'd been studying. This was not what I wanted, but it was something I knew how to do, so I resolved to make the best of it. If it helped keep this business going, then I would do what I could.

"Social media is great, but we need something to direct it to," I said. "We need a website."

"Alexander said no website," Neve said.

"What about just a landing page?" I asked. "An image, your contact info. That's all we'd need. Super minimal."

Neve glanced at the closed door of Alexander's office, even though he wasn't there yet. Eduardo shrugged. "A good compromise," he said. "What Alexander doesn't know won't hurt him."

I set to work. Eduardo showed me how to use the shop's nice digital camera, and soon I was photographing prints, trying to get the lighting right, figuring out how to position myself so my shadow didn't get in the way. "This will be a great way to familiarize yourself with the work we do," Neve had said, and she was right. The shop had some of everything, from letter-pressed wedding invitations to original artwork. There were business cards and monogrammed stationary. There were limited-edition books with thick pages and brilliant colors. But my favorite things were the posters. I couldn't tell what had been commissioned and what Alexander had decided to do himself. Some of them had his signature stamp in the bottom right corner, and those I realized were his own art. Most of them were intricate geometric designs and they were all editions of twenty-five. At last, I dragged a ladder over to the cluster of images that had caught my eye earlier. I had been saving them as a reward.

It was a series, each with an image of a person and a quote by them below. They were all familiar to me because of Mr. Leahey, who was my sophomore English teacher and the first person I ever came out to. He's the one who first told me about Print Shop, actually, after I complimented a framed print that hung over his desk. The coming out was almost accidental, in the form of a love poem in a journal that I thought he would just check off and not read, but instead he wrote, *Love this one* below it and gave me a check plus. Then, *P.S. I have some great queer writers to recommend should you ever want something like that.* It took me a couple of months of blushing and not meeting his eye, but then I finally stayed after school to ask, and he handed me a stack of books that he had apparently been saving for me all that time. I devoured them. When I wasn't sure of myself, those writers were sure of me. I was turning the lens, focusing on Audre Lorde's words that helped me then and still help me sometimes, because even though my friends and family are fine with who I am, I know that plenty of people in the world and in our country are not. Even if they hide it. Even if they pretend they are saying one thing when they are really saying something else. Now the words were clear through my lens—*When I dare to be powerful, to use my strength in the service of my vision, then it becomes less and less important whether I am afraid.*—and I snapped the picture and climbed down.

— — — —

The *Print Shop* handle was taken—no surprise there—so I added the name of our small California city, and PrintShopMartinez.com and @PrintShopMartinez were born. I found the perfect part of the shop to photograph: a weathered wooden table strewn with printed posters and cards, cast in light from the leaded glass window above it. I used it as the home page for the website and simply added the name, street address, and phone number in small Helvetica type at the bottom. As minimal as it could be. Then I got to work on Twitter. I used the wooden sign with its hand-lettered *Print Shop* as the profile photo and then the same table-and-window image as the background. Since I wouldn't be on the clock every day to tweet for them, I wanted to schedule daily tweets out about a week.

"What do you want people to know about the shop?" I asked Neve.

"Well . . ." she said, and I held my pencil to the paper, ready to take notes. "We are not cheap and we are not quick. But we care. A lot. We're attentive—or at least we try to be when we're not totally swamped and I'm not eight months pregnant—and Alexander is the absolute best in the business. We're right for a certain type of client who wants a product that looks truly special. A *discerning* client. We have a solid reputation and a thirty-year history. We champion progressive causes and Alexander has done a lot of pro-bono work—but maybe don't advertise that because I don't want to field a bunch of calls from people wanting things done for free. We use techniques that are almost obsolete not because they should be, but because they take time and care and a level of dedication to master that most people aren't willing to exert. In other words, we're special. And we think our customers and their projects are special." She finished and smiled. "Is that enough to start with?"

"Absolutely."

I had two pages of words and phrases to work with, so I took a seat at my laptop station and began composing our first day's tweets.

We've been around for thirty years but we're brand-new here. Please welcome us with a follow!

We pride ourselves in quality over quantity. With us, you'll find excellence in both product and customer service.

Print Shop: A discerning shop for the discerning client.

Neve heaved herself out of her chair. "Off to pee for the three hundredth time today!"

Just as she got to the bathroom door, the phone rang. I looked at her, wondering if I should answer, but Eduardo picked up. "Yes," he said. "Oh, yes, the banner. Well, Alexander isn't in yet, but I assure you it is our top priority. Right. Yes. Today, yes. I'll let Neve know you called."

A history of progressive printing, I typed, and added the Audre Lorde image. I sat back. How would anyone find us if we had zero followers?

"It was the banner girl again," Eduardo said when Neve re-emerged.

"I really screwed that one up," she said. "And Alexander has the whole Jenkins order to complete today." She eased herself back into her chair.

"One more question," I said to her. "Do we have any friends? Like, businesses that we partner with?"

"Take a look at the client list," she said. "Some of them are well known." She pointed to a green binder on a shelf near me. "Go ahead and look through that." So I spent some time searching for our most recent clients on Twitter and following them. Then I flipped through the binder and tweeted directly at the companies that have hired us and have a following. And one by one, people started following us back.

"Break time," Neve said to me. "You can take between half an hour and an hour; just make note of the time when you leave and get back and deduct it from your shift hours."

"Okay, great," I said. Before I left, I checked the scheduled tweets. One would go out when I was off and then I'd reply to any others that came in and thank people for the follows when I got back.

I got a burrito and ate it on the bright sidewalk patio of the restaurant. I ate fast, not wanting to take too long away. I checked my ex's Instagram and didn't find anything new, and then saw that I'd only been gone for twenty minutes. So I walked up and down the main streets of downtown, looking into the windows of the new stores that had sprouted up in the old, restored buildings. Things there were changing. A lot of the antiques stores were gone, replaced by a hair salon and a boutique. A former photographer's studio where we'd had family portraits taken for a few years was now a wine bar. I began to understand why Print Shop needed to step carefully into the present. The town was changing, and the shop didn't want to be forgotten or left behind.

I was feeling great about how much I'd already accomplished when I got back. Neve and Eduardo were drinking iced tea from tall glasses, each working in silence at their respective stations. They offered me one and I set it carefully next to the laptop and opened Twitter. There were twenty-seven new follows, and a bunch of people tweeting to welcome us. But then a new reply came in.

@PrintShopMartinez *ARE YOU KIDDING ME???*

I clicked on it. It was in response to the excellence tweet that went out over lunch. *Whatever,* I thought. The Internet can be a mean place. I clicked the person's profile. Only three hundred followers, no big deal. But then, a few minutes later, another one came in. *Late AND wrong. How exactly is this customer service "excellent"?*

"Hey, Neve?"

"Yes?"

"I'm sorry to bother you, but . . ."

She must have heard something in my voice because she was soon next to me, looking at the screen.

"Hm."

"Yeah. Whoever it is, they don't have a huge following or anything. What should I say?"

Just then the door bell chimed, and there was Alexander, tall and thin with a slight hunch in his shoulders, gray hair peeking out from under a straw hat and a mug of coffee in hand as though he had come directly from his kitchen table.

"Good morning," he said to all of us, giving me an extra nod that sent a bright spark to my stomach. "And a warm welcome to our new addition. Neve, it will be a busy day; let's get right to the schedule." With that, he turned and ascended the stairs to his studio.

Neve smiled at me and whispered, "Don't worry. I'll make sure he learns your name." She waved toward the computer as though she could banish our disgruntled customer's problem with a single gesture. "Just . . . use your discretion with that. I trust you."

Then she was making her way up the steep stairs, and Eduardo was placing a seemingly endless phone order, and the angry tweets were glaring at me from the screen. I searched for a few businesses' profiles to see how they responded to customers' complaints. I saw lots of "so sorry!"s, lots of exclamation points, lots of personalizations, with people signing their first names or telling the customers the name of the person who would be getting in touch to fix the problem. One of them wrote, *Beth will be getting in touch with you within the hour. She is the BEST!* I realized that would feel good, to have a problem and then be told that the best would be helping me fix it.

I switched back over and wrote, *@LaurenInRealLife So sorry to hear about your experience! Please give us a call to talk to Neve. She will make sure your problem is solved!*

A moment later another tweet came through.

@PrintShopMartinez I'VE BEEN WAITING FOUR HOURS FOR HER TO CALL ME BACK!

Then, like the first cracks before an avalanche:

From someone named @CaliGrrl00: *@LaurenInRealLife @PrintShopMartinez What's going on!? Is this about the banner?*

From @_Micah_Mic: *@LaurenInRealLife @PrintShopMartinez @CaliGrrl00 You didn't hear? They spelled Principal wrong!*

@LaurenInRealLife wrote back, *@CaliGrrl00 @_Micah_Mic I understand that they made a mistake but I don't understand why they aren't fixing it or returning my calls. UGH!!!*

Then, a new person: *@LaurenInRealLife I don't knw you but this sounds like a terrible business & the way they are handling it is even wrse! @PrintShopMartinez*

They kept coming and coming, and I gave it one more try:

@LaurenInRealLife We sincerely apologize for this and are doing all we can to resolve the situation. Please DM or call for updates.

I shut the computer. Eduardo was finally finished with his call. "This banner thing is becoming a real problem on Twitter," I told him.

He showed me his cell phone screen, open to the Twitter app. He'd been following along with everything. "Maybe Alexander was right about all of this. We're an old-fashioned business. This technology may not suit us." He shrugged and tossed his phone on the desk. Then he added, "You've been doing a great job, though. I wouldn't have known what to say."

"Thanks. Maybe when we get her the banner she'll delete the tweets. Or at least say it had a happy ending."

Eduardo glanced toward Alexander's studio. "Maybe," he said, but his voice lacked optimism. I was about to ask why, when Neve emerged and crossed as swiftly as she could to the phone. She flipped through the green binder and then dialed.

"Jessica," she said. "It's Neve. So lovely to hear your voice! No, it isn't ready quite yet but that's why I'm calling. I know we promised it by end of day but Alexander is running a bit behind. I assure you they look gorgeous. We are going to deliver them to your office tomorrow morning. No, we don't mind at all. That will give you plenty of time to have them for the dinner, right? Wonderful. No, thank *you*. Say hello to Meg and have a wonderful night. And please don't worry about a thing." She hung up and dug her thumb into the space between her brows.

Eduardo rose and wrapped his arms around her. "All this stress isn't good for you," he murmured.

"I know. I'll try not to get wrapped up in it."

"Unfortunately, there is one thing you should see." He handed her his phone and she scrolled through.

"Well, perfect." She sighed and climbed the stairs again. She tapped on Alexander's door and opened it but didn't enter.

"We have a Twitter problem."

"I said I didn't want the Twitter in the first place. We've lived without it for thirty years, so it doesn't much concern me."

"It's just, the principle/principal banner?"

"I know. It needs to be done over."

"Okay, so it's on your to-do list? Near the top?"

I heard some grumbled words and then the door shut. She made her way down again.

"We have to go," Neve said to me, hand on her enormous belly. "We have an appointment."

So much swarmed through my mind. Like, should I still leave at five even if there was no answer? And how could they leave me alone with Alexander, who didn't even know my name? But I could only get out the simplest of questions: "What should I tell Lauren?"

"That it's being handled," Neve said, slinging her purse over her shoulder.

"Do you know, like, a specific time or anything?"

"Not yet."

"Maybe just a window?"

"Sorry."

"Are you coming back after the appointment?"

"No, it's four already and the appointment is all the way in Oakland, and with the commute traffic . . ." She looked at me. "Listen.

— 34 —

We try our best. Sometimes we make mistakes. Sometimes we let people down even though we really don't want to. He has this huge order for a longtime client to get through for tomorrow, and then he has this one banner for a new client, and I don't know if it's all going to get done. He's trying. I can't promise anything."

Then they were gone, and I was alone in the downstairs of Print Shop. The front door was locked and the *Open* sign faced in. Twitter was quiet for a moment, besides the occasional *ping* of someone following us back. I had more tweets scheduled but I pushed them out a couple of days so that our bad publicity would have time to die down.

I clicked on @LaurenInRealLife's profile again and scrolled to see what I could learn about her. I saw a lot about school and principals, so I tried to find where it all started. There it was, three months back. *Thanks for electing me to be student rep for the hiring committee for our new principal! I promise to ask tough questions & be your voice.* There was a photo attached and I clicked to expand it, and as soon as it filled the screen I was bowled over. *This girl.* Short shaggy hair and no makeup. A confident grin and a shirt with a picture of John Muir on it, which some people would find so nerdy but I found irresistible. In fact, to my surprise, as I scrolled, I found nearly *everything* about our worst Twitter nightmare irresistible. There were tweets about the final candidates for her school's new principal, urging people to come to the final interviews to weigh in, asking for issues that are important to her classmates. Then there was the announcement: *Couldn't be more excited to introduce Alhambra's new principal. Dr. Joyce Hope will join us at the end of summer!* And in between all of these, there were other tweets, pictures mostly, of hikes she'd taken, close-ups of flowers and plants, blurry bunnies as they hopped across a trail, even a family of foxes. I've read some of John Muir's essays—he had lived in our town, so his books are strewn through the cafés and everyone's houses—but I don't come from an outdoorsy family. Looking at her feed made me want to try walking the hills he used to walk. I wanted to try it with *her*.

I knew we hadn't met.

But I recognized this feeling.

A DM appeared across the screen as I was learning all I could about her.

Have I been forgotten?

No, I shot back. *Not at all. I'm working on it. Will you try back in a couple of hours? I'm really so sorry.*

Suddenly she had answered all the swarming questions from Neve and Eduardo's departure. I would stay past five o'clock. I would stay as long as it took, and it didn't matter if Alexander didn't know my name yet. It was up to me to make this right.

But I still didn't know how to do that. I figured all I could do for now was wait. He'd have to emerge eventually. I kept scrolling to find out more about Lauren. I found more pictures of her and they made my hands shake and my stomach ache in that glorious, lovesick way. Then I made myself do something else. I wasn't even on the clock anymore, so I looked up hiking trails and then John Muir quotes. I set up more tweets even though I technically shouldn't have been working, because something I like about myself is that I care about the things I do. I know Print Shop's Twitter got off to a rough start, but I felt optimistic for its future.

And then, much later, the phone rang.

"Print Shop," I said.

"Hey, this is Lauren." *Her voice against my ear.* My throat seized up. I tried to say hi but nothing came out. "I'm the one who ordered the banner. I've been tweeting with one of you about this."

"Right, that's me," I said. "My name is Evelyn. Evie." Why was I telling her both versions of my name? She had no idea who I was and no reason to care.

"*Oh.*" She sounded surprised or thrown off or something, and I wondered why. "Well, I'm sorry for my rudeness. Just please tell me that my banner is going to be finished tonight. It's already late and I know you guys are closed and it's just . . . it's really important to me. It's for something I've been working on for a long time and if I don't get it tonight I won't be able to use it at all."

"I'm so sorry about all this," I said. "This is actually my first day? Everyone else left except Alexander. He's the printer. He's working upstairs still. I'm actually supposed to have left, but I'm trying to see if I can get this taken care of for you."

"Thank you."

"Sure. I'll let you know when I know more."

As soon as I hung up, the phone rang again. Breathless, I picked it up, expecting it to be her. Instead it was a man's voice. "What a surprise! Who is this?"

"Evie," I said. "May I ask who this is?"

But he just sighed. "Usually I call and let it ring to remind him what time it is. But if he has reinforcements at this time in the evening, things must not be going well. I assume he's holed up upstairs, but if he emerges, please remind him that his husband has dinner ready."

"I will."

He sighed again and hung up.

Then a DM came through.

There was more that I wanted to say but forgot to. So here it goes. I chose your company over other more affordable ones because I believe in local economies, and in supporting businesses whose values reflect my own. I wanted to choose a business right here in town, where my school is and where I live. I wanted to choose a queer business. I wanted to choose an independent business. An established one. Not some trendy new one where I upload an image and they send it to me printed on glass or some shit and delivered via drone like two minutes later and it's great for the welcome party and then goes straight into the recycling. This banner you guys made is really beautiful, and it would be perfect if what I was talking about were the principle of hope and not a woman named Hope who is going to be our principal. I know it's late now and maybe you're the only person left there and maybe you can't do anything. But I need to say that just now when we talked it was the first time I felt truly hopeful about this all day. If there is any chance this can still work out, I would really appreciate it. I'm working at my school tonight to get ready for the welcome party in the morning. I will be here for hours. So no time is too late for me. Okay. Good night for now.

Something in her *good night* made me blush all over again. The intimacy of it. Of course I couldn't know for sure, but I doubted she would have chosen that phrase if she thought she was tweeting to Neve or Alexander. But then I felt foolish for hoping because she had no idea who I was, or that I went to high school a few miles away from her, that we were the same age, that we both liked girls, that the first glimpse of her picture sent a current up my spine, sent my blood rushing, made me think immediately about being kissed by her. It was only my voice, and only for a few moments. I banished the fantasy that my *hello* sent some kind of spark through the phone and reread her message.

I decided to be brave.

— — — —

The stairs to Alexander's studio creaked as I climbed them, and I couldn't help but think of Neve going up and down with her huge belly each day. I didn't blame her for not returning that night. The door was closed and I heard the rustle of a sheet of paper inside. I knocked, loudly enough that I wouldn't have to wonder if he'd heard me.

"Yes?" I heard from the other side.

I opened the door to the studio. I had imagined a room full of metal and paint and machinery, but I had not expected this. I didn't know how the floor of the loft could hold it all. There were so many machines, so many papers, so many tubs of paint, so many metal alphabets in different fonts and sizes. I'd stepped into another world. I felt it. A giant clock on the wall said what I already knew. It was eight o'clock and getting dark, and Alexander was deep in a more important project, and we were running out of time.

"Hi," I said. "I'm Evie."

"Yes, our new hire. Our last new hire was a decade ago. Momentous day, this one." I couldn't tell if he was joking. Nothing about my arrival seemed momentous to him, but being the first employee to join them in so long must count for something. He looked out the window instead of at the clock. "It's far past closing time. Yet you're still here."

"I've been dealing with Lauren . . . She ordered the principal banner? I know it seems like we've missed our chance to get it to her, but it's not too late. She's still working, and I will bring it to her when it's finished." He was still looking at his current project and not at me. He hadn't even so much as nodded in response. So I took another deep breath and said, "I know I'm brand-new and this isn't my place to say, but I just need to say it. Please forgive me in advance. But the way I see it is that we accepted this girl's job, and we took her money, and we gave her something with a major error. She needs it by tonight, and we need to fulfill our obligation to give her what she ordered and paid for."

Alexander ran a hand through his silver hair. His glasses reflected the lamp on his table and then he tilted his face toward me and the reflection was gone. And I could see his eyes. And they were smiling.

"Ah," he said. "A straight shooter. I like that."

He glanced at his watch. "Do me a favor. Call Terry—our home number's on the bulletin board—and tell him I'll be home late. Later. And then let our disgruntled young customer know that we will have her banner to her by eleven."

"Yes," I said. "Yes." My eyes burned and I didn't even feel stupid. I felt like I'd done something right. I made someone listen. And not just *anyone*, but Alexander. Radical, cranky, brilliant Alexander, who believed in art. Who believed in living up to your promises. Who didn't even know what "the Twitter" was but wanted to do the right thing anyway.

"I'm going to need a hand," he said, "after you're finished with your phone calls."

Terry listened to my bad news and then said, "Could have called that one," and hung up.

I picked up the phone to call Lauren, but then lowered the receiver. In a few hours, I was going to meet her. I didn't want to waste any more of our introduction on phone calls. So I DM'd her instead. *Let me know where to find you at 11, and I will be there, new banner in hand.*

Really??? THANK YOU. South parking lot of Alhambra High. Text me when you get here. THANK YOU AGAIN.

And then she gave me her phone number. I copied it into my contacts, full of hope that I'd be using it for a long time, not only later that night.

— — — —

Alexander gave instructions like he'd been teaching all his life. We started by finding the stencil he had cut out of a long but paper-thin sheet of metal. He looked at the *Principle* and laughed, hands on his head, for a full minute, then had me cut and iron a piece of cloth while he cut a new stencil to replace the wrong word with the right one. Finally, we lay the fabric on one of his massive worktables and he laid the stencil over it, the new *Principal* fitting in a space he cut out of the old one. He taught me how to open a can of paint and how to mix it. The most brilliant grass green, the richest blue, the happiest yellow. In the midst of it all, Terry showed up with dinner. Coq au vin for three on ceramic plates with silverware and cloth napkins. Alexander said he was too busy to eat but sat down anyway. Terry asked me questions about myself and I tried my best to sound interesting enough to be worthy of their company. The food was delicious, and I wondered how many nights Terry cooked that way only to walk the few blocks from their downtown Victorian to dine in the dusty shop.

And then we were finished eating and Terry had collected the dishes and left. Alexander made some final touches and placed the banner under hot lamps. I watched the paint change color as it dried. At one point I reached to touch the tip of a letter to test it, but Alexander barked, "Not yet!" It was ten fifteen, but it would only take me a few minutes to get to Alhambra. Each time I thought of parking there and finding Lauren, my heart raced.

Finally, Alexander declared it dry. It was truly beautiful. Like something from the past. Something that would last, just how Lauren hoped it would. I could see it hanging in the new principal's office forever, reminding her of how she had been chosen and the importance of her work.

He folded the fabric into a square. I could see that he still had more to do for his other order, and I understood that this was because of me. The banner printing had taken longer than I thought it would.

"Do you want me to come back and help with the rest?" I offered.

He smiled at me. "I can't afford that much overtime."

I didn't know what to say.

"Just joking. The rest is easy. Drive carefully through the night and I'll see you tomorrow."

"I'm not scheduled again until Tuesday."

"Then I will see you on Tuesday."

The drive to Alhambra High School took less than ten minutes, but my concept of time was off. The red lights were brighter than ever. The sky was dark and the trees rose tall around me. I could hear my own breath. I was aware of everything. And then I was pulling into the south parking lot like Lauren told me to. As soon as I parked and turned the car off, I saw a figure in a lit doorway. *Her* figure.

I climbed out of the car, banner in hand, and headed toward her.

— — — —

"So that's how it started," I say.

I've left out some of the details, of course. Like just how carefully I studied your photos and how they made me feel. But I don't want to hold back *too* much. I want to give this all I can. So I dare to touch the hem of your shirt and add, "I saw this in one of your Twitter pictures. I love John Muir."

You cock your head. "You looked through my profile?"

"I was curious about our disgruntled customer." I can hear the nervousness in my voice but I tell myself it's okay that I'm nervous. It's okay if you can tell how it feels to be this close to you.

I look into your face, allow my gaze to linger. And I see something register in yours: a moment of surprise in your eyes that turns into a shy smile of your own.

"So I should be heading back in. Thanks again."

I nod. You take the folded banner from my hands, take a half step backward toward the bright classroom. And before my disappointment has time to register, before I can wonder if this is all there will ever be between us, you say, "You're coming with me, right?"

HOURGLASS

– – – – – –

IBI ZOBOI

Now

"YOU THINK YOU'RE better than me?" I say while standing outside of Geraldine's, the only fancy dress boutique in town. I'm staring at a mannequin wearing a fitted white sequined dress and she's looking down at me, over the tip of her nose, with a stupid smile on her face like she thinks she's all that.

I look the mannequin up and down, with her bent leg meant to show off the sexy slit in her dress, and those high-heeled shoes that don't even fit. Her hand is held out as if she's supposed to be holding a cocktail or a glass of champagne. Her wig is the worst thing about her. Dolores, the salesgirl, didn't even bother to brush and style it, so this mannequin looks a hot mess.

"Can you please come inside, Cherish?" Stacy says, poking her head out from inside the boutique.

I open the door to the sound of wind chimes, and the scent of cheap perfume and steamed dresses. I inhale because it smells like Stacy's whole house. Her mother's been shopping at Geraldine's since we were both little. My own mother has never bought a thing from here, and neither have I, not even my prom dress. I don't plan to, either.

But Stacy's been dragging me here all week, trying on dress after dress. And I'm her designated photographer. She posts the pics and asks her followers to vote on their favorite look. So, naturally, she gets all the haters who comment on every single wrong thing about her body, face, and hair. And once, even her toes that were poking out from beneath a long gown. But she takes it like a champ. She doesn't care. My best friend, Stacy, has enough ego for the both of us.

"Okay," she says, standing back against the dressing room mirrors in the far end of the boutique. "What about this one?"

The black dress is sleeveless, fitted at the top, flares out at the bottom, and barely covers her legs. "Didn't you wear something like that for the fifth-grade dance?" I ask.

"I sure did. So you think I should be more risqué? I *am* eighteen, you know. So do I show more boob or my butt? Or both?" She holds out two different dresses in each hand. "I got more likes on the pic I posted wearing this one." Without a body to fill them in, one looks like a spiraling slinky and the other looks like a fishing net.

"Stacy, just pick a dress and let's go!" I say, annoyed.

She rolls her eyes and goes back into the fitting room, shaking her booty at me. As the mirrored door swings open, I catch a glimpse of myself wearing a plain T-shirt and jeans—tall, wide, frumpy, and sorry. It's noon on a Sunday and I really did just roll out of bed to shop with Stacy. She wanted to get here before the other girls came into the store.

The prom is next Friday, so mostly everyone at Kingsbridge High has their dresses, tuxes, and limos all set up. But Stacy wants to make it a whole fashion show where she dares herself to find the perfect dress in a small town at the very last minute—and still be the best at everything for the prom.

I turn to the snooty mannequin in the store's window. She has her back to me now. I notice the clearance rack in a far corner of the store and a sign that reads *Plus Size*. A long burgundy gown is displayed in front of the rack—something a great-aunt would wear to her sixtieth-birthday dinner. I've never dared to look through those dresses for something in my size. None of them are like a slinky or a tube or have a slit up the side. None of them hit above the knee or drop down low at the neckline. None of them ooze "hot" or "sexy." None of them are anything I would wear while standing remotely close to Stacy, who is a shaped like an actual mannequin, a straight-up Barbie.

I browse around the store like I've done so many times before. I can't remember the last or first time I wore a dress. So the prom was not an event I wanted to go experimenting with my look for. My own mother lives in her work uniform, or a bathrobe.

I spot a stack of flyers and a small pile of business cards near the cash register. The flyer is a photo of a bunch of ladies wearing long, fitted colorful gowns in patterns I've never seen before—bold and ethnic. The ladies are in all different shapes and sizes. Above the photo reads *Mamadou's African Tailoring: One Size Don't Fit All.*

"What's African tailoring?" I ask Delores.

She shrugs while going through her phone. "Some black man and his son dropped those off. They say they fix dresses."

"Like at the cleaners?"

"I guess," she says.

"So a new black family moved to Kingsbridge?" I ask.

"You should know better than me," she mumbles.

I stare at the flyer once more before putting it down and returning to the conceited mannequin as it stares out of the store's front window. Without thinking twice, I step closer to it and smack it upside its head. It tumbles forward, hitting the window.

"You are not all that," I say.

Delores rushes over to prop it up again. She struggles with the mannequin a bit until it's upright; then she turns and squints her blue-shadowed and mascaraed eyes at me.

Stacy comes out of the fitting room to see my face about to burst into a laugh. She doesn't hold hers in. So we both let out a long, hard laugh as Delores shakes her head and goes back to scrolling through her phone at the cash register.

"Don't hate her 'cause she's beautiful," Stacy says as she walks over to Delores to pay for the slinky black dress.

It's the one her followers voted on a few days ago—the one with slits along the sides that almost show off every single part of her body.

"I don't hate her," I say, side-eyeing the now propped-up mannequin. "She hates me because *I'm* beautiful."

I bat my eyelashes and flash a sexy smile at Stacy and she laughs even harder. For a quick moment, I wonder if she's laughing at the joke or at me.

— — — —

I refresh my e-mail over and over again as I sit in Stacy's passenger seat on the drive home. It's the only thing I can do in Stacy's tiny car, where the top of my head brushes against the car's roof upholstery and my knees are almost curled up to my chest. It's a health hazard riding in her car 'cause I'm six foot five and her two-door hatchback is made for tiny teenyboppers like her—five foot four and only about a hundred pounds. But I still insist on wearing a seat belt even though I feel like I have to fold myself twice over just to get it around my hips. I don't complain. Not out loud, anyway. But I'm sure Stacy can hear it in my breathing—my sighs and grunts. She ignores it, thank goodness.

It's June and I haven't heard back from the three colleges that waitlisted me. But I'm keeping hope alive because there is still a week left of high school. I've started getting a bunch of e-mails about registering for my fall classes at Shaw County Community College, and Dad has already sent in my deposit. Still, I have a cardboard box pushed to a corner of my room full of the stuff I'll be taking with me if I get off any of those waitlists. *When* I get off those waitlists. I'm putting it out there in the universe.

I desperately need to go away for college. And each of those schools are far from Kingsbridge, New York.

"Don't tell me you're checking for homework?" Stacy says. "And if you are, I'm going to your house to throw that overstuffed, raggedy book bag in the trash. High school is over, Cherish!"

"No one gives any homework the last week before school ends. And even if they did, why would you throw my bag out anyway?" I ask, knowing good and well that Stacy never follows through on her threats to make me like her, to make me not care, to make me more . . . fun.

"Because we should be *celebrating*! I really want you to get out of this funk. Cheer up, Cherish!"

This has been her favorite thing to say to me—*Cheer up, Cherish!*—for as long as I can remember. I *am* cheered up. Just, not like her. I'm Stacy's sidekick, her road dog, her ride-or-die chick. And we are nothing alike. That's why we've been friends since the third grade. Even as her different cliques and crews came and went, I was still her loyal friend waiting to hear how so-and-so and this-and-that betrayed her and stabbed her in the back. And with me by her side to tell her how dumb she was acting with a guy, or how cute she didn't look in an outfit, she was leaving Kingsbridge High with a bang—a slammin' prom dress, a new hairdo, and a plane ticket to Oberlin College. She was headed halfway across the country and still, I was her sidekick, *cheering* her on.

"*You* should be celebrating," I say. "I'll be stuck here seeing these same houses and roads and people for the next four years."

"Two years, Cherish. It's community college. You can always transfer after two years."

"Two years is a long time in this town. And besides, we all know what happens to most of the people here—Kingsbridge Elementary, Middle School, High School, and Shaw County Community College. Then the mall or the state prison," I say with a knot forming in my belly because I think I may have just described my whole life in this town—my past, present, and future.

"Don't forget the diner," Stacy adds. "About seven people from our class will be working at Margot's Diner."

I grunt and throw my head back against the seat. "I really should've applied to a safe school. But no. It was either leave

Kingsbridge or bust. And I'm busting right now, Stacy. I'm about to fucking explode!"

"No, you're not. You'll be fine. And you know, you'll have more freedom. Go to the city on the weekends, just like we did a few months ago. And not every single person from Kingsbridge will be going to Shaw. I'm not going to Shaw."

"Rub it in, why don't you?"

She's quiet as she turns up my street and pulls into my driveway. It's sunny out but my little house still manages to have a dark cloud over it, and I'm about to step right into the storm.

"Okay," Stacy says, turning off her engine. "I'm gonna ask you one last time. Please come to the prom."

"No! I'll be fine. Trust me," I say, not wanting to have this conversation with her for the umpteenth time.

"I don't mind if you're my date, Cherish," she says all sweet, slipping her hand into mine.

"Is that how you want to leave Kingsbridge? Letting everybody think we're a couple?"

"That would be kinda badass, you know. All my exes would be so pissed."

"I'm not gonna be part of your lesbian revenge fantasy, Stacy," I say as I open the car door.

"Aw, come on. Please!" She laughs.

I close the door as the passenger-side window rolls down. "You already agreed to go with Alex, right? He's a . . . good guy." I try not to laugh because Alex is like a brother to us. He and Stacy are going as friends since Stacy couldn't get any of her good-looking exes to take her to the prom. Except one. And we're both already clear about why he's not an option.

"You're making fun of me, aren't you?"

"Yes, I am. Just know that you're making *him* look good. He should pay you."

Even I wouldn't date Alex if he asked me. And he has, back in the sixth grade. By that time, I was already half a foot taller than him. Even though he and Stacy are the same height, Alex still looks like a middle schooler. And with heels on, Stacy will look like Alex's mama since he hasn't made it out of puberty yet.

All this was because she promised me not to go with the guy I hated most in this world. The guy *she* once loved most in the world—Brian Price.

Once Stacy pulls out of my driveway, I check the mailbox. Just like every day since waiting on my college admissions letters, I hold the stack of envelopes against my heart and make a wish out into the air that I got into Spelman. The day the letter arrived, and it wasn't either a yes or a no, was one of the worst days of my life. I was stuck waiting. Again.

Inside the house, I rush to the computer to find my little brother, Honor, playing Minecraft. I mush his head and tell him to get out of the way. He doesn't move.

"Come on, Honor, I need to check my e-mail!"

"Check it later," he says, still not moving.

I start to grab his arm and he calls out for Dad. I quickly let go and cover his mouth.

I look around our one-story house and there's no sign of my father on the couch or in the kitchen. So I pinch Honor's arm.

"Ow! Why'd you do that for?"

"Shut up and get off the computer!" I whisper-yell through clenched teeth. "You'll wake up Dad."

I quickly check my e-mail for any news from Spelman, or Hampton, or even Florida A&M. They all waitlisted me. And they are miles and miles away from here—Virginia, Georgia, and Florida. They're historically black colleges that are nothing like my small, white town where my family is one of fourteen black families, and we stand out like four giant oak trees in a forest of shrubs.

My parents and I are over six foot five inches tall, and big. And Honor would probably have his growth spurt this summer since he's going into the seventh grade. The few times we walk downtown together, people either think we're oversize basketball players or freaks. No matter how long we've been living in this town, we never fit in. I never fit in.

And Brian Price was the person who reminded me of this over and over again.

So I'd be hiding in plain sight at an HBCU with all those black kids from all over the country in different shapes and sizes. And I was sure there would be other girls like me—too visible and invisible at the same time.

I check all three of my e-mail accounts. Nothing. Except for a shitload of messages from Shaw County. I ignore them all.

A loud *thud* comes from my parents' bedroom, letting me know that Dad is up and moving about. He swings open his bedroom door and makes his way down the narrow hallway into the living room. The top of his head almost brushes against the ceiling and he has to duck when he reaches the archway leading out of the hall. I search my mind for something to say about the missing groceries before he even asks. But I've gone blank. I stand up instead, ready to head out the door.

"Where you going?" he asks with his usual scraggily voice.

I stutter for a bit. Then I tell the truth. "I forgot the groceries."

He doesn't say anything, but rushes to the kitchen and searches the fridge and cabinets for something, anything. There's a quarter-full carton of milk. There are a couple of cans of beans. There's some leftover roasted chicken, but he'd have to pick at the bones to make a sandwich with the almost-moldy rye bread from last week. I stand in the kitchen and sigh.

It isn't about the food or the money. It's about the time. It's always about time.

My parents watch over people serving time. My brother and I wait for the time that each of our parents would be home together, at the same time. We all coordinate our times to use the car for other things besides getting to work and school. And we wait for Dad's paycheck to clear before we can shop for food—a couple of hundred dollars for groceries before it was time to pay the other bills. So time affected food, affected money, affected me.

Dad bangs on one of the cabinet doors, making both me and Honor jump. Before he starts yelling about time and money and food, I rush out of the house, just as Mama is pulling into the driveway. I walk past her without saying a word, heading straight for Stacy's to beg her to take me to Foodtown.

— — — —

My heart is pounding out of my chest and my throat is dry and tight. Stacy's house is about a mile from my house and I shouldn't have walked it in this June heat. Dad was blowing up my phone and I was ignoring him. I knew he'd want me to come back just so he could yell at me and tell me how irresponsible I am and that I shouldn't even think about going away to college because I couldn't remember a simple thing like buying food for the house.

And that I should stay away from that white girl, Stacy, 'cause she got my head all up in the clouds.

Anything Dad would say to me right now would be out of hanger—anger and hunger. And Mama would be his amen corner, cosigning everything. I didn't need any of that right now.

I spot Stacy's car as I reach her house, a two-story surrounded by a perfectly manicured lawn and rosebushes. I can imagine what she's up to right now—messing with her hair, on the Internet talking shit, or trying on different outfits and adding more mirror selfies to her phone's queue. Her parents' car isn't in the driveway, so I exhale. They try too hard around me. They ask too many questions about my parents, my brother, and school. I won't have to talk to them about college. They will try to fix it for me. They will ask me how can they help. I don't want to deal with that right now, either.

At the curb in front of her house is another parked car, though, a small black one. I've seen it before at school, but I can't place the owner.

I reach the front door, and instead of knocking, I open it. Her house is unlocked during the day. We never do that at our house.

I don't call out her name because I've done this before, walked into her bedroom unannounced. She'll squeal and throw a towel at me; then we'll sink back into our usual shit-talking.

So when I quickly open the door, she's there. On her bed. With a boy.

This isn't the first time. I don't gasp or embarrassingly shut the door. I stand there and stare and make sure that the boy she's with—Brian Price—sees me unmoving and unafraid.

And that's a lie because my insides drop down to the floor, sink to the bottom of my feet. Stacy wasn't supposed to be with him. Not now. Not ever. Not like this.

— — — —

Before

November of senior year was when I wanted to kill Brian Price.

The meme had been going around for two days before it got to me. I didn't know then that Stacy had been the first to see it.

I wasn't always Stacy's designated photographer. She would take photos of me and of us and post them, and I wouldn't care, even if I got comments about how pretty I looked or about my outfit or my hair. None of it fazed me.

Until a Photoshopped meme reached my phone. And I saw my face on a gorilla's body—a gorilla wearing a wig and a dress.

And I didn't run out of school and hide and cry. I approached every single person sitting around me in that cafeteria and demanded that they tell me who did it. I yanked collars, and pulled arms, and yelled in faces. Until Principal Stewart called me into the office and asked me not to bully the students. I didn't show him the photo. I cursed him out instead. I was suspended for two days.

The worst of it all was when my parents found out. They thought I was bullying. I didn't show them the photo, either.

And I wasn't the only one. More and more of these Photoshopped memes kept coming up, and it was easy to trace them back to one fake account. As one of the smallest seniors and one of four black kids in our grade, Alex got it the worst. So when his parents came up to the school and threatened to take it with the authorities, Principal Stewart had to do something.

Brian Price was suspended for a week.

Brian Price had been Stacy's boyfriend since sophomore year.

Brian Price was always an asshole.

Stacy broke up with him because he'd attacked basically all her friends. Me, most importantly.

Everyone knew, especially me, that she still loved him.

That didn't stop him from being an asshole. And she knew that if she stayed with him, she would've been an asshole by association.

— — — —

Now

On the last day of high school, no one shows up to Mr. Randal's Shakespeare class. Well, about ten of us are here and we look like the dumbest kids graduating from Kingsbridge High. If it was Senior Cut Day, no one told us. If there was some sort of after-school party that everyone left to attend, we weren't invited.

I look around at the other familiar faces in the classroom. I know all their names. Some I've known since middle school or elementary school. I've spoken to only five of them. And that was either for a group project or for some silly small talk over the years. One kid's got his head down and is straight-up snoring. Another girl is doodling in her notebook. They all have Senioritis, but a much milder case since they're here sitting in a classroom with me, probably the only senior who is immune to Senioritis.

Senioritis is a plague when there are only a few days left of high school, the prom and graduation are coming up, and no one wants to do shit. Teachers know about Senioritis, too, of course. And the ones who don't care about any of it give us quizzes, exams, and homework assignments. Those are my favorite teachers.

I need a test or a big group project to take my mind off ignoring Stacy, hiding in different parts of the school to avoid her, and not answering her calls or texts.

I fucked up at home with all my chores and standing in as Honor's second mom. The only good friend I had is fucked up. And my whole future is fucked up, too, because I've done all this work in high school and still ended up at a fucking community college.

So for the first time in all four years at Kingsbridge, I take a nap. I take a fucking nap and shut out this stupid world.

My phone buzzes and instead of looking to see who's calling or texting, I turn to the classroom door, because this has always been how Stacy gets my attention. She'd call or text and stand in the doorway waving. This was also how she'd get me in trouble and have my phone taken away by Mr. Randal.

But no one is standing there. So I check to see that I've gotten an e-mail.

It's from Florida A&M. So I ask Mr. Randal to be excused.

I rush out of the classroom and lean against one of the nearby walls and slide down to the floor. I hold the phone close to my heart, shut my eyes, and inhale.

When I open the e-mail, the first word I see is *Congratulations*, and I scream.

My voice echoes in the hallway and kids come out of the classroom, staring at me with my big ol' smile. I stand up, wanting to do cartwheels through the hall.

And even as Stacy starts to slowly make her way toward me, not knowing whether to smile or ask me if I'm okay, I yell out, "I got into Florida A&M!"

I don't read the details, I don't check the financial aid information, I don't know how I'll get down to Florida, but I'm getting the fuck out of this town!

— — — —

Stacy wants to pretend like nothing happened. She wants to pretend that she hasn't been seeing Brian all this time and she's been bullshitting me and everybody else. She asks me to come over and celebrate about Florida. She parks outside my house, honking, refusing to come to the door like always. But not this time. This time, I wait for her to come to me.

This time, she knocks and I open the door and step out.

She's never been inside my house.

"You fucked up," I say.

"He's sorry," she says.

"Since when?"

"Since the moment it happened."

"When I saw that picture or when he got caught?"

"Look, he stopped doing any of it, right?"

"Wrong. He was dead wrong, and you're dead wrong!" I open the door to step back inside.

"Cherish, please," she says, all sweet and with puppy-dog eyes. "Cheer up!"

"Fuck you, Stacy!" I say, slamming the door in her face.

—   —   —   —

I have until Monday to accept the seat at Florida A&M. I'll be losing the deposit Dad sent to Shaw County. He'll have to come up with another deposit, and part of my tuition, and stuff for my dorm room, and my plane ticket.

Still, I let the thoughts of packing and saying good-bye to Kingsbridge wander around my mind. This is not a dream anymore. It's as real as breathing. And it's so close.

But something weighs heavy on my body. This is a moment I want to share with Stacy. I was there for her when she got her acceptance letter to Oberlin. We were supposed to go out to the mall and movies that night. But she chose to stay home. Now I know. She chose to be with Brian, the asshole.

I search through her Instagram feed to see all her posts about what shoes she'll be wearing, her different hairstyles, makeup colors, the works. I wonder who is taking her pictures now.

Then, a new photo pops up.

It's of her and Brian, and the caption: *New Prom Bae.*

I immediately text Alex.

Hey! Are you still going to the prom with Stacy?

He doesn't reply right away, so I head to the kitchen to get started on dinner. Mama had to do the groceries and miss a couple of hours of sleep. I've been making up for my fuck-up since that day by cooking all the meals, cleaning, and helping Honor with his homework. My parents were more than excited about my getting into Florida A&M, but not too long afterward, Dad started crunching the numbers. Still, I had until Monday to just hold on to this bit of happiness for a moment.

No. She's going with Brian.

Did she cancel on you at the last minute?

No. I was never going with Stacy. Who told you that?

Stacy did.

She said I could ride in her limo.

You'll still go even if Brian is there.

Yeah.

Why Alex? You don't remember what he did to you?

Hey. It's a free ride in a limo. I don't have to pay for it.

Seriously? So who are you taking to prom?

He doesn't respond. I wait and wait.

Nobody.

I don't respond. I pull out a package of ground meat and Hamburger Helper. Ten minutes go by before I ask him.

Do you wanna go with me?

No because you don't wanna go with me.

Sorry. I was just . . .

Save it.

Alex knew that he would be a pity date. He was right. The

only reason I was rethinking the whole thing was because of my fucked-up ex-friend and her asshole boyfriend.

I scroll through each of Stacy's pictures and there are more of her and Brian now, as if she's announcing to the world that they're back together, that they're not hiding their relationship anymore, that she doesn't give a fuck about what he's done to her friends because she was leaving Kingsbridge and telling everyone to kiss her ass.

I slam my phone against the counter. Honor glances at me. I look around the house. It feels small. I want to stretch my arms out and push the walls and make everything stretch far and wide because this place is beginning to feel like a prison.

— — — —

The day before the prom, I end up in Geraldine's because I'm going after all. That was the plan from the beginning. Work my butt off, get accepted into an HBCU, get ready to move out of the state, give myself a complete makeover from head to toe, and party like I've lost all my senses.

This was all supposed to be with Stacy's help. This was all planned before that thing with Brian, and before this new thing with Brian.

Since I'm going to be on my own down in Florida, I had to start now. I could pull myself together and be my own damn sidekick, road dog, and ride-or-die chick.

I'd spent a whole night online looking for dresses and creating a private Pinterest board of women with bodies like mine. Models, even. Some with deep brown skin like mine. Their dresses were short and flirty and in bright colors; or they were long and glamorous with revealing slits. The shimmering fabrics hugged their curves and they held their heads high. Confident, badass, and they didn't seem to give a fuck.

I could see it. I could imagine it. I could look just like those women.

I played around with my hair in the mirror. I pulled down the top of my sweater to show off my bare shoulder, and even pouted my lips.

I went from prom dresses to Florida A&M's website, to YouTube videos of current and former students, and I saw myself in each of their faces.

I could see it. I could imagine it. I was going to be one of those students. And I wouldn't hide. I would blend in and stand out at the same time.

I go through five dresses and none of them are like the ones I'd seen on those models online. Dolores takes photo after photo just in case the mirror isn't telling the whole truth. I do look like somebody's aunt or a burnt-out teacher.

"You don't have anything sexy in my size?" I finally ask.

"Sexy is a state of mind," Delores says, still engrossed in her phone.

I try on another dress that fits just right at the top but hits right at my calves, which isn't sexy at all, no matter what my state of mind is.

"Where's your friend? You should ask her."

"She's not my friend," I say.

"Yeah, she is."

"No, she's not."

"Whatever. You'll get over it."

I hold the dress up above my knees, then higher, and higher. I exhale and let it drop down. I could never be that bold. That risqué. I am eighteen now, too.

Stacy's voice flashes through my mind and I wonder what she'd say about this dress, about my body in it. She would squeal. She would jump at even the thought of me wearing a dress.

This is gonna be my revenge. She thinks I'm going to hide in some corner like all the other times she's fucked up, that I'm going to avoid her until she shows up with some gift and I'll fall for it and accept her sorry apology. Not this time.

Dolores comes over to me and hands me a piece of paper. It's the flyer about the African tailor.

"They fix dresses?" I ask, hesitantly taking it from her.

"They do," she says. "I've seen their handiwork. Some of the girls from your school have had their dresses, um, *altered*, they said. And I heard they even make dresses from scratch. It's pretty good."

— — — —

Mamadou's African Tailoring is a few blocks from my house and I was able to take the bus there, even though I had to wait a while for it to come. The store is in a regular blue-and-white frame house with a sign in the front. The door is wedged open and I walk in to the smell of steamed dresses, just like in Geraldine's except there's also a hint of smoked sweetness in the air. Incense, maybe.

Light music is playing and I can't place the instrument—something like a harp, but not. The store is a living room, and at the entrance is a mannequin almost like the one in Geraldine's, except this one doesn't look down the tip of her nose at me. She smiles as if greeting me. She's wearing red-and-gold fabric around her stringy hair, and her dress has loud, bold colors and shapes all over it.

The walls are lined with stacks and stacks of fabric in all different patterns and colors. Three tables holding sewing machines are at the center of the room, and for a moment I wonder if I've stepped into a sweatshop. An older woman is behind one of them, picking apart a dress, and she only smiles and nods at me.

"Alo?" someone calls out, and I jump.

A man wearing a wide and long robe of some sort comes out to greet me. He has got to be the darkest-skinned man I've ever seen in my life. So that explains the *African* part of the store's name.

"You're from Africa?" I ask. I don't think about it. I just stare at his smooth, glowing skin.

"Ah, yes! Senegal!" he says with a deep accent. "You too?"

"Uh, no," I say, laughing. "I'm from right here in Kingsbridge, born and raised. What are you doing here?"

"Eh, my son. He goes to the university. Are you looking for a dress?"

I pull myself together, remembering that I have a day to get this dress. A half day, really, if I was going to get my hair done. I had two hundred dollars saved for this whole thing and I needed to plan and budget both my money and my time. "I heard you fix dresses."

He looks me up and down. I hold my head up high because the walls in this living room store are covered with women who look like me. From Africa, I guess. From Senegal, where they're tall and dark-skinned and gorgeous.

"Where is the dress?" he asks, rolling his r's.

"Well, I thought you had some here that would fit me."

"I don't have time, miss. You see that over there?" He points to the tall and wide table at the edge of the living room where there's a pile of colorful, fancy dresses. I recognize some of them from Geraldine's. "I have to fix by tomorrow. You should come early."

"What are you saying? You can't help me?"

He shakes his head. "After Friday. You come Saturday and we can make dress."

"But I need it for tomorrow."

"Too late, miss, too late."

His phone rings and he steps away to answer it. "You can look around. Maybe you can find something. But I can't tailor it until Saturday," he says. He starts talking in another language.

We don't have too many foreigners in our town, and if we do, they're not usually black. They're not usually from Africa, and they don't make or fix dresses. This Mamadou is going to give Geraldine's a run for her money. There's a rack of dresses in the most beautiful patterns I've ever seen. I'd definitely stand out wearing one of them. But the shapes are all wrong and boxy. I don't bother trying anything on because the thought of going to the prom is slowly fading.

Stacy would know what to do. She would see all this fabric and think of some creative way to put an outfit together for me. I don't have her creative mind.

I start to walk out of the store when a tall boy steps into the doorway. And it's one of the very few times I've had to look up to see someone's face. He's the same smooth, even dark brown like that man. His eyes are warm and friendly. And he has the brightest smile on this side of the Hudson. His teeth are so incredibly white that I can't stop staring at them—his teeth, of all things.

"Alo!" he says with the same deep singsongy voice as that man. This must be his son, the one who goes to the university.

"Hi," I say.

He nods, smiles, and brushes past me.

But I'm not ready to go. "Are you the one who goes to the university?" I ask. "Your father said so."

"Oh, yeah," he says. His accent is nowhere as thick as his father's. "He means college. He thinks every school is a *university*."

"College? Where?"

"Shaw County. We just moved down here from Buffalo so I can go. Since my father has his own business it's easy to move around."

"Shaw County? That's a community college," I say.

He laughs, flashing his gleaming-white teeth. "I know it's not the best, but . . . I'm learning a lot. I'm Mamadou, by the way." He extends his hand out to me.

I take it and it's cool and dry. "Cherish. So this is your store."

"Ah, me and my father are both named Mamadou. Did you find what you were looking for, Cherish?"

"No. I need a dress by tomorrow," I say, knowing that this is my cue to leave, but I just can't. Not yet.

He studies me. I don't do anything with my body. I just stand there. Then, he motions for me to come back in.

He says something to his father in a different language. His father says something in return. Mamadou Junior says another thing, a little bit louder this time. His father agrees or backs off because his voice trails.

Mamadou Junior removes his book bag and grabs a photo album

from a nearby shelf. "Let me know if you see something you like. I can make it for you. By tomorrow."

"You make dresses?" I ask.

He smiles and nods.

Before I open up the album's pages to models I've never seen before wearing those same bright and colorful dresses as on that flyer, Mamadou comes back over to me with a long yellow measuring tape in hand. I just stare at him.

"I need to take your measurements for your dress," he says.

I don't move at first. Then I swallow hard and stand up straight in front of him—chest out, chin up, and head held high. He gently touches my arms for me to raise them.

Slowly, he takes the measuring tape and wraps it around my waist. He looks up at me to make sure it's okay and smiles. I nod.

In my head, I'm texting Stacy about this new boy in town who goes to Shaw County and looks like an African superhero. And he makes dresses. Stacy, he makes dresses!

And she would dare me to ask him to the prom at the last minute.

In just a couple of minutes, Mamadou has measured my waist, my hips, my chest, the length of my arms, and the length of my legs. Then he asks, "Okay. What would you like?"

CLICK

— — — — —

KATHARINE MCGEE

New York City, 2020

ALEXA

"I HEAR IT might snow later," muttered the taxi driver, with a glance in the rearview mirror.

Alexa Faraday didn't answer, just clutched at the tiny data chip she wore on a rubber band around her wrist, as if it were jewelry. She knew she looked ridiculous; but it was comforting, having the chip with her all the time.

The first snow. That had always been Claire's favorite day of the year. *It's when the world feels full of magic, when anything seems possible*, Claire used to say, with an infectious smile. Then she would drag Alexa outside to twirl in the snow, before coming back in to make cocoa with dollops of whipped cream.

Alexa reached up a hand to wipe brusquely at her eyes. It was still hard, thinking about Claire.

I'm going on a date tonight, she thought, wondering how Claire would have replied. Probably something like, "What shoes are you wearing? Send me a pic!" Alexa glanced down at her sodden gray boots. Definitely not Claire-approved.

Well, it was a big deal that she was going on a date at all. She was really only here to experience the Click algorithm firsthand.

Click had launched a few years ago, when Alexa was in high school. Now she was a junior at NYU studying computer science. It had been a normal enough college experience so far, romantically speaking: a few fumbling hookups with guys in the nearby dorms, until her friend Koty asked her out last spring. It had felt so logical—they were in the same classes, liked all the same things—yet when Koty broke it off, Alexa hadn't even felt sad. Which was how she'd known that they'd never really been more than friends the whole time.

A month later, Claire died.

It was a brain aneurysm. She'd had a terrible headache one day and passed out, and then she was *gone*, just like that. It felt senseless and irrational, and even now, Alexa couldn't fully process it. *She wasn't exhibiting any symptoms*, the doctors assured Alexa and her parents in the ER, *there was no way you could have known*. As if that knowledge might somehow make them feel better.

It wasn't fair. Her expansive, impulsive little sister never got to graduate, to go to college, to actually *live*.

After it happened, Alexa had ignored her dean's offer to take some time off and fled straight back here, to school. Her parents were home in Boston, grieving and alone, and part of her knew she should go be with them. Another, greater part of her needed space. That house was filled with too many memories. It was so much easier in the bustling, comforting anonymity of New York.

Still, her dean had called her in again just last week, and strongly encouraged her to take a few weeks of personal leave. Guess they'd finally noticed her dramatic drop in grades this quarter. Alexa had shaken her head and insisted that she didn't *need* time off. Her classwork was only suffering because she'd been pouring all her energy into something else, something that, in the long run, was much more meaningful than school.

But even Alexa couldn't avoid learning about Click. It was everywhere now—in pop-up ads on her phone and enormous billboards outside her dorm room, and in half the conversations she overheard on the subway. *Computer* magazine had even given it a front-page feature. The future of relationships, people were calling it, the answer to modern romance. The greatest data project ever undertaken. *That* was when Alexa had taken notice. She knew better than to believe Photoshopped ads, but data she understood.

Beneath its sugared, glittering promises of happily ever after, Click was entirely data-driven. The moment Alexa joined the service, it swept the Web with surgical precision, finding every last trace of her digital presence: her Facebook posts, the scans of her high school yearbooks, every item she'd purchased or commented on or "liked." Click compiled it all, a web of lingering digital fingerprints, and used that to formulate its famous thousand-item questionnaire.

All that accumulated data, about all its tens of millions of users, enabled Click to predict romantic potential with terrifying accuracy.

Why not? Alexa had thought once she'd read the article. She was trying to code personality analytics herself; it might help her research. And what did she have to lose, anyway?

When she'd finished the survey, the computer had promptly informed her that she had three hundred and four matches in the United States with a compatibility rating of over ninety-five percent; and was she interested in them all, or just the twenty-eight in the ninety-ninth percentile?

Alexa had hurriedly selected the ninety-ninth percentile. The mere thought of three hundred dates made her dizzy.

As if reading her mind, the taxi TV before her lit up with an all-too-familiar ad of a couple rocking on an old-fashioned swing set, their heads tipped back in laughter. They looked beautiful and carefree and charmed. "When it's right, it just Clicks," a cheerful voice-over reminded her. Alexa shrank further into her seat. She pulled the data chip off her rubber band and began snapping it nervously in and out of her phone.

"I'm actually about to go on a Click date," she shocked herself by saying aloud.

The driver gave a hearty laugh. "Good for you! My daughter joined Click last year, and now she's engaged!"

Alexa knew he meant well, but the statement made her even more anxious.

They pulled to a stop. Alexa held up her phone to confirm payment before fumbling for her coat and her purse, then stepped out onto the curb. The door to the restaurant rose up before her, an enormous iron gateway with a scrolling sign that read *The Aviary*. It was trendy and new, with intimidating white tablecloths and French words painted on the walls; the type of place that Click had clearly approved for first dates.

All the "dates" Alexa had ever been on (she used the term loosely) had involved the computer lab or peanut M&M's or sex; or on a good night, all three.

She realized with slight panic that she'd never actually been on a real, grown-up date. And now she was about to go out with someone without knowing his name or what he looked like or anything at all about him, except that Click had decided they were ninety-nine percent compatible.

The thought of the compatibility rating calmed her. Alexa imagined her personality mapped out in binary code, a ghostly string of ones and zeroes, like the instructions for some program about to be run. People were so complicated—sensitive and unpredictable and erratic—but code made sense. Code could be analyzed, and *fixed*.

She hurried through the front doors to the gleaming dark wood bar, grateful that for once she'd arrived early. "Water, please," she murmured.

The bartender barely glanced over as he poured a glass. It was sparkling water, evanescent little bubbles floating lazily toward the surface. Alexa hated sparkling water, but she was wound too tightly to protest. She took a frantic gulp.

"Hey, I think we're supposed to Click."

A boy, with jet-black curls and tawny skin, leaned on the bar next to her. He gave a blazing smile and a bit of a shrug; as if to say, *I know this is the awkward part, but we're in it together, right?* He held up his phone; and on his gloriously shattered screen Alexa saw the telltale yellow of the Click app.

"Um, yeah," she stammered, reaching in her bag for her phone, as if to prove him right. *He* was in her ninety-ninth percentile of compatibility? Boys like that—sexy, smooth, self-assured—never went for girls like her. Already she felt like the butt of some cosmic joke.

"I'm Raden," the boy went on. Alexa nodded, distracted, sifting through her bag with a rising sense of urgency.

Shit, shit, shit. She realized with a nauseous, sinking feeling that she'd left her phone in the cab. And the data chip was still snapped into the phone.

"I don't . . . I can't . . ." All her work—everything that mattered to her anymore—was on that data chip.

Raden leaned forward, his brown eyes lit up with concern. "Are you okay?"

Alexa shook her head. She was about to scream or cry, she wasn't sure which. "I left my phone in the taxi."

"Want to use my phone to call yours?" Raden offered, holding out his iPhone 12.

Alexa took it mutely, her pulse quickening as she tapped out her own number. *Come on, come* on, she thought, praying that the cabdriver would pick up. But no one answered.

"What if you tried to track it?" Raden offered, but Alexa was already logging in, fingers flying as she answered her elaborate series of security questions. Beneath the spidery cracked glass of Raden's screen appeared a map of New York. And there was her phone, a tiny blue dot struggling valiantly against the traffic of the Holland Tunnel.

She looked up at him, knowing this date was ruined before it even began, but also oddly relieved that she wouldn't have to go through with it. It would never have worked anyway. He was so searingly confident and she was—well, herself.

"Can you help me get my phone back?"

"Okay," he said slowly, as if caught off guard by the question. Then he smiled. "I'm Raden, by the way."

Hadn't he already said that? It took a moment for Alexa to realize what he was doing—giving her an opening to provide her own name. She felt even more foolish. "I'm Alexa," she said, as if that explained everything, and started toward the door.

RADEN

Raden Ashby clung to the subway pole, staring in curious amusement at the petite girl before him. She was pretty in a wispy, ethereal way, with fair hair and eyes, and the sort of translucent skin that comes from spending too much time indoors, as if she were still reflecting the glow of her computer screen. A modern-day digital nymph.

She'd looked so devastated, and embarrassed, when she'd asked for his help getting her phone back. He couldn't help but agree, because some part of him loved playing the hero, and hadn't he always bragged that adventures brought out his best work? So he'd hiked his camera bag higher on his shoulder and followed her out the door.

Now they were on the PATH, racing her phone to New Jersey in complete silence. Alexa hadn't said a word since they boarded the train ten minutes ago. There was a single tan rubber band around her wrist, which she kept snapping anxiously against the pale skin of her forearm.

For once, Raden found himself with a girl, with no clue what to say.

There was something weird about this setup, about being told that you were ninety-nine percent compatible with someone before you even met her—before you even knew her name. It birthed too many expectations. It made him wish that he'd met Alexa the normal way: at a crowded bar where they'd have to shout over the music, where he didn't know anything at all about her. And with more alcohol—definitely more alcohol.

Except he knew he wouldn't have talked to Alexa if it weren't for Click. She was nothing like the girls he normally went for, with their dangly earrings and loud voices, wearing short dresses in primary colors. She was something completely different. It intrigued him, and scared him a little, too.

"Why did you sign up for Click?" Alexa asked, evidently thinking along the same lines.

Because of Lauren. He tried to make light of the question. "Already want to know why 'normal' dating hasn't worked for me? Do you ask all your Click dates this early in the night?"

"This is my first Click date." She kept snapping that rubber band, her entire body held rigidly, stiffly, as if she had a glass of water balanced on her head and her life depended on not spilling it. "I signed up because it seemed like the logical way to go on dates, I guess."

The train rattled around a turn. Raden clutched the central pole tighter to avoid swerving off balance, but Alexa reached at the same time. Her gloved hand landed atop his. She quickly shifted away.

"It's my first Click date, too," he admitted.

"Did your friends talk you into it?"

"More like all the brides I've photographed lately. It's how most of them met their husbands." He instantly felt awkward—he shouldn't have brought up marriage with someone he'd just met—but Alexa didn't seem especially bothered by the comment.

Though she might be slightly more bothered by the truth, which was that he hadn't fully gotten over his ex.

He'd fallen for Lauren fast. But then, love came easily to Raden; he was always tumbling in and out of love to varying degrees. He loved the old woman on his block, with her window box full of daisies; the girl who worked at the coffee shop and always slipped him extra muffins; every bride he'd ever photographed. He couldn't take a decent picture of something without falling in love with it, at least a little.

He could still remember the exact moment he met Lauren. It was at an outdoor concert: she'd stood before him wearing jean shorts, holding a bottle of orange soda, craning her neck to see the stage. Raden couldn't look away from the curve of her neck, the delicate row of piercings up the curve of her ear. Finally he'd lifted her onto his shoulders to give her a better view. When he kissed her that night, she'd tasted like the tart orange soda.

Lauren was the reason he'd signed up for Click. As if by finding someone more compatible—upgrading from her, the way she'd done to him—he could prove that she hadn't really hurt him.

The train turned again, and must have hit a cellular hot spot, because all of a sudden Raden's phone erupted in a series of angry buzzing. Dozens of texts cascaded onto the screen at once. Raden glanced down, curious; and his eyes widened when he saw what was written there.

This night just kept getting more surprising.

ALEXA

Alexa squirmed, trying to focus on the brightly colored ads that flickered over the opposite wall of the subway car. But she couldn't help shooting glances at Raden, at the strong, clean lines of his profile, the way his hands gripped tight to the subway rail, his gray peacoat turning his eyes such a deep brown.

She kept having the strangest urge to reach out and grab hold of him, as if to test whether he was real.

"I'm sorry. You really don't have to stay," she said now, feeling guilty for ruining his night.

"It *is* my phone we're using to track yours," he pointed out.

"I know, I just—"

"Maybe I want to be here," Raden interrupted, with a look she couldn't quite read. "Maybe I'm a sucker for impossible tasks."

She didn't know what that meant. "Well, thank you."

"Besides, my best photos are born out of spontaneity." Raden gestured to a dark bag slung over one shoulder, which Alexa hadn't noticed. "I'm a photography student."

"Oh," Alexa said quietly. How . . . unexpected, and curious, that she'd been matched with someone artistic. "Can I see some of your work?"

Raden shrugged and scrolled through his phone to show her a few images, almost entirely of nature: an enormous waterfall, the stars against a dark velvet sky. Even beneath the cracked screen, Alexa could tell they were incredible. There was something bold, almost audacious about them. They practically shouted at you, daring you to look elsewhere.

"Where did you take these?" she breathed.

"The city, mostly."

"New York?"

He grinned. "Shocking, I know. Some of them are in Riverside Park; some are on rooftops."

"So the bridal portraits—"

"I photograph weddings on the side. It helps pay for college." Raden adjusted the strap of his bag. "You'd be surprised how many couples are okay with just a student, given how much cheaper I am than the professionals."

"That's impressive," Alexa said. These looked professional enough to her.

As they emerged on the Jersey side of the river, Raden's phone buzzed with more incoming messages. He pulled it out of his coat pocket with a frown and tapped out a quick reply. She wondered if he was setting up Clicks with the other girls in his top one percent, since this one had clearly become a flop. She shouldn't care, Alexa reminded herself, not when the contents of the data chip were about to be lost. But some foolish part of her cared anyway.

"Here's our stop," Raden said into the silence, as the train rattled up to the Jersey City PATH station.

As they climbed the steps, Alexa couldn't help feeling that Jersey had put out its worst welcome mat specially for her—all she could see were little spots of ugliness, a dried dog turd on the ground, a dirty boarded-up window, illuminated by the dismal light of a flickering neon bar sign.

Then Raden stepped up next to her, and something about his presence, warm and solid and vaguely sweet-smelling, reassured her. As if he'd turned on a light, and revealed all the ugliness to be just her own fear, cloaked in shadows. She took a deep breath, trying to shake the strange urge to cry. *I'm sorry, Claire. I think my project is really gone.*

Don't give up yet, she could practically hear her sister reply. *You might be surprised.*

"Your taxi's exiting the tunnel." Raden held out his phone so she could see the tiny blue dot moving toward them. They stepped out onto the sidewalk, and Alexa's heart sank.

The highway was a four-lane army of taxis as far as the eye could see, like a surrealist painting come to life. Its yellow smear somehow reminded her of the overbright lemon yellow of the Click app.

"Can you call my phone again?" she asked. Her mind was spinning, trying to calculate just how on earth she was going to find her phone in this sea of taxis.

Raden nodded and called her number, and Alexa took off running.

RADEN

"Keep calling it!" Alexa darted between the cabs, moving slippery and quick like a fish through the oncoming traffic, and Raden saw at once what she was doing. She was trying to locate her phone, in a crowded intersection, by listening for her ringtone.

It was so ridiculous that it just might work.

A moment later he heard her phone. "Just a small-town girl, livin' in a lonely world." And he saw it, sitting innocuously in the passenger seat of a nearby cab, flashing and playing that iconic Journey song. He and Alexa exchanged a glance and then sprinted at the same time, both of them dodging traffic. Alexa cried out as a truck swerved around her; and then the cab was in the left-hand lane, already turning into another street, and they were too late.

Raden grabbed Alexa roughly by the shoulders and pulled her onto the sidewalk. "Stop it. You're going to get us both killed," he exclaimed, but she barely seemed to register his words.

"Where did it go?" Her entire expression was bright and tremulous with hope. Raden wordlessly handed over his phone, realizing as he did that the screen was dark.

"You let it die? How *could* you?" Alexa snapped at the rubber band again, and this time she snapped it hard enough to break. It fell in a forlorn piece onto the dirty street.

"Alexa, it's just a phone," he said quietly. "You can get a new one tomorrow. It's not worth getting hurt over." Though to be honest, the way she'd darted through the streets like the heroine of an action movie *had* been kind of badass.

"It's not about the phone." Her voice sounded raw and ragged at the edges. "It's the data chip snapped into it. There's stuff on there that I can't afford to lose."

"What?"

"Claire," Alexa whispered, and burst into sobs.

"It's okay." Confused, Raden pulled her close and wrapped his arms around her, letting her sob until his overcoat was damp with tears. "What do you mean?" he murmured when she finally stepped back, wiping at her eyes. Who was Claire?

"My sister passed away last summer."

"I'm so sorry." Raden still had one hand in hers, and he gave it a little squeeze. Alexa blinked, as if startled by the physical contact, but didn't take her hand away.

"So I've been building this program, for virtual reality. I did all the coding, and the rendering and the interface . . ." she said haltingly.

Raden didn't understand. "What is it?"

"It brings people back to life." At his shocked expression, she hurried to clarify. "Not literally! It creates a hyperrealistic, personalized avatar of a person—it looks like them, talks like them—so you can have conversations with them after they're gone."

"That's crazy," Raden blurted out, and something electric kindled in Alexa's eyes.

"Crazy is losing your sister—your best friend in the whole world—without ever getting to say good-bye," she told him, and he nodded, chastened by the fire in her voice.

"Anyway, it works a lot like Click. It starts by pulling from the person's online presence, to get a sense of their personality so it can mimic them. But the more data you give it, by uploading e-mails or voice mails or anything else, the better the avatar becomes." She gave a shaky smile. "Lucky for me, Claire had a *big* online presence, so the avatar really sounds like her. I've uploaded everything I could find of hers, every message and tweet and post and comment, to create her avatar. I just . . . like talking to her, sometimes. It helps me," she finished quietly.

Raden couldn't even imagine. He felt unshed tears tightening in his throat. "But why is it on a data chip?" he asked. "I mean, haven't you uploaded it to the cloud?"

"The cloud? Where anyone with half a brain could hack it?" Alexa repeated, as if she'd personally hacked multiple things from the cloud, which for all Raden knew she had. "Everyone knows the only really safe way to protect something is to keep it on a hard drive, locally, and then keep the hard drive with you at all times."

Raden wasn't at all sure that everyone knew that, but it didn't seem right to argue. "Are you going to sell this program, when you're done with it?"

"Of course not. I would never try to make money off grieving people." Alexa took a step back, and her eyes were fierce in the golden light of the streetlamps. "When it's finished, I'm putting it online, for free."

"Then we'll get it back," Raden said, and for the first time that night, he felt certain of it. Now that he understood, he would go to the ends of the earth to get that phone, if need be.

"By the way," he added, because he felt suddenly desperate for Alexa to smile, "Journey is my favorite, too."

ALEXA

Alexa took another sip of her pomegranate iced tea and glanced around the Starbucks, which was the same as every other Starbucks the world over; the same harried people rushing in and out, their eyes glued to their phone screens. She still felt a little embarrassed for the way she'd unloaded on Raden. She hadn't even told her parents about her software program. But Raden had taken it all in stride, with a calm determination that softened the edges of her fear. She would find her data chip, because she had to, and that was that.

Raden shifted next to her, drinking his own pomegranate tea. Alexa had been surprised when he'd ordered the same unusual drink as her, but after all, they were ninety-nine percent compatible. On the table next to her, his phone was plugged into her recharging dock.

"I want to see your photos. In real life. Can I buy one?" she asked, voicing her thoughts aloud.

He smiled. "You'd be my first real customer."

"But they're so good!"

Raden's eyes were very warm and very serious. "No one wants to hang art like that anymore. All they want are little square-shaped selfies they can post online."

"I'm sorry." Alexa thought of the bare walls of her dorm room and winced. They suddenly felt cold and austere, and impersonal.

At least she wasn't guilty of posting the selfies that Raden clearly resented so much. No, that had always been Claire's thing.

She glanced down at his phone. The charge had jumped up to three percent. And the blue dot was back—much closer than before.

"Come on!" she exclaimed, and pulled Raden abruptly to his feet.

RADEN

The touch of Alexa's hand sent a shock up Raden's nerves, like a jolt of electricity, as he hurried after her out the door.

It had started to snow. The snow fell like a light dusting of sugar

— 83 —

over everything, blanketing the city in a still, white enchantment. It froze in tiny clumps on Alexa's hair, thickening her eyelashes.

"This way!" She ran forward into the wind. Her ponytail whipped behind her like a snow-flecked banner.

"Did you ever make snow monkeys when you were a kid?" Raden asked as they came to a stop at an intersection.

"Don't you mean snow angels?"

"In my family we did snow monkeys." Raden lifted one foot and tilted his head, looping his arms in an exaggerated pose to demonstrate. "My older brother made it up, and from then on it was always snow monkeys. My parents even gave us banana peels to make it realistic."

"Claire and I used to run outside and try to catch the snowflakes on our tongue. She liked to say that the snow was magic, and if I caught a perfect snowflake, my wish would come true." Alexa smiled wistfully at the memory. Her breath came in visible puffs against the cold night air.

Raden loved the thought of Alexa believing in magic. He wanted to ask what she'd wished for—what she wished for right now.

The light turned green, and she rose impatiently onto her toes. He took a step closer before she could run off again. "Wait," he breathed, and reached a hand toward her face.

ALEXA

Gently, Raden tucked her hair behind her ear. Alexa's breath caught, as if she'd climbed up a mountain and the air was suddenly dangerously thin.

And then he reached behind him for his camera and took a picture. "The way the light hits you . . . this is incredible," he murmured.

The moment his picture was done, she took off running across the street again. Of course it was the light that he found beautiful. Not her. Stupid, stupid to think that he'd been about to kiss her. She focused all her energies on that blue dot, which was so close now, just around the corner.

She came to a halt outside a divey restaurant, *Jersey's Finest Tacos* handpainted on the sign outside. Whoever had her phone must be in there. Alexa kicked open the door, not waiting for Raden, though she could hear his footsteps in pursuit.

Right away she saw her driver, the same one who'd congratulated her on joining Click: He was in line for a freaking *taco*, her phone in its plain red case clutched in his hands.

"Oh my God," Raden said behind her, with a strangled laugh. "Is he about to trade your phone for a taco?"

The driver caught sight of Alexa and smiled proudly. "It's you! I have your phone!" he announced, as if she didn't already know. He took in Raden standing next to her, and grinned even wider. "Is this your Click date?"

See! She could almost hear Claire exclaiming in triumph. *I told you that magical things happen on the first snow day!*

Alexa barely managed a "thank you" as she reached for her phone. She popped out the data chip and held it tight in her hand, so tight that the plastic pressed angrily into her skin. Then she turned back to Raden. "Thank you for helping me get this back. I'm sorry that our date was ruined." She let out a breath. "I'm sure you have other girls that you've Clicked with, but maybe we could . . ."

Her phone kept buzzing nonstop. Alexa glanced down impatiently, and the first thing she saw was a long string of messages from Click. But they didn't make sense.

She let her eyes skim over the first few, and felt a sudden, awful twist in her stomach. *No,* she thought, *it can't be.*

She was supposed to be on a different date tonight, with someone else. Not Raden. Since Click thought she was already on that date, it had opened a chat room for her and her guy, who'd sent a lot of "where are you???" messages. She swiped over to look at his full profile, which was now visible. His name was Kevin. He was at Harvard for mechanical engineering—God, had he come all the way from Boston, just for her? He looked nice, and pleasant. Not to mention boring.

She glanced up at Raden. "You didn't know that you were on the wrong date?" It came out like a croak.

"Yeah. I messaged her when we were on the train, to cancel."

Alexa nodded, swallowing the urge to cry. She didn't fully understand why she was so upset, except that she'd believed that she and Raden *belonged* together, the way she'd believed in magic when she was a child; with a blind, unquestioning faith. They'd ordered the same drink at Starbucks, had the same favorite song! She'd thought that was proof of their compatibility, of Click's genius at work—but it was just coincidence, just random noise in that endless sea of data.

They hadn't Clicked. Raden wasn't in her top one percent of statistical romantic matches; he wasn't anything at all to her, just a stranger who'd been unlucky enough to meet her at a bar, and get roped into a quest for her data chip.

She should have known, should have realized they were so logically improbable together. And yet.

"I'm sorry," Alexa said shakily. She would never have asked him to stand someone up, if she'd known.

"I'm not." Raden grinned. "Like I said, spontaneity leads to good things."

Her heart began to skip in her chest. "I just thought we'd Clicked . . ." she trailed off, and Raden laughed, as if she'd told a joke.

"Alexa. We *did* click. We don't need permission from an algorithm for that."

Her pulse became even more erratic, her chest tightening in a confused mess of feelings. She felt painfully aware of everything—the data chip in her hand, the cold flecks of snow in her hair, the liquid intensity of Raden's eyes. It was as if she were feeling everything for the first time: the way she'd felt after her first kiss, or after she'd built her first working computer program. As if the entire world was raw and new and bursting with possibility.

Raden leaned in and lightly tucked her hair behind her ear, again. But this time he lowered his lips to hers.

This was how it should feel, she realized, as the kiss deepened and the world seemed to fall silent. She rose up on tiptoe, her blood pounding with a wild, furious joy.

When he finally stepped away, she felt a little dizzy. "So," Raden said, holding out a hand, "now that we've found your phone, I'd like to go on a date. Can I interest you in a taco?"

Alexa took his hand, trying her best to ignore the cabdriver, who was giving them an unironic thumbs-up in the corner.

"I'd love a taco," she declared, and grinned. "I hear they're Jersey's finest."

THE INTERN

— — — — —

SARA SHEPARD

"UH, HEY, CLARA." My boss, Grayson, leaned his tattooed arms on my desk. "I have a favor to ask. But if you don't want to do it, I totally understand."

I sat up straighter. "I'll do it."

He looked skeptical. "I haven't told you what it is yet."

It was my second week interning at V, and I still didn't know what I was doing there. Everyone at the record label was constantly in a state of panic about everything—how the new soap in the bathroom wasn't organic, the ineptitude of band managers, some mysterious metric called "Spotify streams." My first day, Grayson had pointed to a couch near the assistant's desk and said, "Just sit there for now." I was given a stack of *Rolling Stones* to read. Four days passed like that. Grayson had promoted me to my own desk, finally, but I'd received no tasks yet. So I'd completed three *New York Times* Sunday crosswords. I composed endless drafts of e-mails to my best friend, Soledad, but I kept deleting them because they sounded so distant and impersonal. Oh, and I hid out in the bathroom a lot, though conversations stopped whenever I walked in. *I'm not going to tell my father that you hate his shitty record label,* I wanted to scream at the congregating girls, the marketing managers and assistant publicists and junior art directors. *And by the way, he's not such a god. He watches Netflix on the toilet. He overuses the word* utilize.

"So we've got a singer-songwriter in town." Grayson fiddled with the button on his collar. His shirt had little dancing skeletons on it—not Grateful Dead skeletons, all top hats and joy, but bony, ugly things that I could picture doing hostile business takeovers and voting unanimously to test their products on animals. These were skeletons with whom my father commingled. "His name is Phineas Cleary. Really amazing guy. He's been traveling the U.S. for weeks for his album. But with so many other bands here for the festival, we're kind of strapped. You can say no—but, well, he really wants to see a psychic this afternoon, and I'm wondering if you could take him."

I blinked. "Wait, what?"

He held up his hands. "Just take him wherever. There's got to be one in the East Village, right? But seriously, I can find someone else. Just say the word."

I sat up straighter. "No, I'll do it."

Two minutes later, after I finally convinced Grayson I was capable, I called Hexa, my old French tutor. After we finished our lessons on irregular verbs or whatever, she'd read my tarot cards.

She didn't even need a guidebook like Soledad. Of course she knew of a psychic. "Best one in town," Hexa said. "I'll pull some strings, get you in today. And by the way, are you hanging in there? I know you must miss her. I know it must be *so hard*. If you ever need anyone—"

"I have to go," I interrupted, hanging up before she could go *there*.

I glanced around and noticed a marketing girl staring at me. As soon as our eyes met, she looked hurriedly away, pretending to be engrossed in her computer. I flushed. So what if I was a leper at V? I didn't want to be there, either. When my father suggested—no, *mandated*—that I work this summer, I thought he'd stick me in the company's legal department. I saw myself filing papers in a dark back room, ordering stuff on Shopbop on the company credit card, feeding organic popcorn to the birds during lunch. It didn't sound so bad. But then he put me at his *record label*. Not that he had any clue, but my favorite Pandora channels were Gregorian Chants, people whispering, and sappy songs from the eighties my mother used to love—John Mellencamp, Bryan Adams. I knew every line of "Run to You."

Still, that didn't mean I wanted to be an outright failure. I was going to show everyone. I was going to kick this psychic thing right in its psychic ass.

— — — —

Two hours later, I stood on a nondescript block on the Upper West Side. A child squatted on the sidewalk across the street, drawing swirls with chalk. Nannies, chattering away on their phones, pushed complicated baby strollers. Three identical curly-coated dogs went after the same chicken bone in the gutter.

My phone buzzed. Grayson. *Just checking in. Call if there are problems.*

I looked up and down the street, avenue to avenue. I didn't have a very good idea of who I was looking for. According to Google, Phineas Cleary was eighteen years old, only a year older than I was. He had two albums out: *Feints* and *Only Then.* The pictures of him online were blurry renderings—arched neck, hair over the face, zigzagging stage lights. Fans commented that his music was "moody" and "dark" and "like a punch to the gut."

"Clara?"

A tall guy had materialized in front of me. He had a yellow-and-maroon scarf wrapped around his neck—very Harry Potter. His wild, thick, blue-black hair was cut in choppy peaks that ended at his pointy chin, and his wide-set brown eyes were framed with the longest lashes I'd ever seen. His expression—an appealing mix of awkwardness, cleverness, and kindness—reminded me of L, the detective from *Death Note*, an anime I was obsessed with when I was in middle school. I'd had a love-hate with L because he battled against a guy who tried to play God, but now I understood why L was so determined. No matter how much any one of us wanted to play God, no matter how much we wished it were possible, the world wasn't supposed to be in the hands of just one person.

"Are you Clara?" The guy's voice was midrange, raspy, and heavily accented. When I nodded, he thrust out his hand. "Grand. I'm Phineas."

We shook. His hand was warm and soft. The tips of his fingers were callused from guitar playing. His jubilance surprised me. I was expecting a storm cloud over this guy's head. A leering crow on his shoulder.

"So are you new to V?" Phineas asked, studying me carefully.

"Uh, sort of." I caught sight of my reflection in a car window and winced. My hair was a snarled mess. My eyeliner was a little smudgy. I was wearing one of my mother's Alexander McQueen dresses, a floor-sweeping maxi with delicate roses embroidered into the silk. I intended to wear everything from my mother's closet this summer. My father had been so quick to bring in cleaners, to haul everything to a charity auction, but I'd managed to stash a few items away.

"Where did you work before this?" Phineas asked.

"Nowhere, really." I wanted to kick myself. I totally screamed *high school student*. The thing I *should* have said, which would make me look older and more sophisticated, was that I'd been at NYU. Studying or whatever. What else did people do in college? My cousin, who went to NYU, took a lot of pictures of his privates and posted them on Snapchat. My other cousin went to UVA and got arrested for jumping out a window onto the hood of a police car.

I awkwardly pointed at the brownstone. "So, um, this is the place."

"Ah." He pushed his hands into his pockets and stared at the building. "Interesting."

"My friend says he's the best."

Someone buzzed us up. There was chipped paint on the walls. A unicycle leaned against the mailboxes. The elevator had one of those pull-across grates that always made me feel like I was in a Hitchcock movie. A man in a white tee, jeans, and socks answered the door of apartment 4B. I felt disappointed—weren't psychics more ostentatious? But Phineas smiled and offered his hand.

"I'm Dan," the psychic said, leading us into the apartment. It was bare except for a futon couch and a small overturned trunk that served as a coffee table. My phone buzzed again. Another text from Grayson. I silenced it. "You can come right through here." Dan gestured to a small door off to the right, then looked back at me. "You too?"

"Yes, come for a reading," Phineas said. "My treat."

"Oh, no." I backed away. "I'm fine."

Dan narrowed his eyes. He hadn't shaved in a couple days. "Are you sure? You could use my help."

"I'm fine," I repeated a little more forcefully.

Dan's face softened. "Well. It's obvious you're suffering a great deal from what happened."

"Nothing happened!" The words lodged in my throat, nearly choking me.

Dan didn't seem to hear. "But just know that someday, you'll be okay. You'll be yourself again. I already see it."

My whole face went hot. A few hideous beats passed. I could feel Phineas staring at me. After what seemed like ten years, I smiled as though clueless, shrugged my shoulders, and plopped down on the couch. "Do your thing. I'll be right here."

Dan gave me a beatific smile, then turned away. After he shut the door, I stared out the window, even though it was just a view of an airshaft, until my vision blurred. My mind felt thick, deep, and soundless. An airless vacuum in deep space.

When Phineas came out of the room, he seemed refreshed, as if he'd just stepped out of a hot shower. I ushered him out of the apartment quickly, lest Dan accost me again. "I'm sorry about that guy," I said when we were back on the street. "He was a last-minute suggestion from a friend."

"Are you kidding? He was totally on point." Phineas's eyes gleamed. "Everything he told me was eerily accurate. He was the best psychic ever."

"So what did you talk about?"

He looked at me square. His eyes were copper-colored, like shiny coins, and they made something inside me shimmer. For a moment, it looked like he was about to say something serious, perhaps about what Dan had said to me.

If it was about me, I decided, I would leave. Right then. Screw V. I didn't care.

But then he said, "I asked for all the upcoming lottery numbers for next year. And which stocks are going to hit. And which team I should bet on in cricket. I'm sick of this songwriting shit. I want to make money the easy way."

My mouth fell open. "Psychics can *do* that?"

He dissolved into laughter. "Of course not. We talked about my goals for the coming year." He hooted some more. "But wouldn't that be nice?" Then he looped his arm through my elbow. "Come on. How about we check out Central Park?"

I blinked. I thought about saying that I needed to go back to work, but then I thought of the stares, my blinking computer screen, and hours of nothing to do. Phineas's coppery eyes met mine, and it was decided. If Phineas wanted to see the park, we'd see the park. I pointed toward the avenue to the left. "It's that way. Let's go."

— — — —

On Seventy-Second Street, Phineas paused in front of the Dakota and remarked that he couldn't believe John Lennon had been shot outside a structure so beautiful. Inside the park, I led him to Strawberry Fields and pointed out the *Imagine* mosaic. There were a few rose petals strewn over the words. I shuddered, remembering the last time I'd seen flowers strewn over a cold, gray slab.

"You all right?" Phineas asked.

"Want to go see the big fountain that overlooks the pond?" I asked brightly, pretending not to hear. "It's been in a million movies."

I walked hurriedly there, avoiding bikers and joggers and an NYPD cop on a Segway. Phineas matched my pace, his arms swinging. "You're a fast walker."

"Everyone in New York walks this fast." I pointed past the fountain to the sun-dappled water, my voice overly loud. "I think I've seen at least ten people tip their rowboats into that lake. So embarrassing, right?"

Phineas's gaze remained on me for a beat, but then he dutifully looked at the boats. Across the water, waiters scurried to and fro at the boathouse restaurant. My mother used to take me there every summer before Shakespeare in the Park. We'd order oysters, which I loved but she hated. I could still picture her face when she drank one down—her scrunched-up eyes and puckered mouth. Sometimes she pretended to choke to make me laugh.

I flinched, pushing the memory away. When I looked over, Phineas was tapping on his phone. Then his gaze fell to a girl across the fountain who was playing a game on a handheld tablet. She kept swearing under her breath and kicking out her legs kung-fu style. "She's really getting into that," I muttered.

"If my mom were doing her family tree," Phineas mused, "that lady would be known as *Addicted to Candy Crush*."

I looked up at him. "Huh?"

He pushed his hair out of his eyes. "My mother is really into our family tree, especially our various traits. But not like, how I got my blue eyes from Uncle Derrick or whatever—more random stuff. She writes it all down. Thinks she's an anthropologist. Has a little book on us and everything. Anyway, it's how I assess everyone these days. And that girl on the bench? Her genealogical marker would be *Addicted to Candy Crush*. Or whatever it is she's playing."

I cocked my head. "What were some other traits?"

"Let's see. *Mean streak*. That's one. Apparently that flourished in Aunt Sadie and passed on to my brother. *Can't stay away from pretzels* is another gem. And *Incredible lung capacity*. I had a great-grandfather who could remain underwater for three and a half minutes, and he passed that on to me. I'm gifted at underwater swimming."

I thought for a moment. "My father has this thing about loading the dishwasher. If our housekeeper hasn't put the forks in just right, he'll do it all over. That's the first thing he goes to when he gets home—the dishwasher, to make sure those forks are all facing the same way. So that could be his. *Forks must all point a certain way*."

He nodded. "My father is like that, except with plants. He won't pull up anything, not even a weed. *Lover of plants, not people.*"

I held up a finger. "How about *Hates the sound of chewing?*"

"Ah, yes, very much a thing." Phineas tilted his head toward the sky and thought for a moment. "And then there's *Won't go out in the rain. Terrible with children. Thinks dinosaurs existed at the time of Jesus.*"

"*Has trouble with map-reading,*" I threw in, laughing a little. At least, I think it was a laugh. It was an unfamiliar sound, coming from me.

"*Picks nose and rolls it into a little ball.*"

I giggled. "*Cleans fingernails with edge of paper.*"

"*Can't remember birthdays.*"

"*Still obsessed with Christmas,*" I said, and then added, "That would be mine." Or, well, that *had* been mine. Before. All at once, I wished it were still mine. I wished loving Christmas still defined me.

He leaned against the railing. Our eyes met, and I felt chills down my spine. There was something so inviting about his gaze. "What's the best Christmas present you've ever received?" he asked.

"A book about Easter Island." My answer was automatic.

He smiled. "Ah, yes. Those *heads*. Who gave you that?"

"My mother." I averted my eyes.

"Ah." Phineas nodded. "She must be good at picking out gifts. Maybe that's her trait."

"She . . ." I stopped before I gave the new, knee-jerk answer. "Yes. That is her trait," I finished. I smiled. It felt like a new light had come into the room. It was nice putting my mother in the present tense again. I liked bringing her back to life.

— — — —

We went into Belvedere Castle and looked at the papier-mâché birds. We walked through the sports fields and watched a game of kiddie T-ball. We raced to the reservoir. I won. We stood at the gate, staring at the tranquil water. The city sparkled over the tufted tops of the trees. The air felt fresher here, and it was almost like I could breathe a little easier, too.

Suddenly, Phineas turned to me. Ran his eyes over my face. I felt a thrill, like I was in a roller-coaster car that had just descended a huge hill. "Have dinner with me tonight," he said.

I was so stunned that I laughed. "What?"

"At my hotel. I'm so sick of restaurants. I'll make you macaroni and cheese," he answered.

"From the box?" I asked.

"Well, yes, because that's probably all I could manage in a micro-wave. If that's okay."

There was a lump in my throat. "O-okay."

He touched my hand. I stared at it, not knowing what to do, and then there was a flicker of . . . *something*. A jolt. "But before that, I have to do something first," he said.

He started down the steps and led me to the little stone area across from Ninetieth Street and Fifth Avenue. Someone standing next to a water fountain waved at him, and I did a double take. Had Grayson *followed* us here?

"Here you go, man," Grayson said, handing Phineas an

instrument case. Phineas grabbed it, slapping him on the back. As I whirled around, a crowd had gathered by the statue of Fred Lebow, the famous runner. Someone was setting up a microphone and several amplifiers. People were talking on their phones. I saw a few girls from the V office gathered by the road, texting and talking. A fan shrieked when she saw Phineas, and others started cheering.

Phineas broke away from Grayson and trotted back to me, registering my confusion. "I'm doing a pop-up concert. I thought of it as we were walking, and Grayson was on board. We leaked details on Instagram and Snapchat an hour ago." He spread out his arms. "Surprise!"

"Oh," I said weakly. I wasn't upset he hadn't told me before—it wasn't like anyone told me *anything*—but I was disappointed that my time with Phineas had ended. Now I had to share him with all these people.

"You'll stay, right?" Phineas's hand was on my arm again. He looked hopeful and almost scared, like he'd done something wrong. "Please stay."

"Sure," I said, managing a smile. Phineas beamed, and after patting me on the shoulder, he ambled to a roadie fiddling with a microphone. A girl passed in front of me wearing a Phineas Cleary T-shirt. Phineas's face was on the front, his brow furrowed in concentration. His eyes looked bottomless.

After a moment, Grayson sidled over. "Going all right?" He'd changed into a Buzzcocks T-shirt, a pair of black skinny jeans, and worn Dr. Martens. There was a cigarette tucked behind one ear, a Bluetooth earpiece in the other.

"It's fine," I said, suddenly noticing that the bottom of my dress was muddy from all the walking.

"I'm shocked Phineas was up for this," Grayson mused. "Usually when he's in town, he keeps to himself. Stays in his room. What did you say to get him to do a pop-up concert?"

I shrugged. "Nothing. Just showed him around the park."

Grayson was about to say something when Phineas tapped the microphone. All heads swiveled his way, including mine. He strummed a chord, then launched into a song. At the very first note, my breath froze in my chest. His voice was molten. The guitar was angelic. Chills danced up my spine; goose bumps prickled my arms.

Everyone else was transfixed, too, staring at Phineas as though he were a newly discovered species. Girls in Phineas T-shirts swayed and mouthed the words. And I found myself mouthing the words, too, even though that made no sense—I'd never heard his songs before now. Suddenly, I realized why: This was an old song from the eighties, "Bizarre Love Triangle." One of my mother's favorites.

I felt a walnut-size lump in my throat. I cupped my hand over my mouth and dove through the crowd, staggering across the street out of the park and coming to a stop in front of a Fifth Avenue high-rise.

I placed my hands over my face, trying to blot out the world, but the sickness and the spinning and the clenching feeling inside me was still there. "Oh God," I whispered, because that cold, airless space in my mind didn't feel so airless anymore. I couldn't stop picturing my aunt Rosie shaking me awake that awful morning. *Clara*, she'd whispered, her voice urgent. I'd known what she was going to say even before I opened my eyes. I'd tried to stay awake through my mother's last night on earth, but I'd failed. My mother was still lying in the hospital bed when Rosie brought me in, but it wasn't her any-more. Her skin was gray. Her lips were blue. There was something so empty about her that I'd stalled in the doorway, afraid, my whole being freezing hard and solid.

"Clara?"

I shot up, peering through blurry, teary vision. Phineas stood on the sidewalk, his guitar still slung across his chest. He was out of breath. He looked so tall all of a sudden. So singularly big in a city of tiny people.

"Wh-what are you doing?" I demanded. "I-is your concert over?"

He shook his head. "I walked out right in the middle of a song. I saw you run off. I was worried."

I turned stiffly away from him, noticing the Metropolitan Museum in the distance, stretching a full city block like an aircraft carrier. "You don't have to worry about me."

Phineas flung the guitar to one side so that it hung purselike on his hip. "*Someone* needs to worry about you."

I turned on him, ready to lash out. Everyone *was* already worried about me, I wanted to say. Everyone stared at me like I was a freak, mostly because I didn't want to talk, mostly because I didn't cry, mostly because I was numb. But didn't they realize I was trying to *spare* them from my pain?

But when I opened my mouth to tell Phineas this, a sob came out instead. It was weak, not much more than a kitten's cry. I pressed my lips together, mortified, and my angry spell was broken. "Go back to your concert," I begged. "Everyone loves you. Everyone wants to hear you. Just go."

"Clara," Phineas said softly, touching my hands. "Listen. The concert doesn't matter. I just . . ." He paused, collecting himself. "I've been wandering around this country, on this fucking tour, for *weeks*. It's lonely. People talk around you, there's always someone there, but it's fucking lonely. And I think you understand that."

A gust of wind pressed against my side. I did understand. The day my mother died, I was immediately surrounded. It was like people thought if I was left alone, I might slip away, too. Even now, whenever I came home, there was a housekeeper there, or a tutor, or the dog walker. Cars waited for me at the curb to take me to friends' houses, activities, volunteer opportunities.

But the company felt lonelier than being alone did. At least if I was alone, I could be myself. I could make my own choices. I could grieve. With people, I was always in this smiling in-between, wanting to cry but feeling I had to put up a front that I was healing.

"You made me feel less lonely today," Phineas said. "You made me feel less lost."

A single bead of sweat dripped down his forehead, dampening his hair. I wanted to be angry, I wanted to be tough, but suddenly I felt dough-soft. "You really left the concert for me?" I asked in a small voice.

"I really did."

"My father runs the parent company that owns this label. You knew that, yes?" I blurted out.

"Yes." He lowered his eyes. "But I only just found out. I asked Grayson who you were before I went on."

"And my mother. Grayson told you that, too?"

His throat bobbed. "I'm really sorry, Clara. I wish I'd known."

The look on his face had shifted into something so heartbreakingly sad, I actually wanted to hug *him*. But then I shrugged. "Well, it's probably better she isn't here to see me working at V. She always kind of hated that my dad had a record label. She thought record labels stole artists' souls."

Phineas just looked at me. A taxi swished by, letting out a loud honk.

"And I'm so much better off, really," I heard myself go on, as though my mouth had separated from my body. "She was always telling me to fix my hair and look nice for company and not to eat with my fingers. Now I can eat with my fingers whenever I want." I grimaced. It sounded so absurd. "Except . . . I don't want to eat with my fingers." My voice cracked. "And I want someone to tell me to fix my hair. I want *her* to tell me. Except I'm supposed to be strong. I'm not strong, though. And it's crap. It's. All. Crap."

I stared at him, challengingly. I waited for him to say something pitying or to ignore my outburst, like my father did, or suggest I needed to visit my shrink, like my father also did.

Phineas's eyes flicked back and forth, as if he was slowly processing every inch of the moment: the smell of the sewer, the sound of the traffic, the glinting crystal collar on the dog passing by. Then he tipped his mouth to my ear. "Before I left school, we were studying volcanoes. Not the way they work, but the cultural stories behind them. I know every volcano myth known to man, not just the ones about sacrifice. There was this one about Pele, Hawaii's volcano goddess. She got angry a lot, and whenever she did, she could make volcanoes erupt. She stomped her feet and caused earthquakes and created other fiery devastations by slamming her walking stick into the ground. You just look at Pele the wrong way and she'd wreak a natural disaster on you. I thought she was awesome. A real *warrior*, you know? A strong woman. She could make shit *happen*."

"Huh," I said, laughing unconvincingly, because I didn't know where this was going.

"I look at you, and I see Pele," Phineas said to me, taking both of my hands in his and shaking them. "You are Pele. You just don't know it."

I stared back at him, wanting to laugh. It sounded like more mumbo jumbo, like his devotion to psychics. And I so wasn't Pele. I was about as far from Pele as one could get. Was there a mealy-mouthed goddess? A scared, defeated goddess? That's who I'd be.

But when he said it again—*you are Pele*—I shut my eyes and tried to imagine it. I tried to picture myself conjuring up high winds, driving rain, even a tsunami.

As I made myself Pele, the wind around us began to blow. And then, like magic, it started to rain. I opened my eyes and stared at the wet drops hitting the sidewalk. "Holy shit," I whispered.

Phineas gaped at me. "Holy shit," he echoed. Then I noticed. A man was hosing off the sidewalk in front of a luxury high-rise, and some of the spray had hit our backs. It wasn't rain at all, just hose water. But still. For those moments, I'd *felt* like Pele. I'd created rain.

I looked at Phineas and started to laugh. And cry, too. Phineas pulled me toward him. My hip hit his guitar, and the strings made a dissonant *clang*, but I barely noticed because his lips were suddenly touching mine. I closed my eyes, my heart thudding so hard it was making me tremble, and I felt him pull me closer, closer, until we were stuck together, until we were melded into one. Then we pulled back and laughed. His eyes crinkled, and the tears ran down my cheeks, and he pressed his forehead to mine and then kissed my temples, my nose, my lips. "It's okay," he said. "It's really okay. It's like what Dan said. Someday, you'll be yourself again. But you know what? That doesn't have to be today."

"Okay," I said shakily. Maybe he was right. I'd felt something today, which was more than I'd done in months. As for tomorrow, who knew? I'd quit or not quit V, I'd reconcile with my father or fall more out of touch with him than ever, and Phineas would move on to perform in Philadelphia and then Atlanta, and maybe we'd talk every day or never talk again. But it didn't really matter right then. All I could think about was that water hitting the backs of my legs and how good it felt that Phineas was here, with me, telling me it was okay.

And how proud my mother would be if she knew I'd just conjured up a storm.

SOMEWHERE THAT'S GREEN

— — — — —

MEREDITH RUSSO

NIA

"YOU'RE NOT TRYING out for a girl part?" Lucian said. His tone was distant as he furrowed his brow and shuffled through cards with pictures of sheep, bricks, and lumber on them.

"I don't think I have the vocal range," Nia said. The tip of her tongue poked through her teeth as, with the delicacy of an artisan, she placed the last of her little wooden meeple atop the pyramid she'd been building instead of paying attention to the game.

"Bull," Lucian said. Nia arched an eyebrow. "Audrey's, like, nothing but falsetto. You could do that."

"Look," Nia said. She sniffed and flicked a purple meeple onto its side. "I feel like the school's barely tolerating the whole bathroom thing. If I start taking roles from the 'real' girls, too, they might burn me at the stake."

"Ah." Lucian pursed his lips and drummed his fingers on a stack of cards. "Yeah."

"Which is why Audrey II's so perfect," Nia said. "It's not a boy or a girl, just a terrible alien space monster, which is totally in my wheelhouse—"

"—transgender student using the girl's bathroom at a local school," the TV blared, drawing Nia's attention across the room where her dad sat with his feet on the coffee table. "A crowd has gathered at city hall to protest the school district's decision. We've got Carlita Fernandez on the—"

"Booooo!" Nia said. She cupped one hand around her mouth and threw board game pieces at the screen. "*Boo!* Change the damn channel!"

"Hey!" Lucian said, snatching as many meeple and sheep tokens out of the air as he could. "Hey, come on."

"How about you watch your language before I watch it for you?" Nia's dad said, turning to her with a look that stopped her in her tracks.

"Sorry, Dad," she said.

"Yeah you are," he said, turning his attention back to the screen and unpausing the DVR. "Throwing things in my house. Throwing your *friend's* things in my house. Pick all that up." Nia wanted to roll her eyes and groan as she did it, but the memory of The Look was still fresh and she didn't dare confront it again, so she did as she was told. Lucian started to help, but Nia's dad snapped to get his attention. "No, no, no. She wanted to act a fool, she can clean it up. She's a big girl, let her do it. You go get a soda and chill with me."

"Hella," Lucian said before disappearing into the kitchen.

"That's not how you use that word! It's an intensifier, not a noun!" Nia yelled, earning a much milder glare from her father, which she returned with a sheepish grin. "What? I love him but he's *corny*."

"It's part of my charm, though," Lucian said, jogging back from the kitchen with a soda and hopping over the back of the couch. He flashed Nia a perfect grin and winked. "Lull them into a false sense of security with show tunes, malapropisms, and European board games, then broadside them with Lucian, World's Greatest Lover."

"World's Greatest . . . ?" Nia's dad said, looking at Lucian like he'd just started speaking in tongues. "Boy, you are *seventeen years old*! 'World's Greatest Lover' my ass."

"That's what she said," Nia said, grinning like an idiot. But her father didn't notice; his eyes were glued to the television. She looked over her shoulder and saw a blond girl in an orange cardigan in front of town hall's big Corinthian pillars, fidgeting and pulling at her hands like someone had a gun to her head just off screen. Nia recognized her. She ran with the Christian crowd and pretty much kept to herself. The junior class alone was 1,300 strong, but Nia was a people person and she always remembered a face, especially one as cute as the blond girl's, though the whole "fundamentalist transphobe" thing certainly took a few points off her cuteness quotient.

"We are all God's creatures—is, uh, what I say, really. But, I mean, if the school lets, um, Nia use the bathroom because he—because she says she's a girl—"

"Dad, *please* change the channel!" Nia said. She threw herself to the floor and groaned, wishing she could fast-forward to graduation and, hopefully, a time in her life when the local news didn't run stories about where she went to pee. She wasn't the only trans kid at her school, of course. Nashville was a relatively progressive city, sometimes, in its way, and the sheer mass of students guaranteed, statistically, at least a handful of people like her. But Nia was the only one with a parent supportive enough to let her transition, and Nia was the only one who had been willing to put her foot down and demand access to the correct facilities—or, well, her dad had when it occurred to him one day that his daughter really was his daughter and his charming, stifling, fatherly protectiveness kicked in. No daughter of his was going to shower with a bunch of teenage boys. Nia pretended not to care about the news report, but they both knew it was a shell, that she only distanced herself because of how scared she was, how apocalyptic the stakes seemed.

"—a real risk to the, uh, biological girls," the girl on-screen continued, her voice quavering, "because then can't any boy come in? It's horrifying."

"Maybe you don't take this seriously," Nia's dad said, turning the volume up to match her voice, "but *I* do. Just because the school's on your side now don't mean they'll stay that way, and we need to keep abreast—"

"I get it, Dad, okay? I get it," Nia said as she returned to picking up pieces.

"Who's Lexie Thompson?" a voice called. Lexie stood up from the fountain and wiped her mouth, craning her neck to scan the crowd.

"No way!" another voice yelled, but this one she recognized: Lucian Jimenez, the boy from U.S. History. She turned toward the voice, Lucian's shaggy mane unmistakable even in the crowded hall, and made her way carefully through the crowd, muttering quiet apologies like machine-gun fire. She found him and a dozen other kids huddled around the bulletin board beside Ms. Gunnerson's drama class. "She didn't even tell me she auditioned."

"Did I get a part?" Lexie said. The entire crowd turned to her, looking more confused than anything, which made Lexie want to melt into the tile and disappear. Lucian grinned and pulled her forward, tapping on a list of names.

"You sly dog, you got *the* part." She followed his finger up the cast list for the school's fall production of *Little Shop of Horrors* to *Audrey* and gasped when she read the name next to it: *her* name.

"But I didn't—" Lexie started, her eyes going wide. "I didn't think. I just . . . You made it sound fun, so I thought I'd try, but I didn't mean to—"

"This is amazing!" Lucian said. He squeezed her shoulder and grinned.

"Yeah," Lexie squeaked. He kept talking, something about rehearsal schedules (how was she going to make room for this *and* church on Wednesdays?) and getting her measurements to the tech theater kids, but to Lexie it was mostly static. Her eyes drifted back down the page, locking on the line just below her name, to the entry for *Audrey II*. The name "Nia Robinson" was right there in black ink, plain as day, but her mind had trouble latching on to it. She hadn't known Nia was auditioning. It hadn't even occurred to her that a transgender would *want* to be in a musical, though now that she thought about it she felt a little reflexive wave of embarrassment because obviously they were people, right? With the same ambitions as everyone else? Her stomach lurched and she started working out the fastest route to a bathroom when Lucian's voice cut through again.

"So you *have* to come with us to Vaughn's farm on Saturday," he said.

"Whose—Huh?" Lexie tucked a strand of gold hair behind her ear and blinked. "Vaughn?" Lucian pointed to a guy nearby with a red kaffiyeh and oversize knit cap who only gave her the faintest nod before returning to a conversation with a girl Lexie didn't know.

"He's the Dentist. He said we can have a party this weekend. It was gonna be small, but now? Preemptive cast party, I think."

"But Nia will be there," Lexie said, her voice barely audible over the crowd. Lexie had seen Nia and Lucian sharing a table during lunch, but they were usually with a crowd. She wasn't sure how well Lucian actually knew the other girl, and she'd always been too nervous to ask. "Right?"

"Ah," Lucian said. He rubbed his knuckle against his bottom lip. "Yeah. True."

"Won't that be weird?"

"Will it?" Lucian said. He turned toward the crows with a shrug, and Lexie noticed an odd tension lurking at the corner of his eye. "You could talk to her about it."

"I think I would die if I tried," Lexie said. She was almost certain she had some kind of anxiety disorder, which would probably explain the constant jitters, the jumpiness, and the nauseous panic attacks, but her parents didn't believe in psychiatry or secular therapy, so she couldn't do much about it except try to breathe.

"You might be surprised," Lucian said, not looking at her. "She's kind of intense, but under that she's a good person. Have you *ever* even said hi to her, actually?"

". . . no."

"Hm," Lucian said, then shrugged again. "Well, it's not like you'll have to talk. She won't jump you or anything. Just promise you'll come, okay?"

"There won't be drinking or anything, right?" Lexie asked. She hoped the answer was yes, there would, not because she wanted to drink (she didn't, because underage drinking was a *crime* and she wasn't a *criminal*) but because it would be an excuse to bow out without seeming rude or stuck up.

"Nah," Lucian said. "The techies usually pregame, but that's it." He looked haunted for just a moment. "Don't cross them, by the way."

"O-okay."

"So I'll see you there?" he said.

"I'll ask my parents," she said, praying her parents would say no. She continued her prayer all through third and fourth periods, barely taking any notes on chemical equations and supply and demand, only stopping her constant entreaties to God when school ended and her mom picked her up. Lexie was normally embarrassed that she didn't have a car, but now it was a kind of relief. If she'd had a car of her own, she suspected she might have just gotten in and driven into the sunset to start a new life at a new school.

"How was your day?" her mom asked when she got in.

"I auditioned for a musical," Lexie said. She expected her mom to look angry, or at least sarcastically amused, but she just looked surprised. "I got the lead. *A* lead."

"That's fantastic! Oh, Lex, you've always been so good in choir—this is *perfect*. What's the play?"

"*Little Shop of Horrors*," Lexie said. That, at least, should get the reaction she was hoping for.

"Hmm." Her mom puckered her lips and tapped the steering wheel for a moment but then just shrugged. "I would have preferred *Joseph and the Amazing Technicolor Dreamcoat* or *Godspell*, but *Little Shop* isn't . . . too bad."

Lexie's stomach bottomed out and her shoulders sagged. She'd *prayed*. She'd prayed *so hard*. Her mother's insistence on moral outrage at every opportunity had dominated Lexie's life for the past seventeen years, but now, when she actually needed it, it was gone. Why had she auditioned for the play? It seemed so stupid and impulsive now, but when Lucian had told her about the story she'd gone home and watched a video of Audrey's song "Somewhere That's Green," and something deep inside her had resonated with the woman from the slums dreaming of a better life. She'd signed up without thinking, and now here she was.

"My parents let me stay up and watch it when I was ten. I developed quite the crush on Rick Moranis," her mom said.

"You *what*?" Lexie balked, this revelation momentarily distracting her from the doom awaiting her on Saturday.

"Oh, honey," her mom said. She shook her head and smiled. "I forget you've never seen your father without the mustache. My type hasn't really changed."

"Mom!" Lexie said. She covered her face and her mother laughed, but Lexie understood she was only delaying the inevitable. Finally, as they passed the vet's office near their neighborhood, she took a deep breath and spoke. "The rest of the cast invited me to a party."

"Oh wow!" her mom said, smiling wider than Lexie had seen in a long time. She felt like her chest was imploding as she realized that God really hadn't listened. "Lexie, that's so *good*! Your first high school party!" Her expression grew suddenly serious. "There won't be drinking will there?"

I could lie, Lexie thought. *I could tell her there will in fact be drinking, and then she'll say I can't go, and I won't have to face Nia.* But she could no sooner lie than a walrus could tap-dance, and she knew it, or she would have just told Lucian she had an important project or something. She *especially* couldn't lie to her own mother—except . . .

"No," she said.

"And you promise you won't have sex?"

"Mom!" Lexie slapped her hands over her face and gasped, though not for the reason her mother probably assumed. "No, Mom. You know I'm not like that." Her mom actually didn't know the extent to which Lexie was "not like that," and she hoped she never found out.

"I know, baby, but you don't know what boys are like." Lexie lowered her hands and blinked. "They can be insistent. Will there be an adult to supervise?"

"I don't think so," Lexie said, her spirit soaring. Maybe she'd say no over *this*. Her mom thought for a while, but nodded as they pulled into the driveway.

"You *are* seventeen," she said. "Your grades are perfect and you've never gotten in trouble." She nodded again, then turned to Lexie and smiled. "I think we can trust you. Just promise you'll check in."

"Okay," Lexie said. Her eyes drifted down to her lap.

"What's the matter?" her mom said. She was half in, half out of the car, a concerned look on her face. "You should be excited."

"It's just . . . Nia's going to be there."

"Who?" her mom said, but then there was a flash of recognition. "You're not sharing a dressing room, are you?"

"She's Audrey II," Lexie said, hating how her mother's eye twitched over the feminine pronoun. "So she shouldn't need a costume." Her mother waved her hand and gave a dismissive shake of her head.

"Just stay away from her. This whole thing should be over soon anyway."

Lexie wanted to ask for clarification on *that*, but her mom was already headed for the front door, and most of her was sure she probably didn't want to know.

NIA

"Please just be nice," Lucian said. "To Lexie, I mean."

Nia reached over without taking her eyes off the road and flipped Lucian's newsie cap into the backseat, too frustrated to laugh at his screech of protest. She'd been shocked when Lucian had admitted that he and Lexie were friendly—she noticed he used the word *friendly* instead of *friends*, as if testing the waters. She knew Lucian had other friends, that obviously they didn't spend every second of every day together and he talked to other people . . . but still, the idea that he'd spent time with that Lexie girl felt like a betrayal. And now they were in a freaking musical together.

"Why should I?" Nia said. She flexed her fingers on the steering wheel. They were only half an hour from Vaughn's farm and the tension was starting to get to her, heating her cheeks and making her back hurt. Thanks to Lexie, the school district was reconsidering its position. They would let her dad know their decision this weekend.

"This isn't a *game*, Lucian," she said. "I can pee in the teachers' lounge during lunch, but I don't have my phys ed credits yet. I *specifically* put them off because I didn't want to change in a locker room with boys. Because I was *scared* of changing in a locker room with boys." She sucked in a shuddering breath through her teeth. "Before her little speech, the school thought it was just a bunch of grumpy old bigots, but *she* made it seem like other students cared."

"You saw her, though," Lucian said, his voice small. "She was practically having a panic attack. I don't think she wanted to be there at all."

"How convenient," Nia said, shooting him a sidelong look. "Have you actually *asked* her what she believes?"

"Well," Lucian said. He rubbed his neck and looked out the window. "Not exactly, no."

"Of course not," Nia said. "Of *course* not. Too busy flirting to give a shit about me."

"That's not fair and you know it!" Lucian pointed a finger at her. "Tanner broke my *nose* when I stopped him from kicking your ass."

"The only difference I see," Nia said, "is that she's using adults instead of her fists." She narrowed her eyes and pursed her lips. "And, of course, she's a cute white g—"

"No," Lucian said, dropping his open palms into his lap. "She's *gay*, idiot." Nia's eyes widened and she cocked her head. "It didn't seem like my place to say it, but *that's* why I don't think she really meant what she said on the news."

"Mmhmm," Nia said, thinking. "She actually *told* you she's gay?"

"No," Lucian conceded. Nia rolled her eyes and Lucian shrugged. "But I really think she is. It's like . . . I don't know. She reminds me of you before a year ago in a lot of ways. You used to get this look like you were starving and you'd just been stabbed all at once, and she looks like that a lot, but, like, whenever a cute girl says hi to her, or when guys in class flirt with her. Stuff like that."

"You could be wrong," Nia said, though the realization that Lucian was a good enough friend to catalog even minor signs of her pain made her feel ashamed for snapping at him.

"I don't think I'm wrong," he said with a grin. "You don't become the world's greatest lover without knowing how to read people."

"Jesus Christ, dude," Nia said, but she was smiling. The GPS instructed her to turn a little late so she looped around a trailer park, feeling the same out-of-place tension she always felt when she was in a rural area. "Fine. *Fine.* I'm still not talking to her."

"What about rehearsals?" Lucian said.

"I'll burn that bridge when I get to it," Nia said.

LEXIE

Lexie spent all Friday evening and Saturday morning worried she would be late. Her parents told her she could only drive their car if she left the phone off, and that they would call her to see if it went straight to voice mail, so she had to write down directions off the Internet, which meant she probably needed to leave early, especially since she wasn't a very experienced driver. The farm was only forty minutes away, but it was technically in a different time zone, which she hadn't known, but when she finally arrived at Vaughn's farm and found it empty, save for Vaughn himself sprawled out in a hammock with a book over his face, she realized her mistake. She wasn't sure if it would be rude to wake him up, so she killed the engine and checked some of her favorite fashion blogs to pass the time.

Lexie didn't actually care about fashion. She wore nothing but hoodies, cardigans, and T-shirts from church. Lexie *did* like girls, though, and this was the only safe way to look at them without her parents catching on immediately, though she doubted they would believe she had any interest in haute couture. Still, the women in these photos, with their high chins and their dark eyes and their movements like hunting cats, seemed more like drawings than real people, like something out of a story come to life. They felt like the guardians of a life she wanted but could never have, a dream she would bottle and hang from the rafters of her heart with bits of twine as she grew up and found a husband and started a family. Looking at them made her soul sing and groan all at once, and she couldn't stop.

A knock on her window caused her to scream and throw her phone across the car as if it had suddenly burned her. She looked up, her chest heaving, to find Vaughn looking down at her with a mixture of confusion and concern.

"Just a—" She leaned down to gather her phone and her purse and banged her forehead on the steering wheel. "*Dang* it! Just a sec."

"Didn't mean to scare you," he said as Lexie stumbled out of the car. He shoved his hands in his pockets and leaned against a knobby fence. Lexie caught her breath and really looked around for the first time, taking in the deep green of the surrounding woods and the vast, open fields laid around the two-story farmhouse. "You looked like you were crying."

"Oh," she said. She made herself smile. "Nah. *Nah*. Just, you know, hanging out. Just chilling. Didn't want to wake you, was all."

"Okay," he said. He jerked his chin toward the trees across the street from the farmhouse and took off down the driveway. "Come on. Since you're early you can help me gather firewood."

"Yes, sir!" she said, snapping off a salute. She'd hoped it would seem cute or quirky, but he just stared at her for a second before giving her a small smile and a nod. She followed him into the woods with her stomach twisting, certain she was going to puke before the party was over. And really, if just meeting the rest of the cast and crew made her this nervous, what business did she have getting onstage? She shoved a bundle of sticks under her arm and closed her eyes, trying to find her center.

"Can I ask you a question?" Vaughn said. She looked up to find him tying his flannel shirt around his waist and pulling his dark, wavy hair into a bun. Lexie recognized that he was attractive in an objective sort of way. She nodded, though she was sure she wouldn't like the question.

"Are you and Lucian a thing?" he said. She blinked. He braced his foot on a branch as thick as her arm and snapped it off, throwing it over his shoulder. "You seem pretty close."

"No?" she said. She wiped dirt off on her jeans and frowned. Boys were indecipherable to her most of the time, but she'd thought Lucian was just being friendly. "Did he *say* . . . ?"

"Nah," Vaughn said. He jumped up and grabbed a low-hanging dead branch and swung on it until it snapped off. Lexie yelped when he fell, certain he was going to break a leg, but he landed with a little puff of breath. He smiled at her and swung both branches over his shoulder. "Just checking." He scratched his chin and swept the ground for more branches. "I think he has a thing for the girl playing Audrey II."

"Nia?" Lexie said, freezing in a kneel with her hand half closed around a bundle of twigs.

"Yeah," he said. "The transgender."

"He almost never talks about her," Lexie said. Oh, *no*. He wasn't just acquaintances with Nia—they were close enough that people suspected they were together, and he'd never mentioned it. Why was he so nice to Lexie? Why did he go out of his way to talk to her in class without acting like a creep? Why did he push her to come today? She thought they were friends. She'd thought he was one of the first friends she'd ever made who she didn't know through either church or her parents, but what? Was he just being polite? Everything inside her felt like the sound of metal on dry ice.

Vaughn just shrugged. "Can you blame him? She's hot. But you know, not my *type*. Come on, let's take this back."

She followed a few steps behind him, her arms loaded with tinder, wondering what Nia would think if she heard Vaughn say that, and whether it was hypocritical to worry about the other girl's feelings *now*.

NIA

Nia was wrapping up a conversation with Constance, the gangly redhead who'd been assigned as Audrey II's puppeteer, when Lucian jogged up with a smug grin. She didn't acknowledge him at first, but then he started dancing on his tiptoes like a kid who needed to pee.

"I'm sorry, Constance," Nia said, "but it seems my son has lost his mind. Can I catch you later?" Constance shrugged and went back to her tribe, the semicircle of pierced, black-clad tech theater kids, and Nia turned to Lucian with a look she thought of as "matronly annoyance." "Yes?"

"I've got *evidence*," he said, leaning forward and speaking in a stage whisper.

"Of what?"

"Look over there." He grabbed her by the shoulder and pointed her across the fire, where Lexie and Vaughn shared a log, him with his legs spread and his hand making languid sweeps as he talked in that laconic drawl straight girls apparently thought was sexy, her watching him and nodding slowly, looking like a tourist who didn't quite understand the language she was hearing. "See? I told you."

"Talking to Vaughn makes girls gay?" she said.

"No," he said. "Quite the opposite: our boy Vaughn is, by every conceivable metric, as desirable as a guy can be at our school without being an athlete."

"I don't see it," Nia said. She frowned and looked at Lucian. "Are you sure you're straight?"

"Shut up," he said. "I'm a student of love in all its forms. He's . . . look, he's tall, good hair, just enough fashion sense to seem cool without accidentally coding himself as gay, laconic in an artsy way, visibly fit, clear skin, and he's got *presence*. Look there and there, at Whitney and Keeley." Nia followed his finger to either side of Lexie and Vaughn, where two of the girls cast for the show's Greek chorus sat on opposite logs. She wasn't sure what he wanted her to see at first, since it looked like they were having completely separate conversations, but then she noticed it: every few seconds they glanced away, with either an obvious look of longing at Vaughn or one of simmering resentment for Lexie. And all the while Lexie just nodded at him absently, glancing at her phone whenever she got a chance.

"Holy shit," she said. This changed everything. "Holy *shit*, you might have a point. Wait here."

"See?" he said. "I told y— Where are you going?"

"I have to talk to her," she said, shooting him a wide-eyed look over her shoulder, the dancing shadows of the late-evening fire making her look like a crazy person.

"But—"

"Too late!" And with that she was gone, striding across the lawn toward the fire.

"Hey," someone said. Lexie looked up from her phone and her heart screeched to a halt when she saw Nia standing over her. The other girl's hands were in her pockets and a smile that must have been fake was spread across her lips. Nia started to speak, but then Lexie realized that she'd never been this close to her before, and now that she looked close . . . Yes, there were the thick eyebrows, there was the skin the color of a fawn's coat, there were the lips as suited for kissing as they were for grinning. She looked just like Arisce Wanzer, the only transgender model Lexie followed online. Lexie wondered if Nia cultivated that look on purpose, maybe did something with makeup because the trans model was an inspiration, or if it was just a happy accident. Either way, she was so spellbound for a moment that she didn't register what the other girl said.

"We were talking," Vaughn said, sounding vaguely annoyed in a way Lexie had learned over the past few hours probably meant he was *very* annoyed.

"Oh?" Nia said with a twist of her head. "Is that what you call it?" Vaughn's eyebrows crawled together, but otherwise he stayed silent as Nia returned her attention to Lexie. "We need to talk."

"We do?" she said. Her mouth felt dry. She wanted to turn inside out, and she suspected she was one wrong move away from throwing up.

Nia nodded. "Walk with me?"

"Uh . . ."

"I'm not gonna murder you," Nia said, her smile shifting into a wolfish grin. "We're not all serial killers. Just most of us."

"Okay." She ran her fingernails across the bark beneath her, clenched her teeth, and, for the first time in her life, decided to face something head-on. She said good-bye to Vaughn, though he was already paying attention to a girl on the next log and didn't seem to notice, and followed Nia away from the campfire, into the growing, ocher darkness of the fields farther away from the farmhouse. When they were far enough away that the tinkle of conversation had faded to match the rustle of the woods in the distance, Nia turned and put her hands on her hips.

"So."

"Uh," Lexie said. She rubbed her arm and shifted her weight from foot to foot, barely noticing as the wind tore strands of her hair out of the tie that held them in place. "It's nice to finally meet you."

"Uh-huh," Nia said, her eyes half lidded. "I'm sure." She pulled her hair back and sighed. "So I saw you on the news."

"I . . . Yeah." Lexie suddenly felt like she was going to throw up. "Yeah, I figured you would."

"And that didn't bother you?" Nia said, her voice like a storm cloud.

"I mean . . ." Lexie took a deep, shuddering breath and forced herself to look Nia in the eyes. "Yes. Yes, it bothered me, but I don't have anything against you, I think you really *are* a girl, it's just . . . what's to stop boys from *saying* they're like you and coming in?"

"Yeah," Nia said, nodding slowly. "Believe it or not, I do actually know how scary the idea of sharing a locker room with guys is. Weird, right?"

"I hadn't—"

"—thought of it that way?" Nia squatted and started pulling blades of grass out of the dirt and braiding them. "No, of course not. Your theoretical problem is much more important than my real, current problem."

"That's . . ." Lexie began. She took a small step forward. "I could talk to the school, help them work out a way to keep you safe."

"Maybe that would work for bathrooms, but what am I supposed to do for phys ed? Cross the entire campus to the office or the teachers' lounge? Change in the janitor's closet?"

"I don't—"

"But if I don't get those credits, my GPA tanks and I can't get a scholarship, without which I can't afford college," Nia said. She swiped her hands on her thighs and sighed. "I was going to go to Lincoln. I was going to be the first person in my family to go to college."

Lexie wrapped her arms around herself, feeling suddenly dirty and small. "Oh."

"Yeah. So thanks for offering to help, but it's too little, too late. At least I know you're not completely evil. That's *something*."

"I want to understand," Lexie said, voice surprising her with its force. "I know I don't know, okay? What I believe now isn't what I have to believe, it's just all I . . ." She swallowed and touched her throat. "You could help me understand. I would like it if you helped me understand."

". . . really?"

"*Really*," Lexie said. "And you might find I understand more than you think."

— 125 —

Was it Lexie's imagination, or did Nia's eyes twinkle a little bit at that? Nia stood and tied a bracelet of grass around her wrist and admired it for a moment, then seemed to deflate. "I really wanted to hate you, but, I don't know, I guess your heart might, *maybe*, be in the right place. And I mean, you're *wrong* about boys following me into the bathroom, and I can explain why, but . . . later." Lexie's stomach untwisted all at once and her cheeks felt warm. Nia bit her lip and scrunched her nose, thinking hard about something. "So you're gay, right?"

"I would *love* to talk about—" Lexie started, but then she registered the final question and her guts twirled back into their knot. "What?"

"You heard me," Nia said. She untied the bracelet and tossed it in the air, watching dispassionately as the wind tore it apart.

Lexie balled her fists and looked down at her shoes, alarm bells ringing everywhere as anxiety inscribed itself into her flesh. She swallowed, hard, desperate not to lose control.

"Wh-what makes you think that?" she said eventually.

"The straight answer would have been no," Nia said, one eyebrow rising as her mouth tipped up in a faint smile, but then she grew serious again. "Now please, be honest with me. How much of you repping your parents' fight about where I pee was actually, *really* real?"

"I don't . . ." Lexie said. She'd never said this out loud. She'd never even typed it, never so much as written it in a journal, and yet somehow Nia saw her. Who else had seen her? She felt naked, suddenly. Was someone going to tell her parents? Did they already *know*, and she was just making a fool of herself? Were they going to send her to one of those camps to try to pray her better? "I . . ." Her throat tightened and her eyes felt suddenly hot and wet and her face twisted up and this was worse than throwing up, definitely worse, but then she felt arms around her and she opened her eyes to find her cheek pressed into Nia's neck, her nose filled with lavender and bergamot hiding just under a blanket of woodsmoke, and the tears faded.

"It's cool," Nia said, her voice inches from Lexie's ear. "I did so much stupid shit before I came to terms with stuff." She pushed Lexie out to arm's length and smiled as she thumbed her tears away. Lexie shivered, fighting the urge to nuzzle her cheek into the other girl's hand (and holy crap, Lexie'd had her doubts about it, but Nia really did smell like a girl, and her skin was so *soft*, and—), all her years of pent-up longing bursting out of her torn seams now, in this moment, with this girl who should have hated her. "I can help you with it. Okay?" Lexie sniffled and nodded.

"Good. *Good*." Nia smacked her forehead and chuckled. "This is, uh, not how I saw this conversation going, honestly."

"I'm glad it did," Lexie said. She rubbed her nose with her wrist. "Could we be friends?"

"Yeah." Nia's eyes glittered in the dawning moonlight. "We've gotta do a show together anyway, right? Might as well." She turned and started rummaging in her bag. "I'll give you my number to make it official." She pulled out her phone and swiped the screen, but something she saw made her freeze in place.

"What's wrong?" Lexie took a step toward her, but Nia flashed her a look so full of anger it reminded her of sitting near the bonfire, as if all the pleasant feelings of a moment before had evaporated.

"Apparently," she said, her voice quavering, whether from anger or sadness Lexie couldn't tell, "I missed a text from my dad."

NIA

"What did it say?" Lexie said, as if she couldn't have *fucking* guessed.

"Your folks got what they wanted," Nia said. She stomped and let out a curse so loud it drew the attention of everyone still at the fire. Like she cared.

"It'll be okay," Lexie said, trying to make her voice as soothing as possible. "Like I said, I can talk to the faculty and—" She held out her hands and moved in for a hug, but Nia held an arm out and gave her a look she hoped communicated even half the rage and hurt coursing through her.

"Don't," she said. "*Don't* touch me. I . . ." She swallowed and wiped her eyes, hating how weak this made her feel. "I know you were just trying to—I know it's your *parents* and not *you*, but you still helped them."

"Could we please talk about—" Lexie began, but Nia stormed past her, back toward the fire. Lucian intercepted her at the edge of the light and pulled her into a hug, and *this* one she gladly accepted. She let the waterworks flow, going limp and soaking his shirt collar and not even feeling embarrassed. He patted her back, and through the anger and the fear she felt a sting of shame for how mean she was to him sometimes, for how she took him for granted even though he was as close to a brother as she would ever have. She slung her arms around him and squeezed so hard he coughed, but she wouldn't let go.

"They changed their minds," Nia said. Lucian's chest muffled her voice, but he still understood what she meant.

"Oh, Nia," he said. He rested his cheek on her head and rubbed his hands up and down her back. "Oh, Nia, *fuck*. We'll find a way to make this work. I'll be your bathroom bodyguard if I have to, dude." He pulled her away, slung his arm over her shoulder, and smiled. She wiped her eyes and sniffled, her face so puffy she could barely see. "I heard one of the techies snuck in some booze."

"Yeah?" she said.

"Wanna see if they'll share?" he said. She leaned against him as they made their way across the lawn to the barn, where the techies went to smoke cigarettes. They were on their way back to the fire in a matter of minutes, two shots of vodka searing through Nia's blood, making her feel . . . well, not better, exactly, but more willing to tolerate her misery. She was looking at the moon, following Lucian and trying to find a silver lining, when he stopped suddenly.

"What do *you* want?" he said.

Nia looked down, and there, standing at the edge of the fire with her blue eyes shining and brittle like glass, was Lexie, her knees together and her phone held like a priceless relic. She held it out like it was some kind of peace offering.

"I think I can make it up to you," she said. Nia looked from the phone to her and sniffed. Lucian nudged Lexie's hands back and shook his head. "Just record me while I talk."

"Go away, okay?" he said. "We can talk on Monday." The corner of her mouth twitched, she nodded, and she started to walk away, but Nia reached out and took the phone from her before she could.

"I want to hear what she has to say," Nia mumbled. She worked out how to open the camera and sat on a nearby log with empty space, watching Lexie through the screen as she strode into the firelight, her steps strong, her chin high, such a dramatic departure from the girl she had seen on the news, the girl she'd held in her arms only a few minutes before.

"Everyone," she said, "I'm sorry to interrupt the party, but I have something to say." All eyes turned to her, and in that moment Nia saw the strength hiding just beneath the identity Lexie had papered over herself. The last year of Nia's own life had been a long exposure of something similar, and she was filled with admiration and affection like warm water, flowing through the spaces her tears had left empty. Lexie gave her a signal, so she hit *Record* and focused the camera.

"My name," she said, her shoulders squared, "is Lexie Thompson. I was featured on a WJRP news report recently where I said that I disagreed with one of my fellow students, a transgender girl named Nia, being allowed to use the girls' facilities." She tilted her head and touched her heart. "I was wrong. I repeated things I'd been told to think because it was easier than speaking up. I said what I was told to say because it made my life easier." She swallowed, closed her eyes, and balled her fists. "Because I myself am gay"—the cast and crew, already enthralled by this, shared shocked glances—"and because throwing her under the bus made it easier for me to stay hidden. But I don't want to hide anymore. I take back my previous statement, and I stand in solidarity with my classmate." The nervous girl returned for just a moment in a wavering, insecure smile, but then she was gone again with a resolute nod. "Thank you."

Nia stopped the recording and handed the phone to Lexie once she'd rejoined them. She sat next to Nia and, while Nia watched, she uploaded the video first to YouTube, then to her social media accounts, and then, after a quick search for their address, sent a link to the same news station she'd spoken to before. When she was done, she let out a long breath, and Nia couldn't help noticing how badly Lexie's hands were shaking. Before she could think twice, Nia slid her hand into Lexie's. Lexie smiled, then fixed her gaze on Nia in a way that made her feel at once like the center of the universe and a moth pinned to a board. A flurry of text notifications erupted from Lexie's purse and she winced.

"No going back now I guess," she said. Nia noticed in the abstract that the party still hadn't resumed, that the only sounds were the pop-sizzle of the fire and the hiss of the wind in the trees, and that a dozen sets of eyes reflected a dozen pinpoints of fire at them as they watched one another.

"Holy *shit*," Nia said. "You *really* did that."

"Yeah," she said, squinting and biting her lip. "I feel like I should be freaking out, but like—"

"—yeah—"

"—and I mean." She squeezed Nia's hand. "Can I just say, and I hope this isn't weird, but you look just like this model I like, and your skin feels really soft, and you smell good, and even before we met I actually admired you a lot, and I'm glad we—"

But before she could finish Nia leaned in and kissed her. Lexie let out a single, surprised squeak, but after that all she heard was applause.

THE WAY WE LOVE HERE

———————

DHONIELLE CLAYTON

THE PEOPLE WHO live on the Isle of Meridien are born with red strings coiled like copper wire around their ring fingers.

I shouldn't call it a string. Or red, even. It's more like a tattoo that mixes with your skin tone, and turns all shades of brown and black and white and everything in between. The coils look a little like wedding rings stacked one on top of the other.

Momma would make me write fifty lines for saying that again. "Trivializing the work of the gods, Vio, will land you straight at the bottom of the sea with the rest of the sinners." But when I was younger, I just thought it was a clever birthmark.

An accident. Of sorts.

But everyone who lives on the island has one. It marks us as belonging to this place.

This is how we find love here.

— — — —

I cover my face with my hand, then let my fingers open slowly to invite the rising moonlight to creep between them. Sometimes when the light hits just right, the red coils scatter across my finger like a constellation of stars. "A love blueprint," Papa used to always say.

I bury three mason jars in the sand. Nestled inside the glass are flickering candles. They surround me like little fires. At the Saturday markets, I sell them alongside my watercolors and Momma's produce. Then I flatten my back against the sand, and the fine grains embed themselves into my tight curls. The waves tickle my feet as I wait for whatever the moon can show me.

This is my nightly routine before Momma starts buzzing so loud about night chores that I can't think anymore. Guests from the island will come soon. As the warm season begins and the islanders stop working, the inns on the leeward side of Meridien will fill. The rest of the vacationers must venture over to us at the Strings of Happiness Inn. They won't be happy, but they'll be here in our squeaky beds, with our mismatched plates, listening to the wind. Momma will be glad to be busy again.

I squint up at the moon. I let my fingers find its light again. Some say that if you look hard enough, the coils will briefly take the shape of the one you're supposed to end up with. A pair of eyes. The outline of a face. The glimpse of a smile. That the gods etched this person's face in the ink that circles our fingers.

I try to see something, anything. I want to be prepared. My sister cried when she met her beloved. She'd just turned nineteen. Her eyes puffed up for weeks, and her honey-brown skin held a flush that turned quickly into bruises. She wasn't ready. She didn't want the coils to disappear from her finger. She wanted to stay with Momma and run the inn forever. Without Papa there to help, she knew it'd quickly fall into disrepair because I wasn't as good as she was at knowing what needed to be done. But her love showed up, and now she's gone to the leeward side. We won't see her and her new husband again until the snow comes.

I listen to the waves now, and for Papa, wondering if the gods told him who I'd fall in love with; if they told the dead those sorts of things about the living.

I want to know how much time I have.

I don't like surprises.

"Papa, you there?" Right after Papa drowned, I used to sit here and wait for him to wash up like a seashell; his broad shoulders and tall frame and big hands spit out by the ocean. But he never came back. The ocean never released him, though sometimes at night, I think I can hear him calling me to join him out at sea. "Do you know anything?"

There's no answer.

I've never *really* given a thought to boys or girls or falling in love with them. I've watched couples check into the inn and hold hands as they climbed our rickety staircase or took strolls on the beach or kissed at the dining room table. I've wondered what love feels like. Another person's hand in yours. Another person's mouth pressed to yours. Another person who has permission to touch you. Momma said people are like streams, and when you meet your beloved, you become a single river flowing in one direction; currents, waves, ripples, indistinguishable from one another.

I don't know if I want that. The thought of having to lose myself in another, shape myself around the form of someone else makes my heart beat too fast, and not the good, excited way. We love so early here. And it feels like there isn't enough time to do all the things I want to do before I have to do the things I'm supposed to do.

I raise my hand again. I have five coils left. I started with ten, and when I only have one left, that's when I'll find my love. Sometimes I wish they'd come back, signaling that the gods had changed their minds, and maybe they'd skip over me. I don't think I'd mind that. I'd gladly sleep in my window nook forever, letting the sun warm my legs, or find a way to leave this island so I can paint a different sunrise and sunset. They say there's nothing beyond our island, but I have to believe there's more. That there's a world where coils don't exist, where I get to choose my own love—or not to love at all.

I watch the sea, anticipating hearing Momma's voice soon, calling out from the wraparound porch, beckoning me to come back inside and help.

The waves bob up and down and crash forward into the sand as the tide comes in. A shoe washes up. Then a jacket. I stand and walk closer to the water. My heart begins to beat faster. Something is out there. I can feel it. Another wave crashes down, and then the tide washes up something heavy.

It's a boy.

For a moment, surprise holds me in place. But when another wave races in and licks at his legs, the spell is broken. I run over and drag him farther out of the water. His black hair is too long, Momma would say, and the wind catches it, slapping it across his face. He's slender and long; all gangly arms and legs and too-large hands and feet. His arms and legs are covered in bruises like he's just survived a fistfight.

I frantically press my hands on his chest and push the water out. Nothing happens. The bones of his ribs feel thin and fragile. I keep pushing down, praying to the gods for him to awaken, until finally he jerks upright. The water comes out of his mouth in sputters and coughs. He rolls over into a wet ball.

I scramble backward.

His eyes pop open and find me. And they're lovely. The kind that curve in the corners like they've been frozen in a perpetual smile. He's very paintable.

"Who are you?" I ask.

"Who are you?" he says through a series of coughs. His white cotton shirt clings to his chest like it's part of his too-pale skin. He doesn't have the usual coloring of a Meridien person. He hasn't been kissed by the sun gods.

"I'm *not* the one who almost drowned."

"I didn't. See?" He props himself up on his elbow, but then keels over again in another fit of coughs. His face pinkens. "I'm all better now," he says, out of breath.

"I should call for help."

"No, don't. Please." He pulls himself up into a seated position. "I don't do doctors."

I frown at him and hope he can see it. "Where are you from?"

I wonder for the briefest second if he's from out there, from whatever lies beyond. But then he lifts his left hand. His ring finger glows like a stick of fire. He belongs to Meridien. He smiles up at me, and it's a nice one, I hate to admit. "I heard that if you stayed underwater for three minutes, you'd be able to see who you'll end up with."

"Did you?" I count the coils on his finger. Five. Like me. It means that there's a chance he could be one of my matches; people with the same number of coils are potential mates. And when the tattoo fades to one final ring, it creates a unique pattern that is identical to your beloved's.

A queasiness settles into my stomach.

He shrugs. "I didn't last long enough. I'm not a strong swimmer."

I hold in a laugh, but it bursts out. "Then it was probably a bad idea to try that technique."

"And what are you doing out here?" he asks.

"I live here."

"In the sand?"

I don't allow his comment to make me smile.

"My family owns the inn on this side. And it's private property—"

"My mother says there's nothing in this world that's really private, and you can't own land. The gods didn't intend for us to divide it up like the food on a plate." He beams with pride like what he's just said is the cleverest thing in the whole world. He stands and stretches out his long and lanky limbs. They make popping noises. He starts coughing again.

"You should go to the hospital."

"It won't help. Aren't we all, like, two steps from death anyway?"

"No," I reply.

He plops down next to me and buries his feet in the sand. "You're trying to *see*, aren't you? I heard the thing about the moon, too. Maybe I should've chosen that one instead of almost drowning."

"Yes," I say. "You probably should've."

"I'm Sebastien Huang," he says with a head nod.

The name lands. "Wait. Aren't you—"

"Yes. I'm the person who tried to leave this island in my aerobird flying machine, which the papers wrongly called a makeshift plane."

"But there's nothing out there." I repeat the words I struggle so often to believe. The words Momma wants to sink into my skin and down into my bones to quiet all the questions I ask.

"How do you know?"

"People have tried to sail away, only to have to turn around because they couldn't find any other land."

"But you don't know for certain. Maybe people haven't sailed far enough. Maybe they give up too soon, and another world is just a little farther ahead." He eyes me.

"You probably shouldn't wish for things that aren't there," I say, and cringe a little because I sound like Momma.

"What's your name again?"

"I'm Viola, but everyone calls me Vio."

"Nice to meet you."

A silence stretches between us as the waves crash in. We don't get the casual wandering visitor. I want to know why he's here on our beach. I want to know what else he's done to find out who his true love is. I want to know why he wants to leave the island. I've never met anyone else with the same curiosity as me.

The island is small enough to know most people, but big enough to be missed if you want to. And Momma always wanted us missed out here on this side. She taught me and my sister to read and write and didn't bother sending us to the school because she thought we'd be ostracized like she was. She said the rest of them would find us when it was time for love.

"I thought I saw a pair of eyelashes," he says. "They could've belonged to anyone, or anything, even a cat."

"The gods wouldn't pair you with an animal."

"I doubt it'd be that bad." He shows me his finger. "Can I see yours?"

I lift my hand to allow him to inspect it. "Looks like you're close, too," he says. "We could be soul mates."

I scrunch my nose at him. "Probably not," I say, even though I'm not sure.

"Maybe the ocean put us together. Maybe the water god knew."

"Knew what?"

"I could've washed up farther down shore."

"It's this"—I wiggle my ring finger at him—"that pulls people together." I want to add that I don't know if I even believe in fate or these coils or love itself. I think of Momma and Papa and how they seemed smashed together like two strong rocks placed too close to each other when they desperately wanted nothing but ocean between them. I can still hear their fights when I close my eyes. It's the reason I first started coming out to the beach at night. Watching the two of them felt like the gods had made a mistake. How had the strings linked two people so wrong for each other?

"But I'm hoping the gods skip me," I say. "Maybe they'll leave me be."

"A life without—"

"Love is impossible," I finish the line we've been taught since birth.

We both laugh.

"Want to come back into the water with me and give it another try?" Sebastien asks.

"Do you have a death wish?"

"My mother thinks so. And the doctors. She's always threatening me with how long I might have left if I don't take better care of myself."

I bite my lip to keep from being nosy and asking what's wrong with him. "Why don't we try something equally dangerous as swimming when you can't?"

"Like what?"

I rub my hands together. "We'd have to touch. Hold hands."

I've never held hands with anyone outside of Momma, my sister, and Papa. The elders of Meridien say that this type of intimacy is reserved for blood relatives and beloveds. They warn us about the dangers that could happen: falling in love with the wrong person, ending up alone, altering the will of the gods, confusing the senses, and losing our fingers. The newspapers print cautionary tales about young teens who disregard the warning. They make sure to include their sad pictures. I've never done it. Then again, I've never had a boy with whom to try.

"You mean . . . ensnaring?"

"Yes. If you let the strings touch—"

"You call them strings?" He hitches a dark eyebrow up at me.

"Strings, coils. What do you call them?"

"Love marks."

"How romantic."

"It's what my mother calls it," he says, and then looks back down at my hand. The moonlight silvers his black hair. "Ensnaring is forbidden, you know."

"I know."

"And you could lose your mark permanently," he reminds me.

"Are you afraid?" I don't care if I lose mine. I'd actually be glad to be rid of it.

"No. I've heard that ensnaring isn't even true. A myth to keep teens from kissing and doing stuff."

"'Stuff'?"

"Yeah, you know."

"I know," I say, even though I don't.

"Other people say it unlocks nexus points mapped out by the gods. You can see possible futures for you and the person you connect with."

I'd heard that, too, from eavesdropping on my sister when she'd have friends over. She was the type of person who people gravitated to despite not setting a foot in the schools on the island. Every girl and boy her age seemed to just know her. The pretty girl from the market. Carolina. This boy is the first one I've exchanged more than a few words with.

"But which future will be true?" I ask.

"I don't know," he says. "Possibly all. Possibly none. There's no fun in knowing exactly how it will all turn out, right?"

"I guess not." I stretch out my left hand closer to him. "So no harm in giving it a try, then."

He finally reaches out to meet it. His palm is callused but soft in the middle. My stomach lifts with a flutter, like I'm a little girl again and Momma is pushing me on the old swing set behind the inn.

We twirl our fingers together, careful not to let the ring fingers touch just yet. His eyes remain fixed on our hands. I watch how his forehead crinkles with concentration, and he bites his bottom lip. He has lovely cheekbones and with some sun could be even more handsome.

"You ready?" I ask.

He nods.

We flatten our left palms together, then let our ring fingers touch. They flush with redness, the blood racing just under the surface. The strings become super red hot. The burning sensation makes my eyes water. Heat and swelling rush in. I almost pull my hand back.

The sky turns cloud white, as if every single shade of night has been leeched out. The beach beneath us dissolves grain by grain, shell by shell, wave by wave. My ears pop, and I suck in a deep breath. It feels like being dunked underwater and held there. The thumping of a heartbeat thunders in my ears.

We swirl inside a kaleidoscope.

—   —   —   —

I know the leeward side of the island by scent and sound: the pollen of the larkspur flowers, the chittering pink birds that cluster in the horsetail trees, the hum of crickets and cicadas, the scent of fried sweetbread. My sandals slip and slide across pebbles under my feet. A bright noon sun presses down on me. I blink until my surroundings sharpen. Sebastien's warm hand holds mine.

"You okay?" I ask him.

"I think. Am I still handsome?"

"Hardly," I reply. He still looks the same as he did before we ensnared. Which is cute, if I must admit it. His hair might be a touch longer. But I can't tell how far we've gone into the future. Or if this is really the future at all.

"Where are we?"

"The high school, I think," he replies.

I've never been to the school before. I've ridden past it with Momma as we made our way to the leeward markets to sell her hothouse tomatoes and buttery squash, and the fresh oysters Papa used to dive for.

The once bustling lanes headed into town are quiet. No trams. No bicycles. No pedestrians. The storefronts display *Closed* signs, and have their curtains drawn.

"Why here?" I wonder.

"Let's go in and find out." Sebastien leads the way forward. His pull is strong and assertive.

"Wait!" I yank him back. "We don't know why we are here, or how to make this stop."

"You wanted to see, right? This is *seeing*. If we turn back, we won't know anything more than we did before. And I need to know." His eyes shine with anticipation.

I gaze up at the school's white limestone roof and matching

shutters. Is this a version of our future? A place without people. Is this how the gods interpreted my desire to be left alone?

Sebastien takes a tentative step forward, then looks back at me with eager eyes. I exhale and join him.

We cross through the doors and into the foyer. Big picture windows offer views of the turquoise sea. Glass display cases hold trophies and plaques boasting student accomplishments. Lockers flank us. Classrooms hold desks and chairs and bookshelves. A banner is draped overhead congratulating graduating seniors. I'd be one next year, if I went to school. But maybe this vision means that Momma will let me go for one year, and I will be able to take a real art class.

Three hallways are roped off. The only one open is labeled *Senior Way*.

We step into it.

"Look," he says, pointing up.

"What?"

"The wall."

We gaze up, and it's covered in superlatives—students nominated as best dressed, funniest, smartest, most likely to succeed.

"It's us."

I search the many portraits and find my face and Sebastien's staring down at me under the label *Worst Breakup*.

Sebastien laughs. "I guess we didn't make it."

"Do you think this is real? Do you think we actually . . . dated?" I ask. It's so far from my reality that I can't even imagine it.

"Seems like it, otherwise why would we be here?"

I feel his eyes. His gaze is hot, heavy, and curious.

"Have you ever had a boyfriend before?" he asks.

"No. Have you?"

"No." He laughs a little, then grins. "But why haven't you? You're beautiful enough, I suppose."

I blush. "Is that *supposed* to be a compliment?"

"I'm not very good at those. I guess I'd make a terrible boyfriend."

"Have you ever had a girlfriend?" I ask.

"A few."

I purse my lips the way Momma does when she smells a lie.

"Well, a few in my head," he adds. "I've kissed three girls. I've found that they aren't into pale boys who miss school and make strange contraptions." He turns his arm around. "Or maybe it's just the bruises."

I nod, for lack of anything better to say.

"My mother thinks I won't be around long enough to meet my love. And the gods doomed my future soul mate to a life without love."

"What's wrong with you?" I ask without looking directly at him. Momma would fuss at me for my frankness.

"They don't know. I've just always been sick."

"I'm sorry," I say, but it feels like the wrong thing.

He frowns. "Ugh. You don't have to say that, and please don't look at me like that." He shrugs. "I knew you'd get all weepy in the eyes. You've got the kind that hold on to tears."

"I do not!" I protest.

"This is why I usually don't tell people."

"Fine. I won't pity you. I won't even be nice."

"Well, if you wanted to kiss me out of pity, I wouldn't say no."

I laugh, and heat rises from my neck to my cheeks like I've spent too much time wandering the beach or picking vegetables in Momma's garden.

"Do you want to be kissed?" he asks.

His words dig under my skin, tickling me and warming me from the inside out. "I don't know."

"You shouldn't die without experiencing it at least once."

"Is that so?" I ask. "And are you going to be the one who helps me?"

"Only if you want—and I have the time right now. Normally, I'm quite busy and important. Can't you see? There are girls—and a few boys—lined up, wanting and wishing that they'd have the opportunity to kiss me. There should be a superlative called Most Kissable, and there you'd find me."

My eyes wander to his mouth. The pink of his lips reminds me of the insides of the conch shells Papa would bring back from the sea for my sister and me. If I were to paint them, I'd use sunset peach and a little ruby red and cream white.

"I've been told I'm a great kiss—"

I press my mouth to his, pushing the words back inside. His mouth is soft and tastes like he's been eating cherries.

The thudding noise returns. Sebastien and I are tugged forward like rag dolls. The walls of the high school disintegrate into white ash around us as everything goes dark.

— — — —

The noise of chattering voices fills my ears. A cool, hard surface materializes beneath my feet. I blink and my surroundings come into view. I'm in front of a floor-to-ceiling window that looks out on a city. Or at least I think it's what they call a city. Nothing on Meridien compares.

I stumble backward, then find my footing and lean forward. I press my cheeks against the glass. Tall buildings reach for a dusky orange skyline. The melody of honking, bicycle chimes, and the opening and closing of doors drifts up from the streets. Bright lights click on as the sun sinks behind behemoths of glass and iron.

I catch a glimpse of myself in the mirror. My once curly hair is straight and flows over my shoulder. Makeup rouges my cheeks. Glasses sit on my nose. I've lost the deep brown color I always had. My skin is a paler shade of brown.

"Where am I? Sebastien?" I whip around to face a crowd.

People buzz about holding champagne flutes and tiny plates filled with food. Huge watercolor paintings cover the walls and hang from the ceiling on clear strings.

A woman waves at me. "Perfecto!" she calls out, and blows me a kiss. "I can't wait to buy another piece."

Another man rushes up to me and takes both my hands in his. I flinch. He smiles and does a little bow. "I'm sorry, I just get so excited when I see you," he says. "A Parisian gallery called just now. They asked to carry two of your paintings. Isn't that sensational? You're a worldwide phenomenon. A godsend. No twenty-five-year-old has ever done what you have. So much youth. So much success. Your watercolors will be hung in every household rich enough to afford them."

"Where am I? What's happening?"

He pats my shoulder. "All the excitement getting to you? I'll go get your very cute husband—"

"Ethan," I say, the name suddenly coming to me.

"Yes, Ethan." He eyes me suspiciously.

I lift my left hand. The coils have been replaced with a wedding band and a glittering diamond ring the size of a swollen cherry.

"Viola Young. Over here. For a picture," someone shouts. A camera flashes. I put my hands up to avoid it.

Viola Young.

My new last name rolls over my tongue.

A handsome young man strides up to me. He's all blond hair, milky-white skin, and green eyes. My future husband.

He sweeps a warm hand around my waist. It feels familiar and comforting, the memory of him lying somewhere deep inside me. "The mayor's here, and even he wants to buy one of your pieces."

I let him sweep me forward, but look over my shoulder, searching the crowd for Sebastien.

The room thickens with people. They pay me compliments and wish me well.

My heart trips over its own rhythm. This is exactly what I want.

To be an artist.

To be away from Meridian.

To know that there are other places in the world outside our island.

To paint other sunsets.

A young man with dark hair grins at me and waves. Sebastien. Or a future version of him.

"Excuse me, just a moment," I say to Ethan. He kisses my forehead and turns to one of my many admirers.

I duck left and right through the crowds. People stop me along the way to offer cheers and a kiss on my cheek. When I finally reach him, I'm exhausted.

"Sebastien!" I almost collapse on him. "Where are we?"

"Your very successful future, it seems." He smiles at me. A silver streak courses through his hair. I touch it.

"I guess I go gray early," he remarks.

"But you're here, so . . ."

"We left the island," he says with a hopeful look on his face. "Something else is out there, and I knew it. I always did."

"Are you still . . ." I hate to ask or utter the word *sick*. Though only four letters and very tiny, so very big.

He lifts a cane in his right hand. "I may be. But I, like, *feel* okay, if that makes sense."

I nod, even though I'm not sure. "Are you married?"

He gazes down at his left hand. "It appears not. I still have my love mark." His eyes hold a sadness.

"Do you wish we didn't do this?" I ask.

"No. Not at all." He takes my right hand. "It's so cool to get off the island. To see your success. This would be an amazing future."

"One that includes you, it seems. So I guess we stay friends after all this."

"And I make it to twenty-five," he says, then turns around in a circle.

I grab his left hand, and the world goes black.

— — — —

My ears fill with a faint beeping noise. It starts light, like the patter of a leaky faucet, only to sharpen into deep, bleating pierces as the world around me settles. The walls hold nothing but whiteness, and a lone window that shows the pink coral sand on the leeward side of Meridien. Seagulls dive in and out of the water. Storm clouds linger in the distance, threatening to stamp out the sun and bring torrential downpours.

My hand twitches. I look down and find a hospital bed and a sleeping Sebastien in it. I jostle him.

"Sebastien."

He doesn't answer.

"Sebastien."

His eyes don't even flutter.

The door opens. A squat-looking nurse trundles in with a tray. Her light brown cheeks are rosy and kissed with a flush. "Oh, dearie, you're still here?" She cocks her head to the side. "You've got to be tired, Mrs. Huang."

Mrs. Huang.

I look down at our hands. There's a pair of wedding rings on both of our fingers.

"What's wrong with him?" I ask.

She looks at me like I've just told her I was from a different planet. "You must need a rest. When's the last time you slept? You've been at his side for so long now. He'd want you to sleep."

"Where are we?"

She inches closer to me, her face scrunched with confusion. "The Meridien Homegoing House, of course."

My heart flutters with panic, and my pulse starts to race. "What is this place?"

"A convalescence home, dearie. You checked him in a week ago."

She pours me a cup of water. "Have a sip. Lack of sleep and hydration can cause confusion."

I gladly gulp it down. It's coolness rushes through me. "Isn't he too young to die?"

"None of us know when our time is up. The gods gave us one gift—to know when our loves would come. The best part of life. It would be greedy to ask for more." She touches her soft palm to my forehead. "No fever. But you've gone all pale and clammy like you've seen a spirit." She scoots a chair up for me to sit in. "You know you can let his hand go. He still has some time left yet."

"Will he wake?"

She nods as she checks his vitals, then gazes down at our hands. "I know things seem bleak right now, but look"—she points down—"you're one of the lucky ones. Your string is coming back. The ink is rising underneath your skin once more. You'll be given a second love by the gods."

I lift my wedding band and find the faint lines of another string just beneath it.

"Can he still be saved?" I ask.

"Only the gods know that." She retrieves a small pillow from the armoire and hands it to me. She pats my head. "I'll be back in a bit. You rest."

My eyelids get heavy. I climb into bed with him. I've never slept beside anyone other than Momma or my sister. But curling up next to his frail form feels familiar. Normal. Muscle memory. Like we've done it a hundred times.

My breathing falls in line with his. Soft and deep.

I wonder how old we are now. Sebastien has a few wrinkles in the corners of his eyes. Though those could be due to his pale skin and the sun instead of years passed. I hold the wish for years in my chest.

I close my eyes and fall into a dream of images. Sebastien running along the shoreline behind my side of the island. A little girl with his black hair and my skin color nipping at his heels.

A tear slides down my cheek.

"You're not crying on me, are you?" a scratchy voice says. "You said you didn't have weepy eyes."

"I lied." I clamp my eyes shut, afraid to open them and see him like this.

He traces a finger over my face. "Let me see them, even if they're full of tears."

I open them slowly, and the tears drop. He catches them with the pad of his thumb.

"Do you regret ensnaring with me?" he asks.

"Do you?"

He has a fit of coughs. I squeeze his hand until they stop. "I swam on the beach behind your inn because I wanted to drown and get it over with. Waiting on it seemed like it had to be worse than the actual thing. But then I heard you. I came to the surface. I saw you set out your candles and the mess of your hair. I listened to you talking to yourself."

I blush.

"I went back under, instead, to see if love was a possibility for me. I had the tattoo. The rings had faded one by one. Maybe the gods did have someone in store for me. Maybe I wouldn't run out of time."

"Well, you had time and love," I whisper.

He forces a pained smile. "I did. We did, and you will have it again." He takes my hand and inches my wedding band back up.

"This could be a lie," I remind him.

"Or it could be true. Either way, it seems we make a decent couple. And I make an *excellent* husband. And we do all the stuff. You know, since we've got a kid and all."

I laugh until it turns to hiccups and more tears.

"Kiss me," he whispers, and I do.

The room fades to black. The bed under us disappears. His heart slows to a stop.

— — — —

The water rushes under me. It's cool and salty, waking my limbs. I sit up. My hair is a tangle of sand and water and frizz. The moon winks down at me.

"Sebastien!" I holler.

I hear his hearty laughter just a few feet away. I race over to him.

"You okay?" I say.

He looks me over once. "Never better."

"You're not afraid of what we just did. Of what we just saw?"

"I'm not afraid of anything," he adds with an infuriating smile.

"You saw your death."

"I saw that I lived. We will all die at some time. And I have time, despite what all the doctors and specialists have told me my whole life." He sits up and reaches for me.

I inch closer. He smooths back my tangle of curls, and I let him without hesitation.

"There's a future where you get everything you wanted," he says.

I close my eyes and think back to what I've seen. The possibility that I get to go to school. That I get to leave the island. I get to be an artist and paint other sunsets. I wonder which, if any, of the visions are real possibilities, real paths, real futures. I want them all to be true.

"But what about you?" I ask.

"Don't you turn into the others and start worrying. You've got that look in your eyes."

"I don't."

He chuckles. It feels like we've had this argument before, and will have it many times again.

"There are so many directions for things to go in. Just knowing that made me feel . . ." His voice quavers.

A door slams shut and a shadow stretches along the beach. "Viola!" my name cuts through the wind. "And just what do you think you're doing out here? And with a strange boy." Momma storms toward us. Her hands are crossed against her chest, and her freckly brown cheeks hold an angry color. "I've been calling out to you for close to an hour. Do you know what time it is?"

The wind catches her scent and wraps it all around me. She's made fresh honey biscuits and brand-new lavender soap for the inn's bathrooms.

I gaze to the left at Sebastien. He looks terrified. I burst with laughter.

"I don't think anything I just said is funny," Momma barks.

"No, ma'am," I say, trying to stop the hiccupping laughs from bubbling up and out. "This boy drowned and I saved him."

"She did," he says, grinning at me.

She clucks her tongue. "This is private property, you know. You aren't supposed to be out here. Let alone swimming."

"I'm really sorry," he replies, ducking his head in the type of shame that appeases Momma.

"Do your parents even know where you are?" she says.

"I suppose not," he admits.

"They must be worried sick. You come on up to our inn and phone them, you hear?" She sweeps him forward. "And, Viola, you've got double chores tonight. I need the salt bags brought in, and the rooms on the fourth floor need fresh linens. The dogs haven't been bathed or walked."

We pad through the sand, each step sinking us a little farther in.

"Maybe I can help," Sebastien offers. And I hope this means he might stick around for a little while. Even if that means he might not be here forever. I've seen three versions of my future tonight. I know, deep down, that all will end in sadness for us. But for the first time, it doesn't scare me that my life could also include love.

"Hmph. By the look of you, boy, you couldn't lift a feather. When's the last time you ate?"

"I'm stronger than I look."

I smile. That he is.

OOMPH

— — — — —

EMERY LORD

I BLAME IT on being the oldest child. I also blame it a little on my parents, who moved my family to the contained, drivable suburbs of Indianapolis. I definitely blame whatever genetics wired my dad to be an Olympics-qualifying worrier.

"Hi again, Dad," I say into the phone. My throat is relaxed, the pitch of my voice cheerful. I am the picture of not annoyed.

"I can hear you rolling your eyes, Cass."

I throw one hand up in the air, though there's no one with me to acknowledge my exasperation. And that—my aloneness—is exactly why he has already texted me four times since I got in the cab. Once was to make sure I was going to JFK, not LaGuardia. C'mon, Dad. New York is intimidating, but I do have basic capabilities.

"Cassidy. Are you there?"

Deep breath. I'm a trained actress, but it takes a toll, pretending I am fine for my parents when I am internally freaking out. "Yes, Dad. I'm walking into JFK right now. I still have my driver's license and my boarding pass."

"Well, I just looked up your flight again, and it's delayed now."

"I know. But only an hour."

"I'm looking at the weather, honey, and I think you should expect more delays."

It's been a sloppy April so far, rain kicking up slush. For me, a pull-your-coat-tighter spring break in New York instead of the South Carolina beach trip some other seniors took. "I *know*, Dad."

I imagine his frown, lit by his tablet, as he switches between the airline website and the weather app. My mom is almost certainly nearby, with an online crossword pulled up and maybe the Anthropologie website, cruising drapey sweaters in the Sale section.

"I'm just saying, keep an eye out for changes, okay? And maybe eat a proper dinner since you're delayed now. I know airport food is expensive, but—"

"Dad, I'm getting into the security line."

"Okay," he says. "I'll let you go."

Will you? I wonder, and I can almost hear it—the distant clang of the next phase of my life, hurtling down the tracks. It's coming. Six months away. And that phase will carry me right back here, for college. Supposedly.

"Bye, Dad," I say, quiet now.

This was a trial run for them, letting me travel to New York alone. Last summer, we did a family road trip to Manhattan, all five of us crammed in a hotel room in Times Square. The second time, it was just me and my mom, for my audition.

It all seemed terrifying and magical, until about three days ago when I realized, sitting at a party in my best friend's dorm, that I have made a terrible mistake. Now it is simply terrifying.

I spent the rest of my trip secretly Googling whether or not you can get deposit money back from a university. Ivy kept asking, "What's goin' on, Cass?" and I didn't even lie. I said, "Just thinking about next year." Then she'd loop her arm through mine and chatter excitedly about how we'll be in plays together just like at home, only at NYU this time.

I settle into the security line behind a tall girl with a long ponytail, as deep red as autumn leaves burning. And I am maybe staring a little bit, because the TSA agent nearby startles me.

"Take this," she says. I automatically accept a piece of red laminated paper. Again, I blame the oldest-child thing. I tend to follow rules.

"Okay. Uh. What is it?"

"Just give it to the agent who takes your boarding pass." She walks away before I can ask for clarification.

Heat snakes up my spine. It has the TSA logo printed at the top and the current time written in dry-erase marker on one of the lines. Did I get randomly chosen for extra screening? My heart thuds like a timpani. See? I'm panicking. I am not equipped for life in New York City. I am not equipped for life, period. Who let me apply for college in the biggest city in America?

No one else is holding a red paper. Not the guy behind me—a

man in a navy suit playing a game on his phone. Not the redhead in front of me. Everything about her—the olive-green duffle bag, her fleece jacket, her tall boots—makes her look like an advertisement for REI. Or like someone who rides horses.

She glances back, perhaps feeling my laser-beam attention.

"Busted?" the girl says, smiling. She nods toward my paper.

"Sorry?" I ask, even though I heard her. I need a moment to collect myself. These outdoorsy girls intimidate me. They always have very clear skin.

"I mean, you're literally holding a red flag. They red-flagged you." She leans in, stage-whispering with a smile. "What kind of intrigue are you part of?"

"Oh, nothing, really." I try to say this in a bored voice. This is my instinct, to switch into a character when nervous. "It's just procedure for those of us in the CIA. We work in conjunction with TSA."

God, *why* do I have to be so weird? Why couldn't I have just said, in a sultry voice, "I'll never tell."

The girl gives me a businesslike nod, thin-lipped. "Huh. Interesting. They don't make us jump through hoops like that at the FBI."

We smile at each other, and it's the strangest thing. Our mouths curling up in such synchronicity that they seem linked. Pleased with our little joke, at the precise same time.

My hand lifts into a wave. "I'm Margaret, by the way. Margaret Carter. You can call me Peggy."

She laughs, a single *ha!* that rings out in surprise. "Oh, sure. I've heard of you, Agent. Thought you'd have a British accent. I'm Natasha."

It takes me a second, but the red hair clues me in. "Romanoff, right? Black Widow. Working with the FBI, huh?"

"That's classified." She pretends to flip her ponytail back.

"Next in line," a TSA agent calls. The girl steps forward, smiling back at me as a farewell.

And I already know: I will replay this short exchange the whole way home, every frame of it. The way she tilted her head toward me, conspiratorial. The mischievous grin. It wasn't really anything—I know that. But sometimes I get glimpses that it might be possible for me. That someday, I'll find someone who gets my sense of humor without a single confused look. Someone who is so beautiful that my hands feel twitchy.

When I step up to the podium, I hold out the mystery paper. The agent accepts it without a reaction.

"I was supposed to give that to you."

"Thanks," she says, taking my ID. I scan my boarding pass, relieved that it beeps right away.

"What was it?"

"Oh," she says. "Just us gathering data about how long it took you to get through the line. Have a good flight."

When I glance over to the other line, the girl has her boots off. I'm relieved to see that she's wearing mismatched socks. They're not woolen hiking socks, either. One has a pattern made of pizza slices. She turns over her shoulder, perhaps feeling my scrutiny again. But she only smiles, as if we're both in on a secret.

Once I'm through the scanner, I look for her once more. She's in full Vitruvian Man, arms and legs wide, as a TSA officer pats her down.

Busted, I mouth at her.

She grins, pressing her wrists together to mime being handcuffed. The agent notices, frowning, and the girl's smile drops. She attempts a solemn look, and I can't help but laugh.

Bye, pretty woodsy girl, I think, wistful.

I grip it, this feeling—so tightly that my fingers ache. It's like trying to hold smoke.

But that's that. Or so I think, as I pick up some snacks and decide on a seat at my near-empty gate. I'm settling my headphones into my ears when I hear it.

"Oh my gosh! Margaret? Margaret Carter?"

It's not the name but the loudness of her voice that gets my attention. Sure enough, the girl from the security line is at the gate across from mine. Going to, per the lit-up sign behind her, Denver. There's an older man beside her, watching as she waves to me. And the girl is giving me a meaningful, wide-eyed *HELP ME* look.

"Hey, Natasha!" I call, looking surprised. It's a neutral enough response.

She's gathering her things, moving—I think—to come sit by me. Yep, she's hauling her stuff over, but with a look on her face that I can't read. Definitely trying to communicate something with gritted teeth.

"You are my savior," she whispers, sitting down beside me. "That guy smells like whiskey and wanted to tell me all about how nervous he gets to fly."

"Get out of town!" I say loudly, with a practiced stage laugh. Hoping the drunk guy can hear me. Trying to sell that we know each other. "I should have known we'd run into each other here!"

"Thank you." She relaxes into her seat, not facing forward but angled toward me.

"So," I say. "They didn't make you go to airport jail?"

"Oh, please. The joint could never hold me." She glances around. "So, Margaret, who are you here investigating?"

She elbows me gently, nodding stage left toward a chic woman in a trench, hair blown out into shiny curls.

"Please. Too obvious. The real villain is the little one."

"That small child? With the unicorn backpack?"

I nod solemnly. "Master of disguise."

We guess at what the middle-aged married couple is bickering about. We speculate that two pilots wheeling luggage past us are sleeping together. We debate the relationship between an older man and a beautiful younger woman. Colleagues? May-December romance?

"Curmudgeonly old spy, training the new generation of beautiful, badass spies," I suggest.

"Agreed. You're good at this."

I should hope so, after nearly four years at the Indianapolis School for the Performing Arts. "You are, too."

She offers up a style of shrug I wish I could perfect—dismissive but elegant. "Art nerd."

Before I can ask what she means, she gestures to the crowd we've been watching. "It's like trying to figure out a painting. Maybe you have a little context—the year it was painted, or maybe you've seen the artist's other work before. But you're largely inferring. It's just paying attention to detail and an educated guess. Why this angle?

What was going on in the artist's life? Sometimes, I think, knowing that for sure takes the fun out of it. I like to speculate."

I don't like to speculate about anything. I like call times. I like a nice, set tempo in a musical number. But before I ask more, she leans away, examining me. "Okay. I'm going to do you."

My heart swells like a balloon, just moments before a *pop!* It takes me an embarrassingly long time to realize that she means she's going to guess what I'm doing here in the airport.

Am I misreading her? Her body language is so comfortable and open. She elbowed me before, like we're old pals who touch all the time. And she brought up Natasha Romanoff. I mean.

I take a deep breath, trying to keep my cheeks from turning pink.

The girl squints at me, and I realize I have had seventeen years to become a cooler person. What have I been *doing* all this time? According to Ivy, I dress like a movie star playing a 1950s professor. I guess that's her way of summarizing that I like blazers and slim-fitting pants but also lipstick. Sometimes I add a silk scarf, and I don't really care what's trendy or not. After you've seen enough Katharine Hepburn movies, whatever is currently in fashion just seems fleeting.

It doesn't help that I keep my regular brown hair at my shoulders, so it can be styled easily for whatever show I'm in. I could have at least gotten some shaggy, French-girl bangs, on the off chance a pretty girl would someday be scrutinizing my appearance for clues.

"You are coming home from"—she pauses, still considering—"A national convention of Model UN. Where you represented . . Ireland. Small, but complex. Lots of history."

My laugh, which was supposed to be light and airy, sounds like a distressed bird. "Nope."

"Wrong? Okay. You were . . . doing a college interview. At Columbia. Where you plan to major in"—she taps her fingers against her lips—"materials engineering."

"Closer." I glance down at my outfit. "Materials engineering. Interesting."

"The thought process had to do with your lipstick," she says, gesturing at her own mouth. "I was thinking, okay, you also look like a fairly precise person. I can see you revolutionizing makeup packaging. Making it recyclable, eco-friendly. But still sophisticated."

"Spring break," I confess. "I was visiting my best friend at school, where I'm supposed to be next year."

"I'm a senior, too," she says, excited. "You're going to Columbia?"

"NYU. Tisch."

"An *actrice*?" She says it in an easy French accent, the *r* sound from the back of her throat. "Huh. You don't seem like the type."

"No?"

"Well, you don't seem like a ham, you know? Always breaking into song at a party, not realizing it makes everyone uncomfortable."

I laugh, loudly, because I go to a performing arts school. I know those types. I am *surrounded* by those types. I am best friends with that type. "I just like taking on other mannerisms. Other identities. Studying how to be someone else."

"Huh. When did you get into it?"

"I guess I was . . . eleven."

Just tell her, Cass. What's the worst thing that happens? She's like: *I'm out of here*? I mean, she's out of here—by necessity—in half an hour anyway.

But, before I can speak, the girl glances down at her phone. "Sorry, hold on one sec. Hi, Mom. Yeah, I'm on time. Okay."

She's placating her mom just as I did my dad, and I know I missed my window.

What I would have told her is that I started summer theater camp in elementary school, and I loved it. Loved the boxes full of costumes, loved the total commitment to roaring like a lion or standing totally still as a tree. I liked memorizing lines, knowing what I was supposed to say and when.

But I knew I was *good* at it in sixth grade. Annabel Warren's birthday slumber party, to be exact, when we all had to go around and say who our celebrity crush was and why. And I sat there, in my pink-striped pajamas, acting my ass off. I said Kellan James, boy wonder of our favorite tween show. The key to my performance was seeming embarrassed to admit it. I stumbled on my words. I said "like" a lot. I glanced at the carpet.

"I don't know," I said breathily, unable to make eye contact with the other girls. "He just seems, like, I don't know. The kind of boyfriend who would, like, be really nice to your younger sister. You know?"

I mean, he *did* really seem like that! I think I actually willed my cheeks to flush. Meryl Streep honestly has nothing on an eleven-year-old who feels very cozy in the closet. Back then, I didn't have the right words for the way I felt anyway.

They bought it completely. And it didn't really feel like lying. I felt powerful and safe, taking on the identity of a girl I simply . . . wasn't.

For years, if Kellan came up, Annabel would waggle her eyebrows at me. She once got me a birthday card with his face on it, which she labeled *Future Husband*.

I came out to her freshman year, and she said, so earnestly, "But there was that whole Kellan James thing."

Oh, Annabel. Sweet, innocent Annabel.

In the end, it was still an inside joke between us. Just for a different reason.

"Sorry about that," the girl says, setting down her phone. She positions herself back toward me. I notice that—of course I do. "I swear, I've been traveling alone for a decade, and she still frets. Okay. Your turn to guess mine."

"Your reason for being in New York?"

"Mmhmm."

"I don't have to guess," I say. "Because I *know*: L.L.Bean catalog photo shoot."

"Oh my God." She covers her face, laughing, but I think she's pleased. "Ha. Yeah, right."

"Am I right? Or am I right?"

"This outfit isn't L.L.Bean. Just Denver-wear. And I'm definitely not a model," she says, motioning as if presenting herself. "I am but a child of divorce. One weekend a month with my dad in the city."

"That's pretty cool, right? Like a New York vacation twelve times a year?"

"Yeah, I like it now. Because when he's busy, which is a lot, I can just go to museums and the park and the theater. I'm not there enough to make actual friends, though. So I'm just a weird, loner art girl. But that's okay. I'll be at Columbia next year."

We talk about friends from home, about summer plans. For me? Working as many hours as I can get waiting tables. For her, unofficial nanny for her younger half siblings. At one point, I make her laugh so hard that she tips her head back.

It can be so freaking hard to tell if a girl is into you or if she thinks she just found a new best friend. I mean, sure, I do have *some* sense of it. But I've been wrong before. Like, a lifetime of crushes on girls who later announce their straightness. Some of the time, I want to side-eye them like, *You sure about that?* But hey. Whatever.

My mom says it'll be easier in college, that not everyone knows themselves as well as I do just yet. That not everyone feels safe or comfortable enough to come out in high school. And I get that; I do live in Indiana, where I have to be careful, too. But sometimes it seems so unfair that I have to wait. Plenty of girls get their love stories starting now, starting years ago. Sometimes I even envy their heartbreak. At least they got to know what it was like, right?

What I get, apparently, is a first date with a girl I met online, who barely spoke to me at the carnival where we met up. On our second date, we agreed that we just didn't click. We did make out in my car, though. That's my romance portfolio.

"Hey," the girl says. We never exchanged real names, and now it's too awkward to throw that into the conversation. "Before, you said you were visiting your best friend at Tisch. Where you're *supposed* to be next year. But you won't be?"

Everything feels so much safer in costume, with adopted mannerisms. So why, sitting here with her, do I want to empty my pockets and show her everything I own? Every flaw, every quirk. The dull coins and gum wrappers, every trivial and unglamorous part of who I am.

"Tisch was always the plan. I got in; we sent the deposit and everything. But now I . . . think it's a huge mistake." The girl tips her head forward just a bit, silently asking for more information. "Ivy's acting-school friends . . . they're all—I don't know. Smart and talented and beautiful. Why did I think I could go there and compete with that?"

"Uh," the girl says, giving me a pointed look, "because you're also smart and talented and beautiful?"

I stare down at my knees, puffing out laugh-air. "Yeah, right."

"Ex*cuse* me," she scoffs. "You *just* told me that I'm good at reading people."

"I guess I thought I was getting the leads in every play and musical because I'm *good*. But maybe I'm just a big fish in a small pond. What if I'm *not* any good, and I'm just driving myself into debt for a career that, like, basically no one gets to have in the long run? I mean, my parents don't have a lot of money, so this is on me. And, God, like . . . just navigating the city. It's so much. Figuring out the subway and trying not to get lost on the streets, and . . ." I trail off, helpless.

"You know what, though?" She's squinting, her gaze somewhere in the crowd. "For the first issue, at least, I think all of us seniors think that."

This time, it's me who cocks my head, wondering if she's right.

"I mean, even if we feel sure about what we want to do—what

if we're wrong? What if it sucks; what if we're not good at it? What if we are, but we still can't get a solid career down the road? It's all unknowns."

"Okay. Then what the heck are we supposed to do?"

She scans the people around us, as if searching in them for an answer. "I think . . . I *think* all we can really do is chase the *oomph*."

I lean forward, thinking I've misheard. "The *oomph*?"

Man, she's pretty. Pale lashes fluttering as she thinks. "Yeah, that thing you feel when you're right where you're supposed to be. That . . . steeled feeling."

Standing in the wings before my first entrance. Drawing my shoulders back, spotlight on me, as the opening notes of my solo sound from the orchestra pit. Total assurance—joy, even, that I can do it. Standing at the piano beside my co-lead in rehearsals, working through tricky, interlocking harmonies. The moments when I can work myself up to impassioned tears.

"See?" she says, pleased. "You know what I'm talking about. Wouldn't you do just about anything to chase that feeling? Wouldn't you keep auditioning even though the girls competing for your roles are going to make you work harder for it?"

"That is"—I say, swallowing—"an excellent point."

Someone gets on the intercom at my gate to announce that the plane is still en route. I sigh, rolling my eyes. "With my luck, I'll be sleeping here."

"Well, then," Natasha says, rubbing her hands together. She wears a thin ring on her pointer finger, gold with a tiny peridot stone that matches her eyes. I want to know what it means to her. Is it her birthstone? A gift? Just something pretty she stumbled across? "I'd better teach you to airport camp before I board."

"Airport camp?"

"Yeah," she says. "I invented it when I was twelve. Stay here."

After I've watched her walk away, I glance at my phone. Two missed calls from my dad, and a text that says *I'm worried*. No kidding, Dad. That is your resting state of being.

I'm typing out a response when my mom calls, a dorky selfie of us popping up with her contact info.

"Hey, Mom."

"Hey, sweetie. Thought I'd check in. Your dad figures he might be driving you nuts." She's probably at the kitchen island, keeping my brother and sister from bickering as they work on homework.

"Only a little. I'm fine. Just sitting here at the gate. Still delayed."

"Poor thing. Delays are no fun, but even worse when you're alone. Is Wi-Fi free? At least watch a movie or something?"

"It's all right, actually. I made a friend."

There's a heavy silence across the line as she, apparently, deliberates.

"No," she decides. "Nope. I don't like you talking to strangers. This is how people get murdered in airport bathrooms and stuffed into trash cans."

"*What?* You made that up. And she's harmless, I swear."

"Wait," she says, breathy all the sudden. "Is it a *girl*?"

Even hundreds of miles away, I can sense her grin, smug as can be. I'm quiet for too long, incriminating myself. "It *is*, isn't it?"

"I've gotta go, Mom."

"You do not! You're literally trapped in an airport with nothing to do. Is she pretty?"

I hold the phone away from my ear so I can't hear her. "Bye, Mom! Love you!"

With my remaining alone time, I consider my options: Text Ivy that I met a girl. (No, can't do it. What if she texts me back after said girl returns, and girl sees it? Or what if Ivy asks something basic like, say, the girl's name?) I could Google *How can I tell if a girl is flirting with me?* (I know from experience that it is not helpful at all.) So, I check my flight one more time, touch up my makeup, and try to convince myself that the girl is actually coming back.

Which she does eventually, a purposeful walk even with her hands full. She's carrying a Starbucks cup, a Rice Krispies treat in plastic wrap, and chocolate-covered grahams.

"I don't get it," I admit.

"You will." Using the empty seat next to her as a flat surface, she cuts the Rice Krispies treat into smaller cubes, then spears one with a wooden coffee stirrer.

"Okay," she says. "So. If you wind up having to stay overnight, you find an empty gate."

She removes the lid from the cup, revealing what appears to be plain hot water. Steam floods upward.

"Maybe knot the sleeves of two sweaters together, drape them over the armrests of these chairs. Definitely pull up a YouTube video of a crackling fire on your laptop. And then . . ." She holds the Rice Krispies treat kabob over the steam. I give her a puzzled look, but it hits me quick.

"Oh my God," I say, laughing.

When her makeshift marshmallow is gooey enough, she presses it onto a chocolate graham.

"Et voilà," she says, handing it to me. "Airport s'more."

When I take it, she licks melted chocolate off the pad of her finger. I almost cough up the bite I'm trying to chew. Instead, I look away, *hmm*ing thoughtfully. "This is impressive."

She gives that same self-possessed shrug. "I'm an impressive person."

Across from us, her gate's intercom announces boarding. The line forms in a rush, which I've never understood. Why sit in that tiny airplane seat any longer than you have to?

"Well, I better get over there," she says, jabbing a thumb at the gate.

"You're lucky. I live here now." I try not to betray that I feel split down the center, realizing I'll never see her again. I might hang on to the wooden stirrer/marshmallow skewer, to remind myself it was real. "Hey, if that drunk guy talks to you again, tell a flight attendant, okay? Seriously."

"I will," she says, solemn. "Nice to meet you, Carter. I'll tell the home office you're as talented as they say."

"Back at you, Romanoff."

She hefts her duffel bag over her shoulder, gives me a half smile before she turns to go.

It settles in, that feeling of total certainty that I will regret what I am doing—nothing—even while I have a chance to correct it. I settle back into my seat, knowing I will wonder forever. That I'll recount every moment to my friends, that they'll scream "Why didn't you ask for her number?"

I won't have an answer. Something I have *longed* for was right there, an arm's reach away. Why couldn't I just lift my hand? Too afraid that I'd have it slapped away, I guess. Maybe it was enough for it to just exist, here and now.

Or maybe that's an excuse I use, to avoid putting myself out there. Maybe I'm just hiding behind the guise of a strong-woman character whose lines I've memorized, without ever making my own, bold choices. I tear through my purse for a pen and paper.

I've gotta do it, right? She started the conversation in line. *She* flagged me down. Have I given her anything concrete in return?

"Natasha, hey!" I say, breathless from hurrying.

She looks up from her phone. The people nearest to her in line are pretending not to eavesdrop.

"Johanna, actually," she says. Is it my imagination—does she look relieved? "Jo."

"I'm Cassidy."

She nods, as if she knew this. Like she'd known me in another life and just couldn't quite remember what name I'd gone by in those years.

"My number," I say, holding out a carbon-smeared receipt. "In case you want to show a New York newbie around the museums next year. Have a laugh at how dense I am about art."

She looks pleased. "It *has* always been my dream to just be weird art girl, instead of weird loner art girl."

"Happy to help. Okay. See you." I say it breezily, acting again—just a little. Trying to be a more confident girl.

"Bye, Cass," she says. The smile stays put.

Back at my own gate, I grin like a fool. But I'm *not* a fool—I know this girl might never text me. Or, if she does, it'll be as friends, and that's okay. She's disappeared into the tunnel toward her plane.

But I still get to keep it—the fact that a pretty stranger patched up my relationship with NYU, like some angel of college plans. That she made my heart feel full of glitter, if only for half an hour. That I got to feel seen.

I'm so lost in it that the buzz of my phone startles me. A number I don't know.

Hey, it's Jo. You're not going to believe this, she says. And I like that. I like that she thinks she knows what I would and wouldn't believe.

I put my music on shuffle when I sat down and this is the first song that came up.

A screenshot of a song called "Pretty Girl at the Airport."

One beat. Just enough for a sharp inhale. And there it is, deep in my chest.

Oomph.

THE DICTIONARY OF YOU AND ME

— — — — —

JENNIFER L. ARMENTROUT

CHEEKS FLUSHED AND stinging from the whipping winds barreling through the near-empty parking lot, I hurried toward the small, two-story county library I'd worked at three days a week for the past two and a half years.

The wind was picking up loose strands of my black hair, tossing them across my face as if it were attempting to blind me. That's what I got for not wearing a hat or taking the time to pull my hair up.

Winter had come early this year to Waverly Hollow, turning the small, barely there town into the North Pole since the day after Thanksgiving. Now that Christmas was in a week, there was a high likelihood that we'd have a dusting of the white fluffy stuff come Christmas morning.

A white Christmas! I thought happily.

I was a big old dork when it came to Christmas. I loved everything about it—the twinkly lights and crinkling paper, the smell of pine and balsam, the music and the movies, and most, I loved all the *hope*.

As soon as I pushed open the main lobby door, the musty scent of books hit me. I tugged off my thick mittens with a smile. I loved that smell. I guessed it was a good thing that I did since I planned to study library science when I entered college next fall.

The library was dead, but that was no surprise. It was a Wednesday night and we tended only to be busy on the weekends.

I crossed the main floor, passing the reference section that saw about the same amount of action as I did. Boyfriendless since the end of last summer, I was officially giving up on the whole dating thing. Not that anyone would blame me, since my last date ended with my fist connecting with Jared Richmond's nose.

Shoving my gloves into the pocket of my coat, I walked behind the front desk, and like I did every time I showed up for work, I headed for the return cart.

Mrs. Singer, the head librarian in charge, always left the return cart for me to handle. Not that I minded. She took care of everything else, so there wasn't much for me to do in the evenings that I worked.

But there was one book in particular that I was searching for.

I bent over and started rooting through the books I'd have to put away later. It didn't take long for me to realize that the way-overdue book hadn't been returned.

The corners of my lips tipped up again.

I straightened as I pulled off the scarf, unsure if the tiny smidgen of relief I felt was absurd. Actually, I knew the answer to that. It was the epitome of ludicrous.

Shaking my head, I went over to the front desk as Mrs. Singer strolled out of the small office, her steel-gray hair smooth and sleek. I slid my backpack off and placed it under the desk. Mrs. Singer was already bundled up, wearing a puffy black jacket and a pale white scarf. Her sparkly purse dangled from her gloved fingers.

"Good evening, Miss Evans."

Before I could open my mouth to respond, Mrs. Singer turned on her heel. Cold air rushed into the library as the door swung shut behind her. And that was it. Off she went, home to her husband of a billion years.

Mrs. Singer wasn't much of a talker.

Scanning the stacks and tables, I spotted two patrons, one by the computers and the other sitting near a window reading. I tucked a strand of hair behind my ear as I grabbed the clear plastic holder that contained a dozen or so index cards.

Our systems were pretty archaic due to lack of funding and the fact that our town was still stuck in the fifties. I mean, we had one high school that served the *entire* county, so our library was like the little library that could.

These cards were linked to library accounts that had overdue books on them. Normally we'd shoot e-mails to the offenders. We rarely ever called them.

Except for Mr. H. Smith.

Getting the way-overdue book back from him had become a personal mission of mine. I'd call him at least once, sometimes twice a week, and he always answered.

And he always had some completely out-there excuse for why he hadn't returned the dictionary he'd checked out four months ago.

Yes.

A *dictionary*.

I was pretty sure he was the only person to check out a dictionary since the Internet was invented.

Pulling out his card, I tapped it off the counter as I picked up the phone and wedged it between my cheek and shoulder.

The phone rang once.

Then twice.

"Hello," the familiar male voice answered.

For some dumb reason, my heart belly-flopped in my chest, which was weird, because this was just about getting a book back, but . . . "Hi. This is—"

"Moss," he answered. "You don't give up, do you?"

I grew up hating my name and the fact that my parents had been hippies who had to have smoked a ton of pot before they came up with it. I mean, my name was Moss. *Moss?* Like, come on. Moss wasn't a name. It was a plant that grew in dank, dark areas. But the way H. Smith said it? I felt my cheeks warm. He said my name like he was whispering some kind of prized secret.

He sounded close to my age. Of course, I knew that didn't really mean anything. I had no idea if this guy was some kind of perv living in his mother's basement, harassing women online while eating Double Stuf Oreos and getting crumbs all over his keyboard. But somehow I knew he wasn't.

"I've missed you," he said, surprising me. Even without a mirror, I knew my pink skin was getting even pinker.

Clearing my throat, I focused on the task at hand. "There is no way you could've missed me."

"And why not?" he replied, sounding amused.

"We don't even know each other."

"I don't think that's true. I mean, at least I feel like I know you." There was a pause. "Just the other day, you told me you hated turkey."

I *had* told him that, though I couldn't remember how that topic of convo had come up. "Yeah, and just the other day you told me the reason you'd been unable to return the dictionary was because you were touring the back roads of France."

He chuckled. "That's not a lie."

"Oh, really?"

"I've been checking them out on Google Maps."

My lips twitched. "And what about the time you told me you haven't been able to make it to the library because you're preparing for an alien invasion?"

"Well, I have been playing *Halo* in my spare time, so it's not like that's a lie," he answered smoothly. "And you know me. You know my deepest, darkest secret."

"I really don't think I know that."

"Yes, you do." His tone was light, playful even. "You know that I like to write. I know that *you* like that I write."

He caught me so off guard that I heard myself stutter out, "O-of course I like that. I do work at a library."

"Mmhmm," he murmured. "And you also know that I just started marathoning *Game of Thrones*."

I glanced up from the phone. The few people in the library were still busy doing their thing. "That's only because you used that as an excuse for not returning the book. You said you were too emotionally wrecked after the Red Wedding scene."

"I was," he exclaimed. "That was a traumatic episode. I mean, I blinked and half the cast was gone. Just *gone*."

I was grinning so hard I was sure there was a good chance he could see it through the phone.

"And I know you cry when those ASPCA commercials come on," he continued.

"Everyone cries when those commercials come on!" I defended myself. "And the only reason you know that about me is because the last time I called, I could hear that song playing in the background. And I didn't start crying. I just said they made me cry."

Truth was, H. Smith was a stranger, but not. From the weekly calls over the last several months, little bits of information about both of us had surfaced. Nothing too deep. He knew I didn't like soda and preferred hot tea. He claimed to drink almost nothing but water and orange juice. We both were animal people. I heard him talk to a dog once, Daisy. Those were the kind of things we knew about each other, and we'd never met.

"Annnnnnyway," he drew the word out. "Have you heard of zelophobia?"

Fighting a grin, I dropped onto the worn stool behind the front desk. He did this every time. Found random words in the dictionary and told me about them. The guy was—I don't know. He was just . . . interesting. "No. I have no idea what that is."

"It's the irrational fear of jealousy." He paused. "I'm not sure what makes the fear irrational, but a zelophobe seems like my kind of person."

"Agreed," I murmured, glancing around the library.

"Did you know *zazzy* was a real word?"

"It is?"

"According to the dictionary I plan on returning, it means flashy and stylish. Can you use *zazzy* in a sentence?"

I laughed under my breath. "My winter jacket is zazzy."

"I'm sure it is," he said, and it sounded like a door shut somewhere on his side of the phone. "Do you know what a zokor is?"

"No, but I'm guessing you're going to tell me."

"That I am," he returned. "It's a molelike rodent that actually looks really fluffy and friendly."

I wrinkled my nose, creasing the skin around my eyes. "I don't know if there are any rodents that are friendly looking."

"Uh, what about Mickey Mouse?"

"Mickey Mouse is a cartoon."

"No shit?"

Another laugh escaped me. "Shocker, I know."

"Well, this conversation is full of zanyism."

"Oh my God," I said, shaking my head. "Does anyone even use the word *zanyism* in everyday language?"

He laughed, and it *was* a nice laugh. Deep. Infectious. He sounded like someone who laughed a lot, and I didn't picture trolls in their mothers' basements as people who laughed a lot. "They should. They'd sound smarter."

"Maybe . . . ?"

"You know what the most interesting word I've found is? I know you're dying to know, so I won't draw it out for you," he said, and I bit down on my lip. "It's *zapata*. It means drooping, *flowing* mustache."

"What?" I laughed.

"Yep. So, I got curious, because who wouldn't be?"

"Yeah? Who wouldn't be," I said, switching the phone to my other shoulder.

"It's actually named after the leader of the Mexican revolution—Emiliano Zapata," he explained. "See. You learn something new every day."

"Or at least whenever I talk to you."

"You probably don't want me to tell you what *zatch* stands for."

"Probably not."

"Just think about how less . . . wordy you'd be if I returned this dictionary on time," he said, this time with an amused chuckle.

"I'm a better person now," I said dryly.

There was another pause. "So, Moss, I was thinking . . ."

After a few seconds, I gave up on waiting. "Thinking what? You're going to finally return the dictionary?"

There was another rumble of laughter. "Maybe. Just maybe."

I felt that swelling in my chest again.

Footsteps drew my attention, and I peered up. Someone was shuffling to the desk with an armful of books to check out. I straightened. "It's been nice chatting with you, Mr. Smith, but it's time to return the dictionary. Our set looks pretty sad without it. Have a good night!" I added, hanging up quickly.

Standing, I pushed the call out of my head and took care of the guy checking out five books on herbology and hydroponics.

Really wasn't going to question that too closely.

Then I tackled the books that had been returned, the mind-numbing task keeping me busy most of the evening. Later, before I closed up the library, I Googled *zokor*, and I had to admit that the brown molelike rodents did look fluffy . . . and friendly.

— — — —

"I don't know why they made us come to school today." Libby sighed as she leaned against the locker beside mine. Her curly black hair was pulled into a tight pouf at the top of her head. "It's a half day and not even the teachers want to be here."

Smothering a yawn, I stared bleakly at the books in my locker. "I wonder if they'll care if I nap through first period."

"Did you stay up watching *Untold Stories of the ER* again?" she asked.

I shot her a grin. "I can't help it. The show is fascinating."

Libby shook her head. "You're so weird."

"You love me," I told her as I grabbed my English book. Libby and I had been best friends since grade school. "When are you leaving for your grandparents'?"

"Christmas Eve eve," she answered with a roll of her light green eyes. "Sigh. No Internet. No cable. The townsfolk are the kind that look at my mom and dad strangely. You know, in *that* way," she said. Libby was biracial, her mother black and her father white. "God be with me."

I cringed in sympathy. "How long will you be there?"

"Until New Year's Eve." She moaned, running her hand along the strap of her bag. "You're going to be home, right?"

Nodding, I pulled out a thin, couple-inch-wide notebook I used for doodling. I wasn't very talented outside of drawing flowers. And I could totally draw a blobfish. Real talent right there. There was just something relaxing about sketching, though. "My grandparents are coming to our house."

"Lucky you. Oh—did you manage to get that book returned?" she asked as I closed the locker door.

I laughed and swung my backpack around, shoving the notebook into it. Libby was well aware of my ongoing mission at the library. "No such luck."

"I think you may as well just give up . . . God, he is so pretty."

Frowning, I followed her gaze and saw her grinning as she stared in the opposite direction. I shifted and immediately knew whom she was talking about.

Quiet Hot Guy.

That was the official name Libby had given him when he showed up at the start of the school year. He was new, and that alone had been breaking news, but add in the fact that he was seriously cute and also seriously quiet? Everyone had paid attention.

Tyler Cox.

I never exchanged a single word with him. He was in my history class, but he sat in the front while I sort of hid out in the back. I didn't see him at lunch, and since we didn't have that large of a cafeteria, I figured he must hang out in the library like some did.

He was a bit of a mystery.

A very cute mystery.

"Why does he have to have better lashes than us?" Libby whispered. "It's not fair."

My lips curved up as I swallowed a giggle. He really did have amazing lashes.

He stopped at his locker. I tried to pretend like I wasn't gawking, but he was really, really nice to look at. So, like the creepers we were, Libby and I watched him swirl the lock on the metal door.

Tyler had a messy shock of hair that was a wild array of auburn and deep brown. It fell forward, brushing his eyebrows. With pale skin that looked like he'd be prone to blushing, those high cheekbones and the cut jaw, he really was more than just cute.

The guy was a hottie.

And he was tall, with the kind of shoulders my gramma would call door-busters. Gramma was also kind of weird.

He started to turn toward us, so I pivoted around, widening my eyes at Libby as my bag thumped off my side. "I really need to stop staring at people."

She laughed. "There are a lot of things you need to stop."

"Like what?" I demanded.

"As if I need to tell you." Eyes glimmering, she grinned as she stepped back. "See you in English."

Wiggling my fingers at her, I lifted my bag up and headed in the opposite direction. I fell into the pack of shuffling bodies, folding my arms across my chest. I dreaded the climb to the second floor. It was too early and I was entirely too lazy—

"Excuse me," a voice called out from behind me.

Wheeling around, I came to a complete stop. Tyler stood a few feet from me, seemingly unaware of everyone passing around and between us.

"Hi," I squeaked like a chew toy. Why was he talking to me? We'd never talked before. Probably saw me staring at him like some—

"You dropped this."

My brows rose as I stared. Goodness. Up close, those lashes were truly amazing. They lowered now, shielding eyes—I wasn't sure of the color. One side of his lips quirked up.

"You dropped this," he repeated, and then lifted his hand, holding the small notebook that now struck me as impossibly uncool. "Thought you might want it back. It's pretty zaz—uh, jazzy looking."

"Did you just say 'zazzy'?" I asked, every part of me stilling. Who would use a world like *zazzy* except . . .

He looked at me like I was an idiot. "Umm, I said 'jazzy.' Stupid joke. Anyway, here's your notebook." He handed it to me and walked away.

I was still staring.

The warning bell rang, tossing me out of my stupor. "Thank you," I called after him.

I stood there for a few seconds, sort of wanting to punch myself. I could talk to some strange, and I mean strange, dude on a phone for four months, but I couldn't say a complete sentence to the one standing in front of me?

Ugh.

I was a mess—a typical walking cliché mess.

— — — —

"Jingle Bells" played softly from the computer behind the front counter, breaking the cardinal library rule, but it was the eve of Christmas Eve, and I didn't think the few people in the library would mind.

One guy was softly snoring by the window, so he didn't get a choice.

Perched on the edge of my seat, I was shading in a giant poinsettia with a red coloring pencil I'd stolen from my younger brother. I glanced at the front doors to see if it had started snowing again, like the forecast had called for. The sun was just setting, casting what I could see of the parking lot into long, cloudy shadows.

Hoping it didn't snow buckets, I went back to the poinsettia. "Silent Night" replaced "Jingle Bells" replaced "Blue Christmas." I had no idea how much time had passed until I heard footsteps approaching me. My gaze flicked up.

And I almost fell out of my seat.

It was *him*.

Quiet Hot Guy. Tyler. I'd never, ever seen him in here before. Granted, I didn't work here every day, but still . . .

"Hey," I said, surprise causing my tone to pitch high. "Tyler."

A lopsided grin formed as thick lashes lowered. "You know my name?"

Heat blasted my cheeks. Was I not supposed to know his name? Did knowing his name make me seem creepy? I kind of felt creepy now. "Well, yes. I mean, it's kind of hard not to—not that I mean anything by that. I mean, this is a small town and you're new—well, newish—and in small towns like this, everyone knows everyone even if they don't know that people know them."

One brow lifted as Tyler studied me.

Oh God, I needed to shut up, but I couldn't seem to stop my mouth. "Everyone knows your name."

Okay. Now I did sound creepy.

"I'm sorry," I said, feeling the centers of my cheeks warm. "I'm just . . . really random today."

"It's okay." One hand curled around the strap of his bag.

I leaned forward. There was something familiar about his voice. I wasn't sure I could chalk it up to hearing him speak in class or the hallways. There was something else, like it was on the tip of my tongue or a thought existing on the fringe.

The grin grew on those well-formed lips, warming brown eyes—dark brown eyes.

And I was totally just sitting there, staring at him like a dork.

I cleared my throat. "So, what can I help you with, Tyler?"

"Actually, I think I can help you." He slid off his backpack and knelt down to unzip his bag. "It's something I think you've been waiting for."

Curious, I watched him reach into his bag and pull something thick out of it. He laid it down on the lip of the counter, and my mouth dropped so far open I was sure I'd catch flies, just like my gramma would say.

A burgundy-and-gold dictionary rested in front of me.

Not just any old dictionary. It was the missing one—the one checked out by H. Smith!

I dropped the red pencil. It clattered off the desk and dropped to the floor. Slowly, I lifted my gaze from the heavy tome to Tyler's chocolate-colored eyes. "I . . . I don't understand."

Tyler was still grinning as he folded his arms on the counter. "I used to live in North Carolina, but my mom met someone at this conference for work. Anyway, after about a year of dating and doing the long-distance thing, they married."

"Okay," I murmured.

He tilted his head to the side. "So I ended up moving here over the summer. My stepfather's name is Harvey Smith."

Harvey Smith.

H. Smith.

My lips parted on a soft inhale.

Oh my God.

"I haven't gotten my own library card," he continued as he glanced down at the dictionary. "So I've been using his, which is linked to his home phone."

"Home phone," I repeated dumbly.

"I know, right? Can you believe he still has a house phone?" He chuckled, and I knew that chuckle. I'd heard it over the phone more than a dozen times. "Scared the crap out of me the first time it rang. Couldn't figure out where it was coming from."

I couldn't speak.

His gaze lowered once more and he ran his fingers through his hair. "Anyway, I was bored one day and found that he'd checked this dictionary out. No idea why. But I started reading it." He lifted one shoulder as he dropped his hand to the counter. "Because why not?"

I blinked slowly.

"Then one day at the end of August, the house phone rang and I decided to answer it," he continued. "It was this person from the public library and . . . I think you know the rest."

I did know the rest, but . . .

But this couldn't be real.

Quiet Hot Guy from school that you never spoke to didn't turn out to be Funny Random Guy who refused to return dictionaries.

Things like this only happened in Hallmark movies, the kind that made Libby cry like she was an angry, unfed baby. They didn't happen in real life, but this was happening. I wasn't dreaming. Tyler was really standing in front of me, and he had the dictionary.

Letting out a little laugh, I shook my head. "I'm sorry. I'm just really caught off guard. I thought I was talking to . . ."

"To who?" he asked, head tilting to the other side.

"I don't know, but not—not you," I said, and then added, "I don't mean that in a bad way, but we've never talked at school and—" Then it struck me. "Did you know who I was?"

"Not at first," he admitted, a faint pink flush spreading along his cheeks. "You actually never said your name until—"

"Until a month or so ago," I said, remembering that call. I sat back in the seat, my hands falling to my lap.

He nodded. "Before that you always introduced yourself as calling on behalf of the library." His gaze flicked away. "Then you said your name and I figured it had to be you. I doubted there were many other people named Moss."

When I looked up, he was staring at the dictionary, his dark brows pinched together and that faint blush still staining his cheeks. It had been him this entire time. I could barely wrap my head around it.

Libby was going to die.

She was going to die and be reborn.

Tyler's gaze flickered to mine. "You never asked my name."

I opened my mouth to deny that, but he was right. I hadn't. "I just assumed the name the card was under was who I was talking to."

His eyes held mine. "Are you disappointed?"

My heart leapt into my throat and the same second my stomach tumbled over itself. I wanted to turn that question over and over in my head, analyze what it could mean. I wanted to dash into Mrs. Singer's office and call Libby.

Of course, I didn't have time for any of that. A flutter grew in my chest. I drew in a shallow breath. "I'm not disappointed."

A slow curl of his lips spread into a smile. "Really?"

I nodded, thinking, *Who in the world would be disappointed?* Part of me kept expecting someone to jump out from behind the stack of books with a camera. Wait. My stomach dropped. "Is this . . . is this a prank?"

His brows flew up. "No. No way."

A kernel of suspicion formed. "Why now?"

Tyler knocked his hair back from his forehead and the strands immediately fell back in place. "I wanted to say something earlier, but I . . ." The blush deepened, and he looked away again, coughing out a low laugh. "I just didn't have the nerve. When I, uh, when I figured out it was you, the girl who sat in the back of history class, I wanted to say something then, but . . ." Another low laugh. "Yeah, I didn't have the nerve."

Leaning forward, I placed my elbow on the desk and covered my mouth with my hand to hide the goofy grin I knew was forming. It took me a few seconds to say, "But you do now?"

"Well, I kinda figured 'zazzy' might've given me away earlier." His gaze slid back to mine and the intensity in those brown eyes snagged me.

"You told me you said jazzy!" I said.

"Yeah, I know. I kind of got nervous when you responded," he said with a shy smile. "I just . . . Yeah, I was nervous."

I couldn't look away. The flutter in my chest increased until it felt like a hummingbird was searching for a way out. Several moments passed, and something . . . something happened in those moments. I could feel the warmth in my face ratcheting up by several degrees.

He rested both hands on the counter. "So, I think it's past time for me to return this to the library." He paused, eyes twinkling. "Especially since you have been so patient."

I laughed as I picked up the dictionary. "I think the word you're looking for is *impatient*."

"Never that," he teased. "Oh, one more thing." Tyler bent down, and a second later he plopped down the only copy we had of the *Encyclopedia of Animals*. "I almost forgot."

A slow grin curled my lips.

"And it might take a really, really long time for me to get through this."

"Yeah, it's a really big book."

"So you're probably going to have to call me to remind me to return it," Tyler explained, his gaze locked on mine. "And I think it's probably a good idea that I get on my own card for this one."

Pressing my lips together, I nodded. "I think that's also a good idea."

"And you know what else I think is a good idea?" Dropping his elbows on the counter, he leaned in. "That I give you my cell so you don't have to call the other number anymore. You know, when you're working . . . or when you just want to talk." He drew in a deep breath while my heart start jumping like a happy kangaroo. "Or if you'd like to grab something to eat."

There was no stopping the smile racing across my face, spreading even wider when the pink in his cheeks increased. "I will defi-nitely use that number."

"Yeah?"

"I mean, I figure I'm going to have to call you repeatedly to remind you to return the book, and I wouldn't want the home phone scaring you again."

His lashes lowered. "You will most definitely have to remind me."

Drawing in a deep breath, I said, "And I'll probably need it when . . . when we make plans to grab something to eat."

Grinning, he briefly looked to the side and then back to me. "Well, that would be just *zazzy*."

THE UNLIKELY LIKELIHOOD OF FALLING IN LOVE

— — — — — —

JOCELYN DAVIES

PART I: INTRODUCTION

THERE ARE TWENTY-FOUR interconnected subway lines running underneath Manhattan. That's over six thousand subway cars, with an average ridership of almost two billion people per year. If you stop to think about it, that makes the chances of seeing the same person more than once one in over thirty thousand—and that's if you're working with a closed system. If you're working in an open system, the chances are even smaller. And the chances of falling in love at first sight with one of those people are even smaller than that.

I know.

I've done the math.

That's what makes this story so weird.

—— —— —— ——

The morning began like any other Monday morning in May, just a month before the end of my junior year of high school. It was one of those days when things just kind of clicked. I didn't hit the snooze button on my alarm; my sister, Aviva, didn't take forever in the bathroom (how much mascara does one *really* need to wear in seventh grade?); and my well-meaning parents (who are deluded enough to think they're pretty cool for parents) didn't attempt to engage me in time-consuming lines of questioning like, "Did you download the new Weekend Warrior album?" (no one downloads albums anymore, *Dad*) and "What did you do to your hair?" (I slept on it, okay??). The line at Brooklyn Bagels wasn't too long. My bagel was crisp on the outside, doughy on the inside, the cream cheese was evenly and sparingly applied (no messy globs that get all over your face and hands), and my peach Snapple was cold and sweet. I glided down the stairs at the Newkirk Plaza subway station. No one was walking slowly in heels in front of me, or eking out some last texts before going underground, or trying to carry a stroller by themselves. My path was clear, my aim was true. The B train rolled into the station right as I swiped my MetroCard.

As the train barreled over the Manhattan Bridge, I took a sip of Snapple and watched the sun come up over the Lower Manhattan skyline. I was going to be on time for school, and things were okay.

And then, something happened that changed my life.

Something that never would have happened if the constellation of minuscule events in my life hadn't aligned perfectly to deliver me to this exact moment.

There I was, taking a perfect sip of iced tea as the perfect sun rose over my perfect city, a city I love, a city that, for once, had conspired to get me to school on time, and I was leaning against the door (I refuse to sit on the subway ever since the incident with the old man who wasn't wearing any pants), looking out the window toward the Statue of Liberty, experiencing the first glimmer of that end-of-school-year feeling, that spring lightness in the air, like fresh laundry. I could feel the rumbling of the bridge rails under the train car, and then a train was passing across from us, going in the opposite direction toward Brooklyn.

And I saw him.

He was standing in the doorway, too, staring out the window in my direction, and when our trains passed, we locked eyes. He had warm, deep brown skin and a flop of curly brown hair, and was wearing a navy-blue zip-up hoodie with a travel-size instrument case—Violin? Flute? Piccolo?—strapped to his back.

He stood up straighter when he saw me, and grinned. His whole face lit up. I didn't have to look at my reflection in the metal-framed subway ads (pro city-girl life hack) to know mine had lit up as well.

And there we were. A girl and a boy staring at each other through the windows of two train cars passing in the early morning light.

The sun rose higher, a radiant ball of light, over the buildings, casting the world (and specifically his face) in a gold-hued glow.

And here is the sad thing about the subway, the one true, sad thing: just as suddenly as someone comes into your life, they are gone. The same constellation of minuscule events that aligned to bring me here are shifting, unraveling, pulling farther and farther away into the cosmos.

And I'll probably never see him again.

— — — —

A month ago, if you'd asked me if I believe in love, specifically the kind that happens at first sight, I would have laughed. I would have told you I believe in facts and numbers. You can't substantiate that love exists by plugging some variables into an equation and calling it a day. Therefore, why should I believe in it? It's not like I could prove it had ever happened to me.

And yet somehow, inexplicably, I couldn't shake the feeling that it just had.

I'm probably extra skeptical this year because I'm taking Mr. Graff's AP Statistics class. That's actually his name. In a class of fifteen, I'm the only girl. You'd think things would be different in 2017, but then again, I read online that the White House wants to offer girls incentives not to pursue careers in STEM, so you do the math (pun intended). The reason, I guess, is that girls can't hack it, and will just drop out eventually to make babies and soufflés. I don't even know what a soufflé is, and I have no desire to push a seven-pound human out of my lady parts until I have at least two degrees and am a pioneer in my field, thanks.

On the morning in question—the *perfect* morning—Mr. Graff was standing up at the front of the room, telling us about the final project.

"This is your opportunity to show the world what budding

statisticians you all are!" he said. Graff is the only person I know who gets as excited as I do about statistics. "Okay." He chuckled. "Maybe not the world. Let's narrow that pool to just our class. As you'll soon find out when you embark on your projects, statistics is all about narrowing the pool of data. You've been working hard all year, and this is your chance to show me what you've got."

"I'll show you what I've got," Alex Coffey said under his breath, and everyone laughed.

"I don't care what you've got, Mr. Coffey, if it's not some excellent math skills." Graff was passing around a stack of assignments. "I'll need to see and approve your ideas by this Friday. You'll turn in your simulated data by next Wednesday. Then you'll have three weeks to gather research, hand in your real data, and write up your final projects. We'll have presentations at the end of the month."

Matt Bloom, who sits on my left, glanced my way and shot his hand up. "Can we work in pairs?" he asked before Graff even called on him. The hand in the air was purely ornamental.

"No pairs," Graff said. "This is solo work." He had finished handing out the assignments and was back at the front of the room. "Ideally there will be some real-life application to your study. And keep in mind that this is worth fifty percent of your grade, so there's a lot on the line here. You're my AP students, and I know you can do it."

A cheer went up from the boys around me. It felt like a scene in a football movie, and Graff had just given us his best coach pep talk.

Clear eyes. Full hearts. Math game strong.

"I want to see some elegant projects, people."

My heartbeat quickened.

Because I knew exactly what my project would be.

PART II: HYPOTHESIS

As Mr. Graff says, statistics is all about narrowing the pool of data.

If I was going to study the likelihood of seeing my mystery boy again, I had to narrow down the variables. For instance, here is what I knew about the morning when we first locked eyes:

1. The place (the third subway car on the Manhattan-bound B train)

2. The time (a weekday morning, 7:37 a.m. Eastern Standard Time)

3. What I was doing (looking out the window on the south-facing side)

Since the subway system is so huge, I had to look for patterns. For instance, when I take the train at random times, I never see the same people. When I take it during rush hour, at the same time every day, the chances of seeing the same people increases.

Take my morning commute. If I'm on time, there's this one couple I always see making out—I think they're a year older than me and go to my school. But if I'm running late, I don't see them.

For my project, I had to assume Mystery Boy followed the same routine every day. If I re-created those perfect conditions, I would be *more* likely to see him. But throw in other variables, and I would be *less* likely.

Hypothesis: Changing the variables of the morning when I first saw him will decrease my chances of seeing him again.

Over the course of the week, I came up with simulated data to support this. On Friday, I handed the whole proposal in to Mr. Graff.

PART III: RESEARCH

Friday night, my family miraculously sat down for dinner together. It's pretty rare that we all end up around the table at the same time. My sister is on the middle school field hockey team, so she always has practice after school. Sometimes I get together with some of the guys from AP Stats to do homework or work through extra-credit problems, or I go to my friend Camila's house for dinner. My mom and dad are in creative fields and sometimes work weird hours. But that night, we were all home. Mom even made her famous pasta sauce (which was actually the Barefoot Contessa's famous pasta sauce).

"So," Mom said, laying bowls and plates out on the round dinner table that used to be my grandma's. My sister plopped into one of the wicker basketweave chairs. The chair scratched against the floor and groaned under Aviva's weight. "Viv," Mom said (pronouncing it "Veev," like we all do), "these chairs were a rare find on eBay. If you break one, I am selling *you* on eBay and using the money to pay for a custom-made new one."

"Mom," Viv said, "that is a really specific threat."

"Well," Mom said, "these are really specific chairs. They're vintage, Aviva."

Pretty much everything in our apartment is something Mom

scored on eBay, or at Brooklyn Flea, or through some design nut she knows from work. She's a prop stylist for a famous interior design blog and just styled their first coffee table book. It was on the *New York Times* bestseller list for five weeks. I don't even think I could calculate the chances of that happening; you have to be really super talented and also all the stars have to align. My mom is a Boss.

Mom adjusted a Shibori indigo placemat, and Viv very slowly and deliberately stood up and then sat down again in a way that was clearly for Mom's benefit. Mom raised her eyebrows. Dad came shambling in in jeans and a flannel. He's a sound engineer for rock bands.

"What's cooking?" he said, and Viv and I groaned. "What?"

"You're such a nerd, Dad," Viv said.

"We're selling Viv on eBay," Mom said.

"Only if I break the chair!"

"Sorry I asked." Dad took a piece of bread and dipped it in olive oil.

"I have a question," I said, interrupting the flow of family dinner-time banter. "How do you know if you're in love?"

Dad dropped the bread in the olive oil.

"Why do you ask, Sam?" No one in my family ever calls me Samara. It's always Sam or Smee or Shmoo (don't ask).

"Don't get weird, Dad," I responded. "I'm sixteen."

"Are you in love?" Mom was making heart eyes at me.

"It's for research," I said. "I'm working on my final statistics project."

"Math," Mom, Dad, and Viv all said, making one collective face of disgust.

"Thanks for the support, guys," I said.

"No, no, we care," said Dad.

"Speak for yourself," Viv muttered.

"Viv," Mom said.

"What's the project?" Dad was serving himself a heaping bowl of penne, Mom fluffed the salad with tongs, and Viv was texting under the table. I could really feel the love.

"I may or may not have fallen in love at first sight with a boy on the B train. I'm doing my final project on the likelihood of seeing him again."

That got their attention. Even Viv put down her phone.

"A random boy?" Viv asked. "Or one you know?"

"Random," I said. Viv snorted her disdain.

"What do you even know about this boy?" Dad said. "He could be a psychopath."

"Or a misogynist," added Mom.

"Or his name could be Demetrius von Snufflemuffin."

"He's a musician," I said, remembering the instrument case. "Also, he looks good in a blue hoodie."

"Well," Dad said, not doing a very good job at disguising his skepticism, "that's romantic, I guess."

"Dad!" said Viv. "Don't say 'romantic.'"

"Okay, why don't you give me a list of approved words and phrases and I'll just read from it like a script?"

Viv brightened. "Really?"

"No, Viv, seriously." Mom passed the salad bowl her way. "You can't write your father a script." Then she added under her breath, "No matter how much we might want to sometimes."

"I'm a human, not an automaton." Dad pretended to look hurt. "Besides, the concept of soul mates was invented by Hollywood for the sake of marketing romantic comedies." Dad took a bite of pasta. "The idea that you have to meet someone in an adorable way in order for it to be meaningful is nonsensical. Your mom and I aren't soul mates. Fate didn't bring us together after some over-the-top series of missed connections. We met at the bar at Webster Hall."

"Excuse me?" Mom said. "Not soul mates?"

"Dad." Viv pushed the pasta away. "No one wants to hear about you and Mom and your gross love story."

I kind of did—strictly for research purposes, of course—but it looked like I was starting to lose the room, so I kept my mouth shut.

— — — —

On Monday, I commenced data-gathering mode.

I catapulted out of bed the minute my alarm went off. I timed my morning routine down to the second.

The train rolled in at a leisurely pace right at 7:12, and I had never loved it more than I did at that moment. I stepped through the doors, and speed-walked to the window I had been looking out the morning I first saw him.

In case you're wondering, I was taking notes on my phone along the way so I could record them in my data log when I got to school. Time. Conditions. Outside factors. So far, everything was going smoothly.

And then—

"Mmm, babe, you're wearing that coconut lip stuff today."

The make-out couple was standing against my door! As usual,

they were so engrossed in each others' mouths that they didn't even see me.

"Excuse me—"

"It tastes like vacation."

"Um, hi, can I—"

More gross smacking noises.

"HELLO THERE." I was practically shouting. The make-out couple turned around and looked at me without saying anything. "I'm doing a school project and need to stand by this window. Do you mind?" The girl stared me down. It's possible this wasn't my finest idea.

"What's the project?" asked the boy.

The train was rumbling along at this point, inching toward the bridge.

"It's kind of time sensitive," I said. "If you'd just let me—"

"If you don't tell us," the girl said slowly, "how are we supposed to know if we want to help you or not?"

I clenched my hands into fists at my sides. Then I sucked it up and told them.

The girl gave me the side-eye, but she nodded at the boy. Without a word, they stepped out of the way and let me have the window.

"Thankthankyouthankyou!" I shouted in their faces as they walked down the train car. "I'll bring you bagels tomorrow!"

"I like everything!" the boy shouted back. There are pros and cons to seeing the same people on your morning commute.

I took my place by the window as we journeyed from the darkness of the underground tunnel into the light.

The sun was shining. I noted this in my phone. There was still a morning haze that hadn't burned off yet, giving everything a sort of dreamy quality. I noted this, too. (The objective weather conditions, not the subjective dreaminess.)

We were cresting the hill when a train barreled toward us from the Manhattan side. My heartbeat quickened. Was I going to see him again? Could it be possible I really *was* in love at first sight? And was I so starved for affection that a strange boy smiled at me and I thought he was my soul mate? Was this because my family didn't like math?

I was contemplating all this when I saw the boy who may or may not have been named Demetrius von Snufflemuffin for the second time.

You know how they say that when you fall in love at first sight, the world kind of stops for a moment? Just as I was registering his dimples, and then the fact that he was wearing the same blue hoodie, my subway car came to a screeching halt. So did his.

Ladies and gentlemen, we are being delayed due to a signal mal-function, we should be moving shortly . . .

Demetrius shook his head. I rolled my eyes. He shook his fist at the heavens. I pretended to weep. He mimed knocking his head against the subway door, then fell down and out of sight.

"Ew," I said out loud, thinking of the many hundreds of strains of germs that blanket the subway. Last year, the *New York Times* published a study, and they found traces of the bubonic plague on some subway poles. Imagine what's on the floor.

The man standing next to me gave me a look. I gave him a look right back. You just can't take any nonsense on the subway.

When I looked out the window again, Demetrius was standing, writing something in a giant spiral-bound notebook.

He held it up, and I squinted to see what it said.

MADE YOU LOOK.

I laughed out loud, then clapped my hand over my mouth. Demetrius grinned. He started to write something else, but before I could see what it said, my train jolted into motion and we were hurtling forward again, leaving Demetrius and his train in our wake.

— — — —

I couldn't think about anything at school that day except Demetrius. (After I entered my notes into my data log, of course.) Here's what I knew I about him so far:

His hair was off-the-charts voluminous.

He may or may not have owned only one hoodie (or had a closet full of blue hoodies).

He played an instrument perfectly sized to strap to your back for a long subway commute.

None of this was relevant to my research.

On second thought, I entered it into my data log anyway, just in case Mr. Graff wanted to know.

— — — —

The next morning, I got up early, while it was still dark. I was out the door as the sky was just starting to glow.

It was too early for the make-out couple. The man who gave me the dirty look yesterday wasn't there, either. In fact, the train was kind of empty, except for a woman in scrubs who was clutching a coffee, her braids swept up in a high ponytail. It was quiet and kind of peaceful. I stood by the window and had a perfect view of the sun cresting over downtown Manhattan. The windows glittered with the sunrise.

Not a bad way to start the day. I wondered, as I always do when I'm up early and see something beautiful I never get to see, if I should consider becoming a morning person.

I didn't see Demetrius von Snufflemuffin, but I didn't expect to this morning, and that was the point.

— — — —

I decided to make the following day my late day, since I had free study first period and this was technically research for a school project. I slept in a little, luxuriating among the pillows after all the hard research I'd been doing. I took my time getting ready, ate a bowl of cereal while reading an actual print newspaper (my parents are into being analog), and even wore boots with a heel so that I would walk slower. The train was *packed* with men and women on their way to work. I pushed my way to my usual window but there was a man already leaning against it, and my bargaining potential was limited this morning as there was literally *nowhere* else for him to go. So I stood directly in front of him, and when we went over the bridge, I stood on my tiptoes to see over his shoulder. A train rolled by on the opposite track, but it was the wrong direction for most commuters this time of day, and the window I was looking for was empty.

In AP Stats, we each updated the class on our progress. Mr. Graff took notes and nodded along, asking questions and helping us fine-tune our data collection. I noted with satisfaction that I seemed to be ahead of a lot of the guys in my class. Take that, gender norms!

When it was my turn to present, a hush fell over the room. The boys lost their minds when I told them I had seen Demetrius again.

"I can't believe you didn't give him your number." Matt had his head in his hands. "You could have held it up to the window!"

"I didn't think of that," I realized. "But if my data is correct I should see him again the next time I'm on time for school. Maybe even tomorrow."

"That's tempting fate," Alex interjected.

"It's not fate! It's math!"

"Wait," said Justin Wu, "why are we calling him Demetrius?"

— — — —

My last class of the day was studio art. Mom had made me sign up for it because she said I was too high-strung and doing something creative would help to soothe my overactive mind. Camila is in the class, too. It gives us a chance to catch up while we smear paint on a canvas.

"Alex's right," she said, dipping her brush into a blob of hunter-green paint. "It's fate."

"It's not fate," I countered. "It's math."

"Why do you think you keep seeing him? Why do you think both of your trains stopped at the exact same time? It's fate, I'm telling you."

"I'll tell you why I keep seeing him. He goes to school in Brooklyn. I go to school in Manhattan. School starts at pretty much the same time every day no matter what school you go to. There are only a limited number of ways to cross between Brooklyn and Manhattan, and one of them is the Manhattan Bridge. See? The pool of variables keeps getting smaller and smaller. If you think about it, how could I *not* see him?"

Camila eyed me. "This isn't an SAT question. We're talking about people. There's room for human error. That number is meaningless, because it exists in a bubble. Human error, Sam. Real life is way more complicated than math."

"I respectfully beg to differ. It was a carefully orchestrated series of perfectly timed events that brought us together in the first place."

"Or," she said, "it was the universe."

"Agree to disagree."

No one understands the purpose of mathematical integrity except for me. And Mr. Graff.

Camila just smiled and smoothed black around the edges of the canvas. She's actually amazing at studio art and will probably be a famous painter one day. I don't know why she puts up with me taking this class with her.

So far it's done nothing to soothe my overactive mind.

— — — —

Over the next few weeks, I immersed myself in my research. I got fancy. I noted when it rained and the trains were slower than usual and people's umbrellas made the floors slippery and treacherous. Or when I made the mistake of trying to open my Snapple while speedwalking down the street and I had to go back to get napkins, or when someone cut in front of me and I missed the 7:12 train by a fraction of a second and the conductor didn't wait. I noted when there was track work, or the train had to reroute over the Q line. I calculated the odds of the same thing happening to him, this boy

I didn't know, at a different subway station, in a different borough, somewhere on the other side of this impossibly big city.

My research was stacking up. I had pages and pages in a Word document saved on the cloud. An Excel sheet full of numbers.

But here's the thing:

I hadn't seen him again.

I didn't understand what was happening. I was doing everything right. My hypothesis was airtight. My math was on point.

Maybe Camila was right. Maybe there was too much room for human error.

Maybe it was the universe telling me it wasn't meant to be.

Maybe Demetrius von Snufflemuffin wasn't ever supposed to be mine.

Maybe we would go on like this, trains passing each other in the early morning sun (not when it rained, I noted), and he would continue to be Demetrius von Snufflemuffin, Mystery Boy. This instrument-playing, cute-message-writing, germ-resistant, navy-blue-hoodie-wearing dream boy of mine.

But maybe it was for the best.

If we did ever meet IRL, then he would become real. And all this perfect stuff I sort of knew about him would be all mixed up with imperfect stuff, the real stuff, the stuff no one wants to know. The stuff that would take him out of the early morning haze of my dreams and into the cold hard daylight of reality.

— — —

I distracted myself by collecting the rest of my data.

I worked on my poster. I made my spreadsheet pretty. I

included graphs and even made some hilarious jokes about Mr. Graff's name.

And then, in the blink of an eye (I mean, it was fourteen days, but who's counting?), there was only one week left. The paper was due Friday. All my research had to be complete by then. Five days to change the course of my life.

Monday I was perfectly on time, but it rained and the 7:12 train arrived at 7:25.

Tuesday my train was rerouted.

Wednesday I ended up being late because Aviva decided to use Mom's curling iron and filled the bathroom with burnt-hair smell.

Thursday I saw him one more time. We both pressed our hands to the glass. I was hoping for something. Anything. Some kind of meaningful connection. *Come on, train. If there was ever a time for you to stall unexpectedly, this is it.* But I had no such luck. The trains went by too fast and we watched each other hurtle off into the distance.

Good-bye, Demetrius, I thought.

Friday the project was due and I was on time and the train was on time and everything lined up exactly right. But I didn't see him at all.

PART IV: ANALYSIS

That was it. The whole thing was over.

I was walking down the hall to AP Stats, about to turn in a killer final project worth fifty percent of my grade. To be honest, I'd never felt so good about a school project before in my life.

So why was I so bummed?

It was a stupid question, because I knew exactly why. I was hoping the numbers would prove that I could trust my weird feeling about this guy. That if I did my research and followed the trail of data, it would lead me to him, and we would meet, and I would know what it felt like to be in love. I would have my answer.

Numbers don't lie, even when the heart does.

— — — —

"Congratulations!" Mr. Graff was once again the most excited person in the room. "You've finished your first step in your future careers as mathematicians!" He was wearing a party hat. "Leave your final papers in a stack on my desk."

I dropped my paper in a stack with the others. It felt surreal. A month of my life, a month of dreaming and working and pinning my hopes on a person I didn't even know, and now it was just another wad of printer paper stapled and shuffled in with fourteen others. It was a piece of me. A real piece. And it was gone.

Next time a teacher asked for a topic with real-life applications, I was picking something with lower stakes.

The boys in my class all wanted to know how my project had gone. They grilled me about the details. Did I see him again? Did we meet? Even Mr. Graff wanted to know. They asked for a sneak peek of the results.

"You'll just have to wait for my presentation on Monday," I replied, cool as a cucumber. Everyone seemed kind of disappointed. *You don't know the half of it*, I wanted to say.

Over the weekend, it rained. Camila came over to do DIY

projects and watch romantic comedies on Netflix. DIY projects are another thing Mom says will calm my overactive mind. She isn't wrong. There's something soothing about repurposing old jeans into something new and useful, so we went to town on denim with scissors as we watched *You've Got Mail*. Viv was sitting in the comfy chair playing on her phone. She didn't look up, but I knew she was listening.

"You see?" Camila said, pointing at the TV while she tore a strip of old denim to shreds. "They live in the same *neighborhood* and cross paths *every day* and it takes forever. But they do meet at the end of the movie." She started braiding the strips together. "Everything connects eventually," she said wisely. She's been talking like that ever since she started watching *Cosmos* with Neil deGrasse Tyson.

It rained and rained and rained, and I didn't leave the apartment for two whole days. My new denim choker was a masterpiece.

— — — —

The sun came out for Presentation Day.

I woke before the sun; I was leaving an extra hour to get to school in case anything went wrong. If I'd learned anything from taking obsessive notes about subway patterns this month, something inevitably would. Happily, my foresight paid off, since my train decided to go over the Q line that day.

On the bridge, I watched the sun come up over the downtown Manhattan skyline, and even I had to admit how pretty it was and how lucky I was to be alive and to call this city my home, blah blah blah. Turning in the project had felt like the end of something, but maybe this presentation was only the beginning. Maybe I'd get an

A, and go on to get a five on the AP exam, and get into MIT, and get a competitive academic scholarship, and this whole project really would be the beginning of my career as a statistician, as Mr. Graff would say, and—

And that's when, as dawn was breaking over the horizon, it dawned on *me* that I'd left my poster at home. Stats was the first class of the day, and I was the first presenter. Everyone wanted to know how my project had turned out. They made me go first.

I checked my phone. It was 6:45. That was why I left extra time. Maybe Camila was right about human error after all.

At Canal Street I got off and crossed over to the Brooklyn-bound side of the track. It was packed, which meant a train hadn't come in a while, which meant something was wrong. My heart started to beat faster and my brain started to do that overactive thing it does, imagining the worst-case scenarios. I had all but convinced myself that the bridge had collapsed when a train pulled into the station, but it was an N train and the conductor was saying something and I could barely make out the words: "No Brooklyn-bound B or D train service . . . take the N to Atlantic and switch there for the B, D, Q, R, 2, 3, 4, and 5 trains . . ."

At that point, nothing, not even subway trouble, was going to stop me from getting that poster. If I couldn't meet Demetrius von Snufflemuffin, I was sure as hell getting an A on this project. I squeezed on between two large men (who didn't take their backpacks off to make room for me or anyone else). The doors closed and I held my breath and we headed back to Brooklyn.

As we made our way across the bridge this time, the sun was bright and the morning haze had dissolved into the air. Everything looked sharper and clearer. I couldn't help feeling stupid about what a big deal I'd made over this mystery boy. People passed each other all the time in New York. Lives intersected and then diverged and went on their way. Once in a blue moon, maybe, an encounter would leave a person's life changed. But most of the time it didn't. And that was the beauty of New York.

Everyone was living out their own stories.

A backpack shoved into me as someone turned around, jolting me, literally, out of my thoughts. No—not a backpack.

An instrument case.

"Sorry," a voice said. "I need to be by the window—"

And then we both looked up, and our eyes met.

It was him. My mystery boy. Demetrius von Snufflemuffin, right there in front of me in all his blue-hoodie splendor. He smiled. I smiled. And suddenly, I got it. I got what all the fuss was about. I got why people took unlikely chances and believed in fate and hoped for things against all odds.

I didn't need the numbers to prove me right. The feeling *was* the proof.

Because I was looking at this boy and all I could think was, this wasn't how it was supposed to happen. I'd planned everything out. I'd done the math. And the good ol' universe did what it wanted to do anyway. I guess the world is bigger than that. There were mysteries yet to be solved. And this was one of them. The day our stories finally led us to meet face-to-face was the day nothing at all went according to plan. The day we met was an anomaly.

And he could have been a murderer, or only looked good in blue hoodies and nothing else, or his name really could have been

Demetrius von Snufflemuffin. But he could also have been a really nice person who looked great in all the colors of the rainbow and have been the kind of guy who isn't intimidated that I plan to win a Nobel Prize before I'm thirty (they don't award them yet for mathematics, but they'll make an exception for me). I'd never know unless I stopped imagining what he was like and actually talked to him. This was my one chance. And I wanted to. I really wanted to.

I opened my mouth to say the most clever thing I could think of.

"Hi," I said. "So, how many blue hoodies *do* you own?"

He laughed. And his entire face lit up. Okay, so it wasn't my finest moment. But we were talking. And that was a start.

PART V: CONCLUSION

Statistics has taught me a lot about life. But I guess the most important thing I've learned is that there's still room for error, and there's a chance things won't go the way you want them to, unless, of course, they do.

His name, it turned out, was Dev. He took the train all the way home to Ditmas Park with me, even though it meant he would be late for school. And since I was going to be late too (thanks, MTA!), I FaceTimed Matt Bloom and gave the presentation of a lifetime from my living room. The entire class cheered when I swung the camera around so Dev could smile and wave, and I didn't even get any points deducted for presenting absentee because, I suspected, I was Mr. Graff's favorite, and also because I wrote this conclusion and handed it in later that day with my most recent findings.

It turns out Dev lives in Manhattan but goes to a specialized arts school in Brooklyn, which was why we passed each other on the train so often. He composes music and can play the scores to all the original Classic Nintendo games. He owns three navy-blue hoodies, but he also owns a gray one and a black one, as well as several other non-hoodie items of clothing in various colors.

But for the entire month of May, he wore the blue ones. Know why?

It was so I'd recognize him.

So I guess in the end, that probably skewed my data. But like I said before, you can't plan for everything.

259 MILLION MILES

— — — — —

KASS MORGAN

I PAUSE OUTSIDE the glass door and take a deep breath. *You can do this*, I tell myself. *This isn't like school. No one's going to recognize you. Or if they do, they won't care. These people have bigger things to think about.* I place my hand against the wall and take another breath. *It's fine. Everything's going to be fine.*

I straighten my tie then check that my shirt's still tucked in, trying to smooth the awkward wrinkles. I bought four different shirts for these interviews, and none of them fit me right. Either the sleeves are too short, or the collar is too tight, or the seams look funny. All I want is to get through this final round, because if all goes well, I'll never have to choose another outfit again. I'll never have to make any stupid choices again.

I wave the temporary pass the security bot gave me over the

sensor, and the door slides open. There's only one other applicant in the reception area, which seems like a good sign. I don't recognize her from any of the earlier rounds, and she doesn't actually look dressed for an interview. She's wearing a plaid shirt and black jeans, and is sitting with one of her studded boots tucked underneath her, clearly unconcerned about leaving a mark on the cream-colored couch.

Actually, now that I think about it, maybe she's not an applicant. Maybe she's someone's friend. Or sister. I always assume that the applicants are only children, for obvious reasons, but that's probably not the case.

I check in with the cheerful receptionist bot at the front desk, then turn around and freeze, unsure where to go. The first cluster of armchairs is way too near the couch. It'd be creepy to sit that close to the girl. But the other cluster is too far away. It would seem like I'm purposefully avoiding her.

I shift my weight from side to side. I have to make a decision. Just standing here like this is even weirder. Quickly, I lower myself into the farthest of the closer chairs, then pull out my tablet so the girl knows I'm not going to try to make conversation.

She doesn't look up, and I let out a sigh of relief. It's fine. I'm fine.

I unlock my tablet and make a halfhearted attempt to start my physics homework. If this thing works out, no one's going to ask me to hand in my assignments before I leave. But I know it's dangerous to think that way. They started with nearly twenty thousand applicants. It's a much smaller pool now, but it's filled with the strongest candidates. This guy I met last time is seventeen like me, but he's finishing up a PhD in engineering at MIT.

There's a thick hardcover book open in the girl's lap. A library book, I realize, catching a glimpse of the plastic wrap on the front. Her eyes don't leave the page as she absently twirls her hair, bleached blond with dark roots. Her focus makes me feel a little guilty, actually, and I'm just about to tackle my first problem set when a flash of movement startles me. Peering over the top of my tablet, I see the girl lower her face to the book and inhale deeply. Like you'd do with a freshly baked cake, or your grandmother's pot roast. Not some moldy library book that's probably been in a hundred strangers' bathrooms.

"You jealous?" the girl says suddenly.

I flinch, as though she's just poured ice water down my back instead of asking a simple, albeit strange, question. She's staring at me with one eyebrow raised, and I feel my throat close up. This has been happening a lot since the incident. It's like my body's way of saying, *Oh* hell *no, we are* not *going through that again.*

After waiting an appropriate amount of time for an answer that's never coming, the girl tries again. "This is one of my favorite smells in the world. Here, want to take a whiff?" She shoves her book toward me. Startled, I lean all the way back in my seat. "Wow, okay. I get that people think real books are old-fashioned, but it's not *poisonous*." She laughs, and I stiffen, bracing for the rush of warm, prickly shame that's become so familiar. But it doesn't come. The girl's laugh is playful but not mocking, and I relax slightly.

"Sorry, I'm not going to let you peer-pressure me into huffing library books," I say, surprising myself. Since the incident, I don't speak without running through the options first, weighing all the potential effects. And, had I thought about it, I never would've said anything like this. Too many possibilities for negative outcomes. She could be offended. Or feel awkward and uncomfortable. Then I'd have to sit here, watching her as she waits for her friend so she can jump out of her seat and whisper about what just happened. And then maybe tweet about it.

But instead of furrowing her brow, or worse, taking out her phone and ignoring me completely, the girl smiles. "'Huff library books'?" she repeats. "I love that. I would totally huff books if I could."

"I saw you do it about ten seconds ago." Right? Right.

"I inhaled the sweet, sweet scent of aged paper, glue, and library dust. I didn't huff the book itself. That would be amazing, though. Imagine stories going straight into your brain!"

I pause to consider this. "I'd rather be able to remove stories from my brain."

"Even now? With everything that's going on?" She gestures around the reception area. "Don't you want to remember as much as possible, in case you're chosen?"

"Like library books full of germs?"

She smiles. "Among other things."

A voice calls from behind us. "Blythe Cohen?" I glance over my shoulder to see the receptionist bot standing next to the door. It's a newer model, one that uses the right inflection to ask questions.

To my surprise, the girl unfolds her legs and stands up. So she *is* a candidate, I realize, feeling foolish. I almost stutter an apology for misjudging her, but stop myself just in time. She doesn't know I'd written her off as a friend or a sibling. Though sometimes, I feel like the people around me *can* read my thoughts, like my awkwardness is written right across my face. It was certainly clear enough in the video.

The girl picks a bag up off the floor and slings it over shoulder. "Good luck," she says with a smile.

"Yeah, thanks. You, too."

The girl walks toward the bot, which has glided from the desk to the door. "Blythe? Right this way, please."

Blythe Cohen. Why does that name sound familiar? I do a search for it and my eyes widen as they land on the results. Right. She's the girl who invented that pioneering technique for cleaning up oil spills. When she was twelve years old. She was on all these talk shows, and even got to meet the president. I guess in that light, her casual demeanor makes sense. She's pretty much guaranteed a spot on this thing, if she wants it. But *why* would she want it? Why would a girl with the opportunity to make Earth a better place be willing to leave it all behind?

I have to wait for another ten minutes before the receptionist bot calls my name and leads me into the conference room. Ten people are already seated at the long table, although I only recognize a few of them. There's Lauren, the program director. Tessa, the psychologist who evaluated me. And Cheung, the engineer who oversaw some of my tests, including the one where I had to put an engine together underwater.

"Philip, good to see you. Please take a seat." Lauren smiles warmly and gestures toward one of the empty chairs. I nod and try to sit without doing anything too awkward.

"Thanks for joining us for the final round of evaluations," she says, glancing down at her tablet.

"I'm happy to be here." For the first time, I don't fight the tingle of excitement spreading through my body. This could really happen. In a few months, I could be leaving all this behind. I won't have to finish that useless history term paper. I don't have to make up excuses for why I'm not going to graduation or—my stomach twists—*prom*. Instead of spending the summer earning money for college and exchanging e-mails with a randomly assigned roommate who wants to bring his therapy iguana with him, I'll be preparing for the greatest adventure in history.

"As you know," Lauren continues, "you've been monitored extensively throughout this process. We're not just interested in your scientific aptitude, though that's certainly an important element."

A blond woman leans forward in her chair. "That device you designed for collecting water is very impressive. Particularly since you had no time to prepare."

I nod. "Thank you." There's no reason to tell them that I've spent most of life learning how to survive in extreme situations. In the jungle after a plane crash. In an urban wasteland after the zombie apocalypse. When I was younger, it was a way to cope with my anxiety. I guess I thought that if I was smart and prepared, nothing could hurt me. But recently, it's become more fantasy than nightmare. I *want* to use the skills I've developed. And not just to save my life, but to create a brand-new one. I'm ready to start over, to devote myself to something that matters instead of staying here, floundering in a world that fits me as badly as my new shirts.

Lauren continues, "It's also essential that your personality complements the other members of your team." She glances back down at her tablet. "You scored a ninety-one in empathy, which is good, but suggests that you might have a difficult time sacrificing an individual for the good of the group, if necessary."

My stomach lurches at the word *sacrifice*. I remember some of the terrible questions the psychologist asked me. What would I do if we started to run out of oxygen during the trip? What if none of the seeds we brought were viable? How much medicine would we give to someone who was close to death?

"Your overall leadership score is only sixty-eight, though that's not a huge concern, as long as we balance the team properly. And . . . let's see . . . problem solving: ninety-one. Patience: fifty-seven. That one could be a problem. But certainly not a deal breaker. Flexibility: eighty-two . . ." She goes down the list, and I do my best to maintain a neutral expression. It's not the most fun thing in the world, being analyzed like this, but it's got nothing on the 534,656 comments on VidHub.

Lauren places her tablet on the table, then turns to look straight at me. "After this, you'll complete your last evaluation, and then the committee will meet to make their final selections. So, Philip, I'm going to ask you one more time. You're sure you're ready for a one-way mission to Mars?"

Images flash through my head. Saying a tearful good-bye to my parents. Joking with the reporters at the launch, knowing that it doesn't matter what awkward things I say because I won't be around to see people making fun of me online afterward. Climbing those stairs, strapping into my seat, and feeling the violent rumble of the rockets. Watching Earth fall away and the sky fade as the windows fill with stars. Knowing that the next time I set foot on solid ground, it'll be in a world without oxygen, but also one without VidHub followers. Where only intelligence and bravery will matter.

"I'm absolutely sure."

— — — —

I meet with a different psychologist this time. James. He's a cheerful youngish guy with dreadlocks, wearing a tie and the kind of immaculately pressed shirt I'm pretty sure you only get from having a team of house elves dress you every morning. "As we explained during your previous briefing, the final evaluation is a test to see how well you deal with isolation and boredom, and how you get along with others in close quarters." He lets out a small laugh. "The shuttle is going to feel pretty small during the six-month journey."

"I'll be sure to pack deodorant," I say, wincing slightly when James gives me what I refer to as a "courtesy smile."

"Okay then, follow me."

He guides me down a series of hallways, the last of which leads to a set of frosted glass doors with the words *Isolation Chamber* etched onto them.

"Did you guys build this just for this mission?" I ask, trying not to let any hint of apprehension creep into my voice. Being stuck in a small space is one thing. Being alone with my thoughts for twenty-four hours is another.

James shakes his head. "We use this to evaluate all members of the space program. Though it's a little different this time. We're putting you guys in there two at a time, to see how you interact during a stressful situation."

"What's stressful about sitting in a room for twenty-four hours?"

"When was the last time you sat in a room doing nothing for *one* hour? No phone. No computer. No TV."

"I think you're underestimating teenagers. We might be addicted to technology, but we're also lazy. This sounds like a vacation to me." It sounds like a dream, actually. I've spent the past few weeks staring at my phone like it's a bomb that's about to explode. Or rather, a bomb that's already exploded and will continue to do so indefinitely.

James raises an eyebrow. "I'm not speaking from my experience with teenagers. I'm speaking from my experience with human beings."

"Everyone all set?" a cheery voice calls. It's Tessa, the other psychologist. When I see who she's walking with, my stomach lurches. It's the blond girl from the reception area. "Philip, this is Blythe, one of the other finalists. You're going to spend twenty-four hours in the isolation chamber together so we can see how you work together as a team."

"We've met," Blythe says, grinning at me. "He accused me of pushing drugs."

"What? No," I sputter, blushing as I catch James giving me a strange look. "That's not what happened."

"Well, this is already off to an interesting start," Tessa says with a smile. She waves her badge over the sensor on the wall and the doors hiss open.

The isolation chamber is a tiny square room that looks like a futuristic jail cell. It's completely bare except for two padded benches wedged against the walls, and a metal table with two large bottles of water and a stack of protein bars. We file inside, filling the space between the two benches. "Bathroom's right there," Tessa says, pointing at a room the size of an airplane lavatory. I make a mental note to go easy on the water. And the protein bars, for that matter.

Tessa and James go back outside to make room for a medical technician, who hooks me and Blythe up to sensors to track our heart rates and brain activity.

"I don't want any of you to be shocked when you start reading my mind," Blythe jokes as the technician places a sensor against her temple. "So you should know that there's always a part of my brain writing Harry Potter slash."

She doesn't look like the type of girl I imagine staying home on Saturday nights to write Harry Potter erotica. She looks like she belongs on the dance floor of some underground club, dancing wildly to a band I've never heard of. I can imagine her hair flying, her hips swaying. *Get it together*, I tell myself as I feel my pulse begin to speed up at the thought. Thank God I'm not hooked up to the heart-rate monitor yet. I take a few deep breaths and regain my composure before it's my turn to get wired up.

"You're all set," Tessa says a few minutes later, after the technician leaves. "If you need anything, you can press the red call button by the door. Otherwise, we'll see you in twenty-four hours."

"See ya," Blythe calls cheerfully while I nod, wondering how the hell I'm supposed to get through twenty-four hours without saying anything dumb.

The door slides closed, and all the lights go out except for a dim recessed bulb in the ceiling. Blythe flings herself onto one of the benches with a loud sigh, and I sit gingerly on the edge of the other, wishing there were a little more space between us.

"So how many times have you done this?" she asked, turning onto her back and stretching out her legs. There's something strangely intimate about seeing a girl lie down like that.

"Done this?" I repeat. "Been in the isolation chamber?"

"Yeah. This is my third time."

"Oh." I pause. "This is my first time." I wonder what that means. Whether she's ahead of me in the rankings, or whether it's just a scheduling issue. "Who were the others? The other people, I mean."

"The first was a girl named Maddie. She was really nice. At least, I think she was nice. She didn't talk very much."

I wonder how Blythe is going to describe me after this. *He seemed nice. At least, I think he was nice. He didn't talk much except to make awkward jokes about drugs.*

"The second time was with this guy Jordan. He thought the committee was listening and analyzing everything we said, so he refused to talk about anything but chemistry, physics, or astronomy. I'd be like, 'Hey, Jordan, can you pass me a protein bar?' and he'd be like, 'Did you know that this protein bar would only weigh half an ounce on Mars? The gravitational force is only thirty-eight percent as strong as Earth's.'"

"So they're *not* listening to what we say?" I ask, wondering if perhaps this Jordan kid was onto something. I can't afford to mess this up.

"They probably are. But I don't think it's to see how much Mars trivia we can drop in conversation. They want to see our interpersonal skills, how we deal with boredom and stress and stuff." She jumps to her feet suddenly. "Do you want to have a dance contest?"

"What? No." Just the *thought* of dancing in front of another person makes my heart race, which kind of sucks because now the committee is going to think I'm not comfortable in small places. Which is really unfair, because I'm not claustrophobic, and I doubt dance parties are going to be part of the Mars mission. Unless Blythe is also selected.

"Why not?" Blythe raises her arms over her head and sways her hips from side to side. It's not quite as sexy as the move I'd imagined. But much cuter.

I suppress a smile. "Well, for one, there's no music."

"Oh, that's not a problem." She clears her throat, tosses her head back, and starts to sing loudly and off-key. "I'd stop the world and meeeeeelt with you." She continues to shake her hips and wave her arms while she sings, and despite myself, I laugh.

"What *is* that?" I ask.

"It's Modern English. What? Don't you like eighties music?"

"No, not particularly."

"That's probably because you haven't listened to enough," she says, flopping back on the bench, slightly breathless.

"I wouldn't have pegged you for an eighties music fan."

"Why? What you have pegged me as?" Blythe asks eagerly, sitting up again.

I stiffen, realizing too late that I've sent us down a road with too many conversational landmines. "Nothing. I don't know. Sorry, that was dumb."

"No, tell me. I'm curious."

"I don't know . . . I guess I assumed you listened to cool indie stuff."

"Like the Starfish Amputees?"

"Maybe. I've never heard of them."

"Yes!" She reaches out to give me a high-five.

Confused, I tap my palm against hers. "What did I do?"

"The Starfish Amputees are a made-up band. It's a game I play to see whether people are poseurs or not."

"Isn't that kind of mean?" I ask hesitantly.

"I don't think so. I never call them out on it or anything. I'm not trying to embarrass anyone. I just like to know, for myself."

"I guess that's fair. So what are your favorite fake bands?"

"Oh . . . there are so many, it's hard to choose." She holds up her hand and begins counting off with her fingers. "There's the Amphibious Gentlemen, the Hip Hip Hoorays, Baking Soda Stars, Toadstool, Third-Grade Talent Show." She shakes her head. "They were so good until they sold out."

"I don't know. I really like that Christmas album they did. The one with the guitarist from Dead Poseur's Society."

"Good one."

My eyes have adjusted to the dim light enough that I can see her smile, and the sight turns my stomach from a solid into a liquid, just for a moment.

"That's one thing I'm going to miss," she says wistfully. "Going to shows. That moment when the band you've been waiting for all night comes onto the stage, and their opening chords release something inside of you." She sighs. "I don't think there's a better feeling in the world. When the bass kicks in, and you can't tell if it's coming from the speakers or your own heart. And you know everyone else feels the same way, and you're all connected by the music."

I don't say anything. I've never been to a concert, so I don't know that moment she's talking about. And if I'm chosen for the mission, I probably never will. But that's okay. There's a lot I'm going to miss out on, but plenty more terrible things I'm going to avoid.

"Are you okay?" Blythe asks.

"Yeah, I'm fine," I say quickly. "So why do you want to leave, then? I hear the music scene on Mars is pretty quiet."

She shrugs, but there's something forced about the gesture. "Some things are worth sacrificing for." She lets out a long breath. "Okay, instead of talking about the things we're going to miss, I think we should list the things we're happy to leave behind. I'll start . . . Let's see . . . mosquitos."

"Really?" I say. "That's the best you can come up with? *Mosquitos?*"

"It's the first thing I thought of! I have more. But now it's your turn."

"All right . . . um . . . okay, the typing dots."

"Like when you're texting?" Blythe asks.

"Yeah. I'm not going to miss seeing those dots, and that knot you get in your stomach when they go on for too long, and you know the person you're texting keeps deleting their message and starting over."

"I hadn't really thought about that. But yeah, I guess we won't be texting anymore."

"Just good old face-to-face contact."

"Or helmet-to-helmet contact," Blythe says, "if we're outside. Okay, it's my turn. I'm not going to miss . . . unloading the dishwasher."

"Shopping."

"Hay fever."

"Dancing."

Blythe laughs. "No way I'm giving up dancing."

"You can do whatever you want. But no one's going to make me feel guilty about not dancing. No more bar mitzvahs, *quinceañeras*, sweet sixteens, weddings . . ."

"Sounds like you've had quite the busy social life."

"I've been very busy awkwardly standing on the edge of the dance floor, pretending to check my phone," I say.

"We're definitely not leaving awkwardness behind. What could be more awkward than living on top of six strangers?"

"Lots of things. Trust me."

In the dim light, I see Blythe's expression change. "Like what?" she asks softly.

My heart starts pounding a warning. *Don't tell her.* This is my best chance at a fresh start. I can't ruin it now. Not this early. I force a smile. "Nothing. I was just making a joke. A stupid one, I guess."

"Can I ask you a personal question?" she asks. I nod. "Who are you most worried about leaving behind?"

"My parents," I say as something deep inside my chest cramps. "What about you?"

"My grandmother. But she's really old, so I'm not sure how much time we would have together anyway. I know she'd be proud of me if I'm chosen, but I can't imagine saying good-bye to her."

"What about your parents?"

"They both died when I was little."

"Oh," I say. "I'm so sorry."

She gives another one of her practiced shrugs. "Two fewer people I'll make cry if I leave."

"Yeah," I say quietly. I've never seen my parents cry, but when I told them I'd made it to the final round, there was a look in their eyes I never want to see again. Something worse than tears. Like I'd yanked on the threads holding their hearts together and broken them somehow. "That's one thing I'm ready to leave behind."

"What? Crying?" Blythe asks.

"Letting people down, I guess."

We're both lying down on our benches now. There's only about two feet of space between us. I don't think I've even lain this close to a girl before.

A shrill, piercing wail rips apart the silence. I gasp and jump to my feet, heart racing. Blythe lets out a yelp and also jumps up, but she loses her footing and crashes into me. I put my arm around her to steady her. "What the hell is that?" I mutter.

"It's a fire alarm," Blythe says, lurching toward the door. There's no handle on this side, so she bangs on it a few times. "We have to get out of here."

I hurry to stand next to her. "It's okay. Just relax. It's probably just a false alarm. And if it's a real fire, they'll come get us. No one's going to forget about us."

She keeps banging on the door and pressing the call button, as if she hasn't heard me. "Let us out. Let us out!"

"Blythe," I say, speaking her name aloud for the first time. "It's all right. You need to calm down. There's no smoke. The door isn't hot. Everything's okay. It's probably just a drill."

"There is. There is." She spins around again and resumes banging on the door with one hand and pressing the call button with the other. "Why isn't anyone answering?"

I take a breath, and I can smell it now. Smoke. Slowly, so as not to panic Blythe, I stand up and walk around the tiny room, sniffing. It's not coming through the door, and I don't see any vents.

"You smell it now, don't you?" There's no accusation in her voice. Only fear.

"Yeah. I smell it. But there's no reason to freak out. This is a brand-new building. It'll have state-of-the-art sprinklers and fire doors. We're going to be fine."

"We're going to die in here," she says, her voice breaking.

Without thinking, I pull her toward me and wrap my arms around her. "No, we're not. I promise," I whisper into her ear. She's trembling, so I tighten my hold. But I can't ignore the fact that the smoke is growing stronger. I look around the dark room, desperately scanning it for something to use to break the door. But there's nothing. That's the point of the isolation chamber.

That's when it hits me. This is part of the test. It has to be. That's the only explanation for why they've left us in here with the alarm blaring. The smoke isn't from a real fire. They just want to see how we'll cope.

"This is part of the test," I say. I try to take a step back so I can look, but she holds on tighter. "We just need to relax, to show them that we don't panic in emergencies. It's all going to be okay."

"But the smoke . . . The fire's coming closer." She's right about the smoke. It's not just the smell anymore. Real smoke is filling the room, burning my throat every time I inhale. But I know it's all being carefully monitored. There are people watching our vital signs. They're not going to let anything happen to us.

I lead Blythe over to the bench and lower her onto it. "They're just trying to scare us," I say.

"Are you sure?" she asks, trembling against me.

"I'm sure. All we have to do is stay calm." I run my hand up and down her arm, and after a few moments, she stops shaking.

The alarm stops suddenly, leaving a ringing in my ears. Slowly, the smoke starts to dissipate. "You were right," Blythe says, letting out a long sigh. "Thank God."

I realize my hand is still on her arm. "Sorry," I say, jerking it away.

"Sorry for what?" She tilts her head back to look up at me.

"For . . . I don't know . . . sorry, just forget it."

Blythe sits up, and tucks her legs underneath her, but doesn't move away. Her knees are touching my thigh. "Philip, are you all right?"

"Yeah. I'm fine, totally fine."

"Why did touching me make you freak out?"

"What? I didn't. I mean, *it* didn't." My heart thuds frantically, and I try to turn away, but she puts her hand on my face and gently brings it back around.

"Tell me." I feel the warmth from her fingers seep through my skin, melting something inside me. She traces my cheek with her hand. "You can tell me."

And to my surprise, I do.

At first, I can't make it through a whole sentence without stammering or stumbling. It's like my body is clinging to the words, and

I have to drag them up through my throat one at a time. But after a few minutes, the words start to pour out of their own accord.

I tell Blythe about the girl I'd liked since middle school, Ava. How I somehow worked up the nerve to ask to her prom. I explain that I was so nervous, my palms were too sweaty to hold my phone, which dropped and broke in front of Ava before I'd even had a chance to say a word. I tell her how I managed to stammer my question. Kind of. How it took three tries for Ava to understand what I was saying. The pained look that crossed her face when she said no, like I'd just asked her to do something revolting. How, to my horror, a wave of nausea crashed over me, and I end up throwing up in the trash can. Right next to Ava's locker.

Blythe doesn't say anything. She just takes my hand and squeezes it as I speak.

"Of course, someone filmed the whole thing and put it on Vid-Hub. I'm sure you saw it," I say, then continue before she has a chance to respond. "*Everyone's* seen it."

I remember exactly where I was when I realized what had happened. I was sitting in the kitchen, having a snack, when my friend Alex sent me the link to the video. It was just a few hours old, but it already had more than twenty thousand views. I couldn't breathe. I couldn't move. All I could do was stare as the view count skyrocketed. It hit fifty thousand before I got up from the table. And the comments . . . thousands of people calling me a loser, telling me I was going to be a virgin for the rest of my life.

But that wasn't the worst part. It was the memes. My face was everywhere. I couldn't go online without seeing a photo of myself throwing up into that trash can. By the next week, there were over ten million views and it was all anyone at school could talk about. Even some of the teachers.

I drew in a shaky breath. "I couldn't sleep, couldn't even get out of bed. Eventually, I stopped going to school. My parents tried everything. Bribes. Threats. Promises. Then, about two weeks after the . . . incident, I heard about the Mars mission."

"I'm so sorry that happened to you," she says, tightening her grip on my hand. "People will move on eventually. They always do."

I shake my head. "Not soon enough. Not before I go to college. Can you imagine trying to make it through freshman orientation? I heard there's a *mural* of me somewhere at Princeton."

"So don't go to Princeton. They're all dicks anyway."

"You know what I mean. Besides, it's . . . it's not just because it went viral. I've always known there was something wrong with me . . . I just didn't expect the entire world to find out all at once." As the words leave my mouth, something in my chest cracks, releasing a wave of pain.

"No, Philip, no," Blythe says, her voice soft. She wraps her arm around me, and I lean into her. "There's nothing wrong with you. *Nothing.*" Her face brightens. "You know what I think you should do? You should make a response video!"

Just the *thought* of making a video makes me feel clammy and nauseous all at once. "I know you're some kind of genius, but that's actually the worst idea I've ever heard in my entire life."

"I'm serious! It'd be really powerful. You can make a statement about not living in fear, how it's better to fail than never try at all."

"Yeah, maybe. I'll think about it," I say, to get her off the subject. But I know there's no chance in hell of me ever doing something like that. "What about you? Why would a girl with every opportunity on earth leave it all behind? I saw you on all those talk shows when you were younger. Everyone who meets you loves you."

To my surprise, her face falls and she shifts away from me. "I don't know . . . I know this sounds weird, but it just hurts too much," she says quietly.

"What do you mean? Are . . . are you talking about your parents?"

Blythe shakes her head. "No. I mean, watching what we're doing to the Earth. What does it matter whether we can clean up oil spills if the ice caps have all melted?"

"That's ridiculous," I say. "If you care so much about the environment, you have to stay and fight. You can't give up."

"I don't see it as giving up. I have the chance to help build a brand-new society on an untouched planet. This time, we have the chance to do something right, and I want to be a part of it."

I stare at her, sifting through the countless arguments popping up in my head. But as I catch sight of the sparkle in her eyes, the words fall away. This is what she wants, what she's decided. "They'll be lucky to have you," I say, smiling. Besides, the last thing I want to do is convince her to pull out.

Blythe takes my hand. "They'll be lucky to have *you*. I just wanted to make sure you're in it for the right reasons."

"You mean, not as a way to get out of prom?"

She cocks her head to the side. "Well . . . if we're both selected, we can organize the first-ever prom on Mars."

"I am *not* traveling two hundred fifty-nine million miles to join the Martian prom committee. Besides, it'd be pretty pointless without music."

"I can take care of that." Blythe grins at me, then starts to sing, the same terrible song she butchered earlier. "I'd stop the world and meeeeeelt with you," she croons before moving on to the next verse.

Still holding her hand, I stand up and pull Blythe to her feet. She gives me a confused look, but doesn't stop singing. Without saying a word, I wrap my arms around her waist and begin to sway in time to the music.

She finishes the song, then rests her head on my shoulder. "You're less terrible at dancing than you lead people to believe."

"Maybe I just need some practice," I whisper into her ear.

"I suppose that's one way to stay busy on a two-hundred-fifty million-mile journey." She lifts her head up to look at me. "Though it might be hard in zero gravity."

"Only one way to find out." I tighten my hold, and then lift her off the ground, spinning her through the air while she laughs.

— — — —

I don't know exactly how it happens. I guess the dancing tires us out, because at some point, we collapse onto one of the benches, breathing heavily. We eventually fall asleep like that, curled around each other on the narrow bench. The only way for us both to fit is for me to wedge myself between the edge of the bench and the wall, but I don't care. I feel like I could stay like this forever. Even if the entire left side of my body has gone numb.

When the lights go on, we have just enough time to disentangle ourselves and stand up before the door slides open.

"Hello again," Lauren says cheerfully. "Everyone okay in here?"

I exchange a quick glance with Blythe. "Yeah, all good," I say.

"Great." James smiles. "We're just going to take each of you off for a quick debriefing, and then you'll be on your way."

Blythe turns to me. Her hair is rumpled, and there's more eyeliner under her eyes than on the lids. She looks beautiful. "I'll see you later," she says.

I nod. "Yeah, see you later." But I don't want to wait another four months to see her, so as Lauren starts to lead her away, I call out, "Hey, Blythe?" She turns around. "Want to get coffee or something after this?"

She smiles, and warmth floods my chest. "Yeah, that'd be great."

I try to rein in the manic smile threatening to take over my face. "Great. I'll meet you outside."

James leads me away in the opposite direction, and a few minutes later, I'm seated at the long table in the conference room again. Except this time, only Lauren is there.

"You did very well in the isolation room," she says as soon as I've lowered myself into the chair.

"Thanks. The fire simulation was pretty brutal, though."

"I know. But it's essential that we see how you perform under pressure. As, I believe, you figured out fairly early." She gives me a knowing smile before glancing down and her tablet. "Of course, the real test was to see how you and Blythe worked together. And I'm pleased to say that our predictions were entirely correct. You two complement each other perfectly. Your dynamic is exactly what we're looking for on the team."

Excitement fizzes through my chest. *Oh my God*, I think. *This is it. I did it. We did it. I'm going to Mars! Blythe and I are going to Mars.* I don't think my smile can get any wider.

"Oh, dear," Lauren says quickly. "I suppose I should've been clearer. I apologize. While you're a very strong candidate, Philip, I'm afraid you weren't selected for the mission."

Her words land like a punch to the gut, knocking the air out of me. "But you just said . . ." I trail off.

"Yes, it's a difficult situation. You see, we can't just think about the group dynamic for this mission. We have to think about how the new colonists will interact with the team we sent six months ago. There's a young man on that team we think will do well to balance out Blythe's exuberance, but we wanted to make sure before we made our final selection. Luckily, you and he have nearly the exact same personality markers, so we figured you'd be a good test case."

The air still hasn't returned to my lungs. I can't talk. I can't breathe. The room starts to spin, and I place my hands on the table for balance. "So . . . I was never a real candidate?" I finally croak.

"Oh, no, of course you were! You made it all the way to the penultimate round. But we only brought you in for *this* round so we could keep evaluating Blythe. Sorry to mislead you. We very much appreciated having you here. We couldn't have chosen Blythe without you. She should be very grateful."

I take a deep breath. "Can . . . can I tell her all this when I see her? We're meeting after this."

Lauren shakes her head sadly. "Oh, dear, I'm sorry, Philip. Blythe's on her way to the shuttle. Tessa put her on the helicopter a few minutes ago."

— — — —

In a daze, I stumble through the rest of my brief conversation with Lauren, then manage to make it out of the building before I collapse onto a bench. My heart is beating so fast, I can barely catch my breath. The words *she's gone* echo through my head. She's going to Mars, and I'm never going to see her again.

I know, rationally, we only spent twenty-four hours together, but something happened in that room. We had a real connection. We had real *potential*. My heart cramps as I imagine all the things we'll never do together. Exchanging wondrous looks as we stare out the shuttle window, taking in the dizzying beauty of space. Holding gloved hands as we step out of the craft and set foot on a foreign planet for the first time. Laughing and exploring and dreaming and—

My phone buzzes. For one brief moment, I think it's her. She could've asked for my number. She would've wanted to say good-bye.

My stomach plummets. It's my mom.

How'd it go?

I'll wait until I get home. I want to see her face when I tell her I'm not going. That's one good thing, I guess. The chance to see her crying happy tears for once.

I let out a sigh and tilt my head back. It's a beautiful, sunny spring day. The sky is an uninterrupted stretch of clear blue. There are no clouds. No helicopters. Blythe is already gone.

If I'd been chosen, I'd be on the helicopter with her. I can picture the two of us huddled next to each other, giddy with excitement as we learn about the next stage of our adventure.

The mission was the only thing getting me out of bed in the morning. It's what gave me the strength to go back to school to face the cloud of laughs and whispers that followed me everywhere. What the hell was I supposed to do now? Finish my homework?

Apply to college, where I'll spend the next four years watching girls cringe when they pass me?

There's nothing wrong with you. Nothing.

Even if she wasn't lying, there aren't other girls like Blythe out there. Most girls would rather make out with a garbage can than with me. I would know. About a million of them said so online.

I feel the familiar prickle of morbid curiosity, the same one that compels you to stare out the window when you pass roadkill. I want to know how many views it's up to. I need to know if the entire planet has now seen the video twice, or if once was enough. Before I can stop myself, I've pulled it up. Twenty million views. Awesome.

I scroll to the most recent comment and brace myself for the jolt of fury or shame I know is coming. But to my surprise, it's not a terrible comment. I can tell right away, because the cruelest ones are always written in all caps.

Philip is adorable. I'm kicking myself for not kissing him when I had the chance. He's destined for great things, I know it.

I jump to my feet. As I'm standing there, staring dumbstruck at my phone, another new comment pops up. *I wish he'd make his own video. I'm about to go on a pretty scary trip and need something inspiring to watch.* The username is ISpeakModernEnglish.

Everything in my body turns fizzy, every cell tingling. I need to write back, even if it means ten million people are going to fill the rest of the thread with cruel comments. But then I hear her voice in my head, clearer than I've heard anything before. *You can make a statement about not living in fear, how it's better to fail than never try at all.*

I take a deep breath and let my finger hover over the most

terrifying button on VidHub, *Go Live. Just pretend she's the only one watching*, I tell myself, pressing it. A light starts blinking, and to my surprise, a strange feeling of calm washes over me. "Hi, everyone," I say. According to the number on the screen, more than ten thousand people are watching. "My name's Philip. I figured it was time for you to meet me . . . the *real* me . . . so here I am. So, hello to everyone out there who's watching, whether you're in the U.S., Asia, Europe, wherever. Or even if you're on Mars." I pause and smile. "Especially if you're on Mars."

SOMETHING REAL

— — — — —

JULIE MURPHY

"HAVE YOU EVER been on TV before, June?" Daria asks as she brushes a matte coral blush along the line of my cheek where a cheekbone would go if mine protruded.

"Mm-mm," I practically grunt, trying my very best to tell her no but also be still, because I've never had my makeup professionally done and I can only imagine it involves staying perfectly still.

Daria, the lanky Asian makeup artist, is one of those human beings who looks like she's not wearing makeup and probably doesn't even own a hair dryer, but for whatever reason she's been entrusted with the job of preparing my face for camera—and rightfully so. The girl is damn good at her job. With my rosy cheeks and double chin that not even obscenely overpriced foundation can hide, I look like an airbrushed cherubic version of myself. All that's missing are wings and a bow and arrow.

Okay, but really, self-deprecation aside, I look pretty amazing. She added a touch of bronzer, too, that suddenly made me look much more like my father's daughter than I ever had before. I'm the result of my Irish mom and my Mexican dad. Somehow I ended up with all mom's complexion genes, while my brother is a more natural mix of the two.

Daria shields my eyes as she sprays my curls with a sugary-sweet hair spray before brushing out every last light brown ringlet into glamorous waves that look as foreign on me as a football helmet.

"Impressive," I say.

Daria winks. "The power of transformation."

The trailer door swings open as a production assistant rushes inside and guides a stomping girl to the chair next to me.

"Here's the other one," says the PA.

"Do we have an ETA on Dylan?" Daria asks.

The PA shares a meaningful glance with Daria's reflection in the mirror. "We're gonna get some intro film on these two for now."

Dylan. I have to remind myself to breathe. For the first time, I glance over to the other girl. And it is immediately apparent that I don't have a chance in hell. The other girl wears thick-soled Dr. Martens and fishnet stockings seamed up the back. Her midnight-blue crushed-velvet babydoll dress swishes around green-bean-like thighs. Her long white-blond hair is streaked with black and sits piled into a sloppy bun on top of her head. On me, her whole look would look like I got in a cage fight with a clearance rack at Hot Topic, but on her, it works. Really well.

The girl is the exact opposite of me in every way, but worst of all, she's my competition.

Three years ago, I would have been the person flipping through channels at home, briefly landing on *A Date Come True* and snickering at the contestants for a moment before settling on reruns of *The Simpsons*, *King of the Hill*, or *Bob's Burgers*. (If I were religious or whatever, my holy trinity would be Lisa Simpson, Bobby Hill, and Tina Belcher.) But all that was before Dylan. His legal name is Timothy Dylan Wachowski, but when his manager discovered him and his tiny little garage band, he became a solo act simply known as Dylan. To be honest, his name could be Wallflower Zambino Bubba and my love for him would still be just as endless.

I've had plenty of crushes, but none of them compare to the pain that is falling in love with someone's every word, every note, and feeling like they can both fix you and break you all in one song without you ever having even met them. Not once. It's the kind of pain you've either got to shut out entirely or embrace completely. I guess you can call me a glutton for punishment, or you can just refer to me by my official title: June Smith, President and Founder of the Official Dylan Fan Club International. Yeah, I've got it bad.

Which is why I didn't even have to try out for *A Date Come True*—a show where totally normal, achingly average-looking people compete for dates with their most beloved celebs. Nope, the producers went to the pain of tracking me down, and no matter how hard I tried, I couldn't say no.

"I guess now is as good a time as any for you two to meet," says Daria as the door swings shut behind the PA. "June, this is Martha. Martha, this is June."

I lift my gaze to say hello via the mirror. Martha turns to me, though, before glancing into the mirror. Awkwardness explodes in my chest. Why didn't I just turn to her instead of insisting on communicating via our reflections? Why didn't I say hi immediately the moment she walked into the trailer?

"Hi," I finally sputter.

"Hello," she responds, her voice cool. And I don't mean hip. I mean even and self-possessed.

"So you're the competition, then?" Heat spreads beneath my skin, and I wonder how long it will take for the blotchiness to surface above Daria's amazing makeup. If I'm this much of a mess just meeting the other girl, what's gonna happen when they put me in front of Dylan?

But then Martha smiles at me with her lips still pressed together, and something about her expression soothes me. "I guess so," she says. She shrugs. "Maybe we've already won just by being here, though."

If I close my eyes, her voice feels like warm water being poured on my head, like when you're getting your hair cut and the stylist presses the nozzle of the shampoo bowl right against your scalp.

Daria clears her throat. "Martha was one of sixty thousand girls who tried out."

"Wow," I breathe.

"And I hear you didn't even have to audition," says Martha. "Sounds like a head start to me."

I laugh a little too deeply. "Trust me. I'm gonna need all the advantages I can get."

Martha smiles into the mirror, and it's easy to forget, for a moment, that she's my competition and that tons of production people are waiting outside to film me in all my awkward glory. As I meet Dylan. *The* Dylan. Oh my God.

I watch as Daria freshens up Martha's face, but just barely. Martha's bone structure alone has already done half the work for her. I force myself to really study my transformation in the mirror. For a moment, the smallest bit of logic nudges its way into my brain, and I realize that Dylan has no idea who I am. Well, other than what they tell him. But besides that, I can be whoever I want to be. He doesn't know the girl who showed up here this morning in leggings and a baggy fleece with uneven skin and frizzy hair and a double chin. All he'll ever know is the finished product. The perfectly made-up face and the lush waves cascading over my shoulders. There's no hiding the double chin, but to be honest, I don't hate it all that much to begin with. When I walk out of this trailer, Dylan will see the upgraded version of me in my long-sleeve navy maxi dress and suede booties. So maybe you can't take the awkward out of the girl, but you sure can hide it.

— — — —

"Okay!" shouts Jill, a petite white lady and the head producer on set. She's the one who reached out to me about the show in the first place. She wears all black and is barely tall enough to hop into her director's chair sitting across from me, but her voice compensates for whatever she lacks in stature. "We're gonna get some intro footage. June's first. Everyone, shut the hell up!"

Daria fusses with my hair once more, twisting my waves so they frame my face just so.

"Five," says the burly cameraman just behind Jill's shoulder, "four, three, two, and action."

Jill clears her throat. "June, we're going to ask a few questions. You'll look just over my shoulder the whole time at Zeek behind me. Got it?"

I nod. Four cameras are trained on me, ready to capture me at every angle, which is only slightly horrifying. I have to squint to see beyond the looming lights that feel like the heat lamps my brother uses for his pet lizard, Ralph. Just beyond Jill, Daria hovers with her belt full of brushes, and a few feet behind her sits Martha, who offers me a short wave.

"Now, we'll edit my prompts and questions out, so it just looks like you're talking to the camera. If you fumble, just start over or pick up where you left off. The magic happens in the cutting room."

I nod, trying not to focus on how dry my mouth suddenly is.

"So tell us about your role with Dylan's official fan club."

"Well, I started the Dylan Fan Club, and at first it was just a message board and not really anything serious or official. And this was back when Dylan was just beginning to get big hits on YouTube. So when he got picked up by Galaxy, his label, they reached out and asked if I'd be interested in making things official, and before you know it, we've got chapters all over the world and a really intense site with everything from a merch store to a fan-fic archive."

Jill nods, and I think her smile is telling me that I am not totally bombing this thing. "Now, I hope you don't take any offense to this, but you seem really normal."

Behind her, Martha laughs. My eye catches hers and I laugh, too.

"Well, I am normal? I think? I mean, would I even know if I wasn't? I guess I'm my own normal?"

Jill smiles, but this time it's not in an encouraging way. "No, no, I just meant, you don't strike me as the fangirl type. You know, I've been producing this show since season one and we've seen it all, so it's just . . . refreshing. And I'm kind of wondering what made you start the fan club, if you wouldn't mind talking a little about that."

"Well, Dylan did covers for a while. At least at first. And I was into his sound and stuff, but it was his first original song that really got to me. 'Me Against the World.' Those lyrics, they were, like, immediately seared into my brain. It was almost like all the words in that song existed inside of me, but Dylan had somehow grouped them all together and sorted them out. And not only that, but he could freaking sing. That video of him in his dad's basement. Just acoustic. Nothing fancy. I would turn that song on and close all the curtains in my room and just lie there in the dark. I should've felt so alone, but I didn't. And I wanted that feeling all the time. But Dylan's one person." I laugh a little. "I'm not some psycho who's going to stalk him at his house, so I decided to find people who felt just as alone as I did. I guess I just thought we could be alone together, or maybe—just maybe—we'd find that we weren't all that alone to begin with."

I stop for a moment to let Jill speak, but her eyes are wide and she's just nodding me along.

"So I guess I don't really come across as the type of person who would start a fan club, but I think we'd all surprise ourselves to find out what lengths we might go to to re-create and savor the moments that make us feel like we have purpose. There's no shame in that."

"Good," Jill says, her whole body leaning in. "Now, paint me the picture of your perfect date with Dylan."

At the mention of his name, my whole body tingles. "Well." I gulp loudly, and suddenly the cameras and the lights . . . all feel so warm. "I love divey little restaurants that look like they can barely pass health inspection, but are actually, like, really good and authentic. And then maybe Dylan would take me to see his favorite band that no one's even heard of yet. I mean, of course I'd love for Dylan himself to play me something on the beach or something crazy, but I think that what the last few years have really taught me is that there's something really telling about the music someone else shares with you."

"Wow," says Jill. "Kid, you're a natural. All right, Martha," she shouts. "Your turn!"

I stand up, and Daria squeezes my elbow before whispering in my ear. "You probably didn't notice, but the whole damn crew was hanging on your every word, and we don't impress easy. I think you got this date in the bag."

I turn to her, my whole face lighting up. "Dylan will see that? How does he even decide?"

"Well, maybe, but the decision is more in the hands of the—"

"Daria!" Jill snaps. "Let's get some powder. This girl's T-zone is lighting up like a runway."

Daria grimaces and runs off toward Martha. With no one to guide me, I hop up into the empty director's chair behind Jill. I'm eager to get to know my competition.

"Okay," says Jill in a voice so low I can barely hear. "Just take it slow, and if this gets to be too much, we'll take a breather and pick back up again. You're in the driver's seat. Just like I told you a few weeks back."

She's been prepped for this? Immediately, I feel somehow threatened. I know this is just a dumb TV show and that none of this is real, but because at the heart of all this reality-TV-show bullshit is a real moment with Dylan—hopefully all to myself—for me to tell him how much his music means to me. And Martha seems to have some kind of connection with Jill, which I can only conclude is an upper hand.

Jill continues. "This is a vehicle for you to tell your and Marisa's story, okay? And I know it will mean so much to Dylan, too."

Martha nods quickly. "I'm ready."

"Martha, you have a special connection to Dylan, don't you?"

She takes a deep breath. "I've never been the kind of person to dig through all this trash music on the Internet to find the band no one's ever heard of. That's cool if you're into that. But I guess my jam has always been more books and fashion. I can blow some serious cash on first-edition Nancy Drew books and handmade jewelry. But Marisa, my older sister . . . she's one of those people that's always ten steps ahead. Or she was." For a moment, Martha stares down into her lap as she rings her hands together. "She was the kind of person who was always dragging me to dinky little clubs to see bands she swore would be the next big thing. And sometimes she was right."

In spite of myself, I can't help being a little bit mesmerized by Martha. I wish she wasn't the competition. It's not even that she's a threat; I just don't like the feeling of being pitted against her.

Jill nods. "Good. She sounds great. Was Marisa a big early fan of Dylan?"

"Oh, yeah." She smiles, her eyes a bit glassy. "She loved that damn song."

"'Me Against the World'?" asks Jill.

"Yep, that's the one." The silence that follows is heavy, like Jill's given some kind of cue that Martha hasn't picked up on or doesn't want to.

"You said Marisa *was*? What happened?"

"She was so stubborn. Our parents told her to go to community college for a semester or two to figure out what she wanted to do or where she wanted to go, but she couldn't see that logic. She wanted the *experience* of going to college. So my parents agreed to send her to Portsmith, a little liberal arts college an hour outside the city. She was driving home for Election Day—"

"Election Day?" asks Jill.

"Yeah, my dad is one of those people who votes in every single election, like down to school boards and city treasurer, and it's sort of, like, programmed in us to vote and be really obnoxious about it, too. He was born and raised in Cuba, which means he didn't take civic responsibility lightly when he became a citizen."

"That's sweet," Jill tells her in a too-sugary voice.

"Marisa was driving home to vote and to watch the results roll in. It was a midterm election, but lots of congressional seats, so our dad was, like, really geeking out. And it was Marisa's first time to vote. Dad bought fancy cupcakes and my mom made some decorations and even got some champagne for us all to share."

I'm hanging on her every word. I know this has nothing to do with Dylan or his music or this stupid date we're competing for, but if Jill is out to make good TV, she knows how to get it done.

"Wrong-way driver," says Martha so simply. Like she's said those exact words a dozen times before. "It was instant. She was gone. There was no pain. That's what the paramedics told us. I think that's supposed to make it better, and it's not like I wanted her to be in pain, but I kind of wonder if she would've preferred to know the end was coming. To just have a minute or two to prepare herself." She shakes her head, her gaze looking far past the camera now. "I think I've had too long to think about this now."

Jill nods sympathetically. "I'm so sorry, Martha. Is your sister—sounds like she was wonderful, by the way—is she the reason you're here for a chance to meet Dylan?"

"Well, technology . . . it's either a burden or a curse. We were able to figure out what song she'd been listening to at the time of—when it happened. And it was that song. 'Me Against the World.' That's back when it wasn't even popular yet, so I didn't really think much of it other than that it was nice to just know what she was listening to. But then Dylan's career blew up, and that song . . . it was every-where."

"Wow, I imagine that must have been rather difficult for you."

Martha nods, her gaze unmoving. "At first. At first, it was miser-able. I couldn't escape it. But it wasn't going anywhere. So I had to make the best of it. That meant being an optimist for once. Opti-mism was always Marisa's job. And I guess I just had to force myself to see the song as Marisa's way of always being there for me. Maybe that sounds cheesy, but it worked."

"Perfect," Jill tells Martha. "You're doing great. Now, one last thing. If you win this date with Dylan, what is it that you want to say? Look right at the camera."

Martha nods, gripping the armrests of her chair, and looks straight into the camera. "I'd tell him 'thank you.' I'd say 'thank you for giving me Marisa's last gift. For giving me a way—a tangible way—to hold on to my sister forever.'"

Jill stands and begins to clap like a freaking maniac. Nausea washes over me as I'm reminded that this is just entertainment. Jill might as well be locked away in a writers' room orchestrating this whole thing via a script. But this isn't fiction. This is our lives. This is Martha's life. I'm going to be sick.

I stand and whirl around on my heel, prepared to storm off to . . . I don't know exactly where, when I am confronted with a holey-T-shirt-clad broad chest.

Slowly, my gaze lifts like I'm a marionette and someone is pulling the string attached to the center of my head. I gasp.

Dylan takes off his silver aviators and says, "The party has arrived."

— — — —

I would like to say that the first words I said to Dylan were something to the effect of how thrilled I was to meet him or how much his work has meant to me, but instead it was more of a word salad: "Much tall you are."

I've been sitting by the craft services table for an hour and a half now, contemplating each and every single one of those words. It's been a constant stream of crew members grazing past as they each tell me we should be back to filming any minute now.

It'd be a lie if I didn't admit that I was just slightly disappointed to find that after his initial hello, Dylan has been squirreled away in a super-fancy trailer with a security guard stationed outside the door. Some silly part of me thought that maybe I'd get to hang out with Dylan during downtime and we'd develop a rapport. Maybe we'd have inside jokes. I shake my head, and roll my eyes at my own naïveté.

"Hey!" says Martha as she plops down next to me. "You found the food. Good place to set up camp."

I wrinkle my nose. "I'll be the first to admit that I'm pro-food, like, all the way, but my nerves have got me way too anxious to even gnaw on celery sticks."

"Oh my God," she says, leaning in toward me, her hand resting on my thigh for a moment. "Me too."

I smile at her gratefully. I'm so glad she's not the version of my competition that existed in my head. I didn't know what I expected from my competitor. Cattiness? Bitingly rude? But Martha is just good. And I think that maybe she deserves this more than I do.

"I'm sorry about your sister," I tell her.

She half smiles. "Me too." After a moment, she adds, "She would die all over again if she knew I was here doing this."

I cough, not sure what exactly to say.

"That was a bad joke, huh?" asks Martha.

I let out a short laugh. "Well, it wasn't exactly a good one."

She shrugs. "Me and Marisa always had a vicious sense of humor. I think she'd approve."

Something inside me unlocks. Something I didn't even know was locked away to begin with. I have this wonderful and scary and heart-stopping feeling that I could tell Martha my most hideous thoughts and my most ridiculous hopes and she'd just sit here like she is right now, unfazed. And that's sort of a wonderful thing if you think about it.

"All right, ladies," says Jill as she power walks toward us. "We've got you all set up for the challenge portion of the show. So let's head over there and Daria will freshen you up."

"Cool," says Martha. "What's the challenge?"

Dread settles in the pit of my stomach. This is the part I've been most anxious about. There's always one challenge. Sometimes it's a race or an obstacle course or trivia or some type of competition, but whatever it is, it always ends poorly, with at least one of the contestants being humiliated.

"No can do," says Jill. "We like for the on-camera reaction to be as authentic as possible."

She walks off, and then turns, beckoning for us to follow her.

"Yeah," Martha says under her breath, "because the first thing I think of when I think of *A Date Come True* is authentic."

I hiss out a knowing sigh that surprises me. And then it doesn't. I don't even know if I should be here anymore. I've barely even seen Dylan anyway. I take a deep breath, trying my best to shake off the negativity.

A few minutes later, we find ourselves standing in a studio with white curtains concealing the walls around us. And Dylan is there, too.

Daria flutters around touching up our makeup before dedicating her attention to Dylan.

"Nate," says Jill, bringing over a man in a perfectly tailored tux. "This is Martha and June, our competitors for this episode."

Nate doesn't really need introductions, though. He's the host and face of *A Date Come True*. There's something comforting about the way his makeup settles into the creases around his eyes. Not everything is as it appears on TV. That's for sure.

Nate's smile dazzles as he winks at the two of us, reminding us that he's a pro charmer. "You nervous?" he asks. "Don't be nervous." He holds up his hands for us to see. "You're in very good hands, I swear."

After he walks off, Martha and I turn to each other, and in unison say, "Gross."

We break out in a fit of giggles, but we're cut short by Jill. "Let's do this thing. We only want to do one take here, so bring your A-game, people!"

Nate takes his position between Dylan and Martha and me as Jill counts down to action. "Okay, we're back," he says.

I feel my whole body straighten as I realize I'm on camera again.

Nate turns to Dylan, his voice as smooth as a radio host's. "Now, Dylan, you've thought long and hard about our challenge this week, haven't you?"

"Oh, yeah. Totally," says Dylan. "I guess you could say I cooked up something really cool."

"Let's drop the curtains, shall we?" asks Nate.

All around us the tall white curtains *whoosh* to the ground and Martha and I find ourselves in a state-of-the-art double kitchen with brand-new stainless-steel appliances. Over one side hangs a sign that reads *#TeamJune* and the other side has a sign bearing *#TeamMartha*.

My anxiety washes away for a moment as I realize that—Oh my God!—this is a cooking challenge! I can cook. I can really freaking cook. I've got this shit in the bag.

Then I look to Martha, her eyes huge and full of terror. My

stomach twists into a knot as I'm reminded that my success is her failure. It's not that I feel bad for her or think she should win by default on account of her sister. There's just this nagging feeling inside of me that wishes we'd met in real life.

But this isn't real life.

"Martha," says Dylan. "June."

My name! He said my name! Some animalistic instinct in my brain switches on and I turn into a monster fangirl with blurred vision for anything that isn't Dylan. *And hey, don't forget about the freaking cameras*, I remind myself.

"I'm a total foodie these days," continues Dylan. "But back when I was just a little kid, my favorite meal was dinosaur-shaped nuggets with ketchup. So I've decided to ask you ladies to blend my foodie love with my old-school fave and make me some panko-crusted dino nuggets with ketchup made from scratch. You've each been given the same ingredients, and there may or may not be a few red herrings in there."

Nate laughs. "A woman's place is in the kitchen, am I right?"

Dylan snickers quietly.

I nearly gag. Martha and I exchange a look. *More like misogyny, am I right?*

"Right," says Nate, "so you'll each have five minutes of Wi-Fi time sponsored by Tunez Headphones, and then you'll each have one hour to re-create Dylan's childhood dish. Aaaaaand your five minutes starts now!"

"Cut!" shouts Jill. "I should force you to do a retake for that sexist bullshit you pulled, Nate, but we'll just cut it in post."

Nate shrugs and walks off to his dressing room. "You can't get rid of me, Jillybean!"

I realize that I have a quick moment to say something to Dylan besides how tall he is. I take a step toward him. "Hi," I say. "Your, um, music means so much to me." When I say it out loud like that, it sounds so much more generic than how it actually feels.

He turns to me, sliding his sunglasses on. "I would hope so." He laughs to himself. "I mean, that's why you're here, right?"

I force out a dry chuckle, but I can't ignore the disappointment settling in my chest. "Yeah. Totally."

"Oh, but thanks," he adds just as he's swarmed by people armed with cell phones and itineraries.

As he's quickly whisked away, crew members buzz around us like bees, changing the lighting for our contest. My throat goes dry, and my stomach feels suddenly heavy. It's that same feeling I get when I'm driving somewhere and I know—I just know—I've taken a wrong turn or missed my exit no matter what my GPS says.

"Okay, girls," says Jill as she hands us each an apron and ridiculous chef hat, both emblazoned with the show logo. "It's just like they said. You get an hour to cook and five minutes on the Internet with these bad boys." She hands over two tablets, provided by sponsors too, I'm sure. "We'll start rolling in a bit, and we won't interfere, really, unless there's an emergency. Oh, and uh, no talking to each other during this or trading secrets or something." She smiles. "Not that you'd want to, right?"

We both nod.

After she walks away, Martha looks to me and says,

"Fuuuuuuuuuuuuuck." It comes out like one of my brother's long burps that he does on command.

I laugh. "It's just a dumb challenge," I tell her. "Dylan doesn't really care if you can cook." Or maybe he just doesn't care in general.

She shakes her head. "You don't get it. I really, really can't cook. And not to be a total pain in the ass, but I'm a vegetarian, too. Just the sight of raw meat makes me want to puke." The color begins to slowly drain from her face.

I take a step closer. "Listen," I whisper, my lips nearly brushing against her hair, "I know we're not supposed to be helping each other, but just, like, do what I do."

For a brief moment, she squeezes my hand. "I don't know how much that will help, but thank you. I really appreciate it."

As we're carefully positioned with our tablets and notebooks in our own personal kitchens, facing opposite each other, cameras hover around us. I search for things like baking instructions and tips for breading and ketchup recipes. I'm not sure what Martha is searching for, but she looks downright manic.

As our time ends, our tablets are taken away and we're left with our notes, our ingredients, and our intuition.

I decide to bake instead of deep-fry—mainly because I think it might be easier for Martha to follow along. I start in on the chicken, pounding it into submission. I search my supplies and come up with a few different shapes of dinosaur cookie-cutters. I push through the chicken, using my weight. It's not easy, but it works.

As I mix my bread crumbs and beat my eggs, I glance over to Martha, whose once beautiful velvet dress is covered in flour, despite her apron. She mumbles a stream of curse words, and I try to offer an encouraging smile, but she's lost in her frustration. I feel awful for her, but the camera guys seem to be really into her cooking-nightmare meltdown.

I don't think that cooking is specifically for women, but in my house, my mom was always the one in the kitchen. It was her happy place, and she let me share that with her. But unfortunately, the kitchen was her one and only happy place in our house, so when she split when I was in seventh grade, her kitchen became mine.

Nothing about being on camera makes me comfortable, but being in a kitchen can almost make me forget that millions of people will be watching me from the comfort of their homes in a few weeks' time.

As our hour fades into minutes, I put the finishing touches on my ketchup, including a sprig of parsley.

"Time!" Jill shouts.

Martha and I wait in silence for a few minutes as Dylan is summoned from his trailer. We both look and feel like messes.

Nate and Dylan stand between Martha and me in front of a table with our presented entrées. Mine is a pile of dinosaur nuggets—some more misshapen than others—alongside what I hope is not-totally-disgusting ketchup made from scratch. And Martha's dish is fury personified. On her plate is one uncooked chicken breast covered in ketchup with a giant chopping knife sticking out of it.

I sigh. There's no competition. One is edible and the other is decidedly . . . not.

We quickly regroup, and Daria swings through to lightly powder our faces, but she takes no pains to hide the mess we've made of our hair and clothes.

"Well," says Nate as the cameras begin to roll again, "I guess we won't be doing a blind taste test this time."

I look to Martha and can practically hear her gulp.

"Uh, yeah," says Dylan as he chuckles nervously. "Looks like some kind of horror movie over there."

Martha shrinks back a little. I guess there's a chance she could still win, but it doesn't look good.

"June, let's give your dish a go," says Nate.

I nod and hold my plate for the two of them, and they each swipe a nugget through ketchup before chomping down.

"Hey, this is pretty great!" Dylan says, his mouth still full.

"My wife's gonna kill me if those bread crumbs have gluten in them," says Nate. "But it was worth it!"

I roll my eyes.

"Cut!" shouts Jill. "Let's get the girls all cleaned up and ready for the rose gazebo."

Daria waves for us to follow her back to the makeup trailer, and once again Dylan is ushered away by a crowd of assistants and managers.

I practically jog to catch up to Martha. "Hey, are you okay?" I ask.

She shakes her head, but says, "Yeah, I'm fine."

"It's just a dumb TV show," I tell her as we come to a stop at the trailer, the door swinging shut behind Daria.

Martha turns to face me, and I can see that she's pressing her lips shut in some attempt to hold back tears. She shakes her head again before finally bursting, tears streaming down her flour-coated cheeks. "I just thought that if I came on this show, and won some dumb date with this ridiculous singer who I don't even really like . . . I just thought it would give me some kind of closure." She uses the tips of her fingers to press under her eyes, like she's trying to push the tears back in.

I reach for her sticky hands and hold them tightly in mine. "That's not silly or dumb or whatever," I say. "I can't even imagine what it would feel like to lose a sibling. Shit. I don't even like my brother and I'd still be a wreck."

We stand there for a moment, hand in hand. We're just two people who were randomly driven together in the most ludicrous of ways by some reality TV show that I can now say, without a doubt, is more fake than it is real. But standing here with her. This is real. There's just something about her that makes me feel like we could really be something to each other in real life. For reasons I don't know how to explain, Martha makes every nerve in my body light up like a Christmas tree. It's like when Joey Scheck kissed me after eighth-grade graduation and for the first time ever I felt like my life was a movie and I was finally the star.

"I don't know what's going to happen with this ceremony, but I hope that there was a reason for all of this," I finally say. "And maybe it's not something you'll understand anytime soon."

She looks up and squeezes my fingers tight before giving me a floppy shrug. "Or maybe I will."

The door swings open and we startle apart, like we've been caught doing something much more than holding hands. "Ladies! I can't do my job without your faces!" says Daria.

— — — —

We look much more glamorous than we feel. In the makeup trailer, we gave ourselves glorified sponge baths in an attempt to rid ourselves of sweat and kitchen smells before Daria performed transformations on each of us.

My waves have been refreshed and lay perfectly over my shoulders. Wardrobe has put me in a royal-blue chiffon dress that sweeps the floor. And Martha is downright stunning in a lacy burgundy dress with a trumpet skirt.

After a few hours of waiting to be beckoned, we're driven on a golf cart to one of the far-off lots behind the studio. The set looks like a small town square with a gazebo, and the whole place is dripping with twinkly lights. I recognize it as the usual backdrop for the rose ceremony. For some reason, it hadn't occurred to me that this was a set and not some tiny little town center outside of Los Angeles, but it's just as fake as the rest of the show. Still, it's hard not to get swept up in the beauty of it—if you can manage to ignore Jill's shouting and all the grunting camera operators.

Nate is in his signature tux and Dylan wears his same holey jeans, but with the added touch of a slim-cut, flat, black button-down shirt.

I think I'm going to win. How can they even pick Martha after the kitchen fiasco? But do I even want to win anymore? It's hard to imagine my "date" with Dylan doing anything more than ruining the version of him that lives in my head. The version of him whose voice cradled me, letting me know that even in my darkest hour, I was not alone. Already, there's this sense of mourning settling inside me that I can't quite explain except to say that maybe the version of Dylan I'd built up in my head never existed at all. It's nearly impossible for me to even recall the edge-of-my-seat excitement I felt this morning at the prospect of this moment.

Nate and Dylan wait for us on the steps of the gazebo, where a propmaster stands with one yellow rose.

Dylan wipes his brow as we take our places. "These lights are killer, huh?"

I squint up at them, but they don't seem so bad to me. Not any different from the interview lights at least.

Nate pats his forehead to avoid messing up his makeup. "Yeah, they must be testing out something new."

Dylan cringes a little and calls out, "Lissa, we gonna wrap on this soon? I'm not feeling so hot."

"Yeah, babe," someone answers from behind the sea of crew and cameras. "One and done. We're out."

Dylan nods as Nate lets out a loud burp.

I reach for Martha's hand one last time, and her fingers intertwine with mine. "Almost over," I whisper.

She winks. "Maybe it wasn't such a bust after all."

Jill counts down, and our hands drift apart as we await our completely unreal reality-TV-show fate.

"Ladies, our time together has come to an end, and in just a moment one of you will move on to a very romantic one-on-one date with Dylan." Nate gestures to Dylan.

Dylan steps forward, the rose in his hand, and says, "I've had so much fun getting to know you both."

Getting to know us? Our paths barely even crossed.

"And I want you to know," he continues, "that I didn't make this decision lightly. June, I'm so impressed by your dedication to not only me, but to my fans. Mega fans like you are what keep me going. And you slayed the kitchen challenge this afternoon. And, Martha, I feel like, whoa, for you and your family. It means so much to me that the last thing your sister heard was my voice. It's so, like, meta."

My skin crawls at the thought of that information feeding his ego.

He holds his stomach for a minute before adding, "But after what happened during the kitchen challenge today, it's hard for me to tell if your—" He burps into his fist. "Excuse me." And then again. "—if your heart is in it. Oh fuck. I feel like shit. I think I'm gonna—"

And then I swear to God, everything that happens next occurs in slow motion. Dylan projectile vomits in my and Martha's exact direction. The only thing that saves me is Martha pulling me out of the path of puke.

"No, man, don't do that," says Nate. "You're just gonna make me . . ." And then Nate is puking, too.

Crew members and posse members crowd both Nate and Dylan, and Martha and I are pushed back even farther, reminding us both how very unimportant we actually are.

"Those gross-ass chicken nuggets!" Dylan moans. "It's food poisoning. That bitch poisoned me!"

I turn to Martha, my eyes wide.

Her hand flies up, the back of her palm pressed to my forehead. "How are you? Are you feeling all right?"

I shake my head. "I was too nervous to eat all day."

She laughs. "Me too."

I clap a hand over my mouth, stumbling back. "Oh my God. I poisoned Dylan. *The* Dylan."

She waves off that notion. "Psh. He'll live. They're probably pumping him with fluids and gold as we speak."

We both take a minute to glance around. No one is looking for us or checking on us. It's almost . . . a relief.

Martha takes my hand. "Let's blow this puke show!" She pulls me with her to a golf cart with the keys in the ignition.

She slides in behind the wheel and I take my seat next to her as co-captain. "I gotta get out of this dress," I tell her.

"Me too. I feel like a total stranger."

As the sun sinks down behind the horizon she speeds off toward the makeup trailer where we left our street clothes.

We both take turns changing inside the trailer, and when we're done, it's like a makeover reveal on a TV show except this time, it's more of an un-makeover, where we just reveal ourselves. Our regular, normal, everyday selves.

I stand beneath the dusky sky in my leggings and gold flats in my favorite dress—the bright yellow one covered in all kinds of food from, hot dogs and hamburgers to sundaes and doughnuts.

Martha slinks down the steps toward me in the same stompy boots she wore earlier today and a short body-hugging violet knit skirt with a black T-shirt that says *Do no harm, but take no sht*. She's the type of person who if you don't want to kiss her, you probably want to be her. And I think I definitely want one of those things.

"There you are," I say, my words coming out breathier than I expected.

"Here I am," she says.

A speeding golf cart stops to a halt next to us. "I was looking for you two," says Daria, looking paler than I remember. She slumps against the steering wheel and groans.

"I'm so sorry," I say. "We just had to get out of there."

She shakes her head. "Trust me. Things got pretty bad back there."

"What do you mean?" asks Martha, taking the final step down.

"Well, I guess we all ate whatever Dylan and Nate had and it was like a Puke Convention. Not a pretty thing," she says.

"Wait," I say. "So it wasn't me? I didn't poison Dylan and Nate?"

She shakes her head. "No way. No how. We think it must have been the crab dip from craft services." She shakes her fist at the air. "Damn you, delicious crabs!"

I laugh. Even when she's been puking her guts up, Daria manages to be somebody I want to be friends with.

She gets out and stumbles past us up the stairs. "You two had better head home. Jill will call you once she can pull her head out of a toilet, but my guess is we're scrapping the episode." She pauses for a moment, realizing that this might be crushing news for us. "You two were great, though. Really. I meet lots of shitty people on this job, and you both made my job a breeze. Go have fun tonight. For me."

Martha turns to me, one brow raised mischievously. "You got plans for tonight?"

I bite down on my lip, forcing myself not to blurt something ridiculous, like *I have to run an update on the fan site*. "I had a date," I finally say. "But looks like I got stood up."

"Still a good night for a date," she says, taking my hand. "I've got a car."

I take an instinctive step toward her, like the only thing driving my body is nature. "What do you want to do?" I ask.

And then she kisses me. Right on the lips. I expected it, but I didn't. It's the perfect mix of want and surprise, which aren't two things I often find in the same place. She pulls back, lingering for a moment, her lips hovering above mine. "Something real," she says.

SAY EVERYTHING

— — — — —

HUNTLEY FITZPATRICK

TO YOU HE'S *that boy*.

The one who breezes through the door of the diner, blowing in fresh air and the pale green smell of still-distant spring. Always with the usual crew, the ones from the lacrosse team, full of high spirits and themselves. Your own age—you guess—but somehow younger—carefree, dead sure that the world is theirs to enjoy, with every intention of doing that. They swarm, laughing, jostling shoulders, into the biggest booth at the back, four on one side, four on the other. That boy sits on the outside, closest to the aisle. The others grab menus they don't need, since they always order the same old things. Burgers, fries, milk shakes, hot apple pie overloaded with ice cream.

All he ever gets is iced tea. Straight up, heavy on the lemon slices.

Almost indistinguishable in their lacrosse clothes, those boys could be any team from anywhere. Except that when they wear their blue-blazer-and-khaki uniforms, it's easy to know what school they come from. Private, preppie, one town over from here. In a different turn of fate, you would have been there, too. You might've been as carefree. No worries about money, certain someone would pick up after you. With a wince, you remember when you were like them, your major concern that the girls' uniforms were ugly.

The boys sweep through their meal—it barely takes ten minutes—crowd out, on to the next good time. That boy moves aside to let them go, flicks a glance toward you, as you hover by the cash register. He catches your eye for a moment, then ducks his head to take a long pull from his straw, the tea reduced to watery ice cubes by now.

You walk up to his booth, heart hammering—why? You do this ten times an hour during your six-hour shift! But he's always left with his friends before. Have they given him money this time or assumed he'd pay? "Rich kid" rolls off him like an overdose of Axe body spray.

He's been looking down, long lashes fanning his cheekbones, but glances up when you drop the check on the table, lips parting as though he's about to say . . . what? Without a word, he flips his wallet from his jeans, pulls out cash. Bill after bill, slides them toward you.

"This is the first time I've gotten a sixty-dollar tip on a two-dollar glass of iced tea."

Leaning back against the fake red leather of the booth, he gestures to the spaces where his friends had sat. A hasty scan shows you they'd barely covered their tabs, with bonus scatter of extra coins.

"You gave me too much," I say.

"I'm good at math. You deserve more."

"It's your job to compensate?"

"It's my choice to even the score." His husky voice is even, practical.

"No way." You push most of the money back across the table, curl your fingers down, ashamed of your bitten nails.

"Waitress! Hell-ooo! I asked for honey mustard on this omelet. This is Dijon!"

You look over to see Maeve, your boss, make a guillotine-style chop against her neck—*no fraternizing with customers*—then jerk her head toward table five with their burning need for honey mustard. On an omelet. Dear God.

He's made no move to take the cash, now concentrating on smoothing out the wrapper from his straw, giving that job more attention than it deserves. "Look . . . I won't overtip again. I won't tip at all, if that bothers you. But whenever I come here, you never sit down. I'd like to see you at a movie or a restaurant. Having fun."

"Are you asking me on a date?"

"Would that be your idea of fun?"

"I don't know. I don't date."

A flick of . . . something—pity?—passes like a hand over his face.

He sets his elbows on the table, looking at you straight on as you stack up plate after plate.

"It could be a test date. If you don't like it, you never have to do it again. Not with me, anyway. How about tomorrow? I could pick you up at your house? Or—"

"Hey, girl! This coffee's stone cold. Do something." It's the crabby guy at table nine who always takes up a four-person table by himself.

Do something.

"I get off at noon Saturdays. You could meet me here."

Not at your own home. Not now. You used to love having friends over—watching their faces as they saw where you lived. As if that defined who you were.

Wherever this boy comes from, you're willing to bet it isn't a second-floor walk-up with bad plumbing.

"Really?" His voice incredulous, almost cracking, like he can't believe he's gotten your agreement. As if he'd had more arguments lined up like ammunition, ready to fire.

"Sure." Your answer's braver than you are.

His slow smile transforms his face from striking to drop-dead gorgeous, the corners of his eyes scrunching as if you're sharing an in-joke, dimples you hadn't seen before bracketing his lips. You're looking straight at him now—for the first time. Everything you've noticed before came from sideways glances. Hair long enough to curl around the backs of his ears. Generous lower lip, thinner upper lip that qualifies that generosity. Faint purple shadows under his eyes, suggesting sleep doesn't come easily. Eyes that can't quite make up their mind—blue with a ring of brown-green around the pupil—or is that gold? Chameleon eyes.

Maybe they tell a truth about him. That he'll be whoever he needs to be, depending on the setting or situation. Something you should remember.

You step back, your bussing tray sharp between you like a gray plastic shield.

"You might want to tell me your name, so I don't have to call you Test Date."

"Sean."

He raises his hand, as if he's going to shake yours, old-school polite, then changes course and brushes it through his hair, blue-black in the harsh overhead lighting of the diner.

"Emma Greene."

"Oh, I know *your* name."

That takes a beat to process. Why? You don't know his.

"Tomorrow, then?" He's reaching over now to gather his friends' remaining plates together, as if cleaning up the table fast will make tomorrow come faster.

You map the pulse beating in his throat, the dip and curve of the smooth skin above his collarbone, oddly mesmerized.

You look up to find him studying your face for heartbeats that pulsed longer than heartbeats should. Then you look away again.

"Tomorrow. But, so I know, what will we talk about? I don't know a thing about you."

Sean slides out of the booth. Flashes that smile. "That's what tomorrow's for."

He's out the door before you even notice he's left the entire tip on the table.

— — — —

"If you can't be good, be careful," your best friend tells you.

"That's your advice, Jen? What are you, a health teacher from the fifties?"

"I think that covers it pretty well. Text me if he's a psycho or a loser."

"*So* not helpful."

"Just quit being the Caution Queen. Take risks."

"Risks haven't turned out well for my family."

"For your *family*, not you. Emma. Babe. Go be seventeen."

After five years, you'd think you'd be able to separate your roots from your wings. Still hadn't happened. You're afraid it never will.

— — — —

You don't expect a bright purple car, not from a boy whose entire wardrobe seems to consist of his lacrosse jersey or school uniform or white shirts and baggy khakis. Sean has his back to you, tossing things into the car's backseat. You walk up next to him and clear your throat. He doesn't seem to hear you, so you clear it again, louder, step closer.

He straightens, his gaze traveling slowly up your legs to your face, flushes a little, smile shy now. "You came."

"Of course. I said I would. It's not like I was going to skulk out the back door of the diner to avoid you." You sound a little bitchy, your words shoved between you as if you still had that tray as a shield.

He shrugs, offhanded, then his words come in a rush. "I never take anything for granted."

Turning away, he scoops a pile of catalogs—Victoria's Secret, Sephora, a few copies of *Teen Vogue*—off the seat and tosses them in the back. "Sorry. This will just take a moment. You'll have to shift the seat back. I forgot how long your legs are."

You're slightly taller than Sean, you notice now. So long legs are . . . a good thing? Bad thing? God, this was part of the reason you don't date. You need a translator, and you can't afford one.

After you climb in, he pulls open the glove compartment, drops a handful of jewelry into it. A necklace, a few unmatched earrings, a tube of lip gloss.

You crane your neck to see if there's anything even more disturbing in the rear seat—discarded condom wrappers, kicked-off high heels, lace thongs. Instead, more catalogs, a flowered scarf, hair scrunchies, a pink hoodie.

"How many girls have you had in this car?"

"Wha-at? Oh—no. Nothing like that," Sean says, shifting into reverse. He isn't good at it. Grinding sound. "My sister's car."

A shot of relief. He's never given off that player vibe.

"That's why it doesn't exactly throb with testosterone."

"Yeah, I've found regular gas works better. I had to sell my own car. Which did not have a stick shift, obviously. Carrie's crazy possessive about this thing. So, learning curve."

"You're learning to drive this on a first date?" You almost bite your tongue. "First" implies there will be at least a second and possibly many more.

"If I'm asking you to leave your comfort zone—not to mention the whole inexplicable 'I don't date' thing—the least I can do is meet you halfway. No worries, though. I watched a bunch of YouTube videos on Mastering a Standard."

"Seriously?"

"Nope. But, Emma, I got this."

He brakes fast at a four-way stop, nearly stalling out.

Instead of getting pissed, or embarrassed, Sean laughs. "Maybe I haven't got it. Can *you* drive a stick?"

"I can."

"Go for it." He pulls over onto the shoulder of the road, settles comfortably into the seat you vacate, folds his arms, completely at ease, no ego on the line at all.

"Ummm . . ." you say, after driving for several silent minutes. "How'd you know my name, anyway?"

"Superior espionage skills."

"So I'm with a spy?"

He shifts in his seat, rubs a hand against his jeans. Nervous?

"You could say that. Although your *first* name is, in fact, on your name tag at work."

"You might not be a good spy, since you just revealed your secret."

"Good point. But trust me, I've got more."

"I hope so, because that one isn't going to take this conversation very far."

Sean chuckles. "Why don't you tell *me* a secret? Like . . . *why* you don't date."

"Or I could maintain my air of mystery and you could tell me another one of yours. Like where we're going? That would be a good thing to reveal right about now."

He points left. Then right. Then a sharp left . . . over a short wooden bridge that rumbles in a way you remember so clearly it reverberates in your bones, onto a familiar graveled road.

It would have been easier to drive straight off a cliff.

—   —   —   —

You're out of the car faster than the speed of thought, looking up, swallowing hard, arms locked tight against your waist.

Except for the distant heave of the ocean, the air's so still, deep silence everywhere. As if no one's lived here for ages. As though it all fell into an enchanted sleep when your family drove away.

There it is. Three-tiered like a wedding cake, rose-red brick covered with climbing ivy. Home.

"I loved this house."

You've forgotten Sean until his warmth comes up beside you, the back of his hand brushing yours.

"Yeah," he says, on a sigh. "Me too."

After this, it takes only an inhale to get it.

"Sean . . . what"—your voice shakes—"what's your last name?"

"Lowell." He shoves his fists deep into the pockets of his windbreaker, much too thin to hold off the harsh March wind whipping off the bay.

Your throat constricts; you have to suck in air to get the words out.

"Look, Sean *Lowell*, I don't want to do this. Whatever this is."

He steps closer, hands splayed, apology-style. "You have every right to be pissed. I was afraid—I knew—if I told you the truth you wouldn't come. I mean—why would you?"

"Why am I here now? To meet your parents? See how they've redecorated?"

He stares at you for a second, bites his lip, blinks. "A movie and a nice dinner seem sort of inadequate, considering the whole my-dad-destroyed-your-family-financially thing. Please, Emma. I can do this today—only today."

"Do you *get* how creepy that sounds? *All* of this is creepy. You wanted to see me have fun—that's what you said! Instead of—I don't know—mini golf—you've lured me to my old house with God knows what agenda."

"Mini golf's really overrated. It's like paintball, looks so great in the movies, but— Okay, never mind . . . no luring, I swear. I'm just asking nicely. If you want to leave, I'll drive you back this minute. No matter how things look right now, I swear, I'm a normal person."

You look up at the house—your old corner room with its high-arched windows. The widow's walk at the top, fenced in with black wrought iron, where you and Jen used to pretend you were captaining a ship, or pace, waiting endlessly for your mythical boyfriends to come back from sea. That life you barely remember, with no boundaries, no money worries, no limits to anything and everything you could hope for.

Sean hunches his shoulders against another quick whip of wind off the water.

"So you knew who I was all along?" An even worse thought occurs to you. "Are you doing this for your father?"

He shakes his head. "No! God, no. At first I just got that you were this gorgeous girl with great . . . iced tea—then I found out your last name and thought . . . Shit, this sounded so much better in my head. Emma—Dad ripped off a lot of people. But you're the only one whose house we lived in. I wanted to give you . . . something."

The wind has risen high enough that his words seem to blow away the minute he speaks them. You hear them, though, as clearly as you've seen the headlines. Rupert Lowell—"Billion-dollar con man." The arrest. The upcoming trial.

Sean's *father*.

"You mean something more than a sixty-dollar tip?"

"I wanted you to . . . notice me. I didn't know where to start. In retrospect—not there."

"*Notice you?* Have you . . . *seen* you?"

Christ, Emma. "He's cute" is very much beside the point.

"Too busy looking at you."

Despite yourself, you crack up. "Oh my God—that's the cheesiest line I've ever heard."

"But you laughed," he says. "So there's that. I haven't even seen you smile at the diner."

"I *never* saw you looking at me."

"I'm a spy, remember? Practiced at stealth. If not at driving stick or asking a girl on a date."

You search his face, almost squinting to see past his color-changing eyes to what might not be changeable about him. To look beyond the looks.

He can probably feel you wavering. Pushes one last time. "No one's here. Please."

"So it's just you and me, alone, in a deserted house. What could possibly go wrong?"

"It's already gone wrong. I'm aiming to get it right."

Sean ushers you in, holds open the door like he owns the place—oh, that's right, he *does* own the place.

You look around the kitchen, shiver. It isn't cold—it's that the house seems like a ghost ship, and you're the ghost in it. With all that money, the splashy lifestyle his parents had—society queen, high-rolling financier—you'd have thought everything would have been redone, possibly dipped in gold or wallpapered in thousand-dollar bills. But the pale turquoise walls, the piney wooden cabinets—unchanged.

Sean shrugs off his windbreaker, passes it to you. You have the sudden sense that if you said your shoes pinched he'd kick off his own, give them right over.

"This way." He holds out a hand—as though offering the same sort of comfort as the coat, in a different form. You take it, without thinking. If you think, you'll probably leave right now.

The staircase is just beyond the kitchen. The banister you used to slide down. You've walked through this house so many times in your head in the past four years.

"Wait. We're going upstairs? Where the bedrooms are?"

Sean's gone one step ahead of you but he stops and turns back now. "Um . . . yeah . . . I have something to show you. I mean, something you might need and want—Jesus, that's just as bad."

Now you're both laughing, too loud in the quiet house, harder than the moment deserves—giddy—both of you—with a nervous need to release crazy tension. Then you fall silent. Look at each other in the half-light. It's unknown territory—all of this—except that it isn't. Except that it's your home. And Sean strangely doesn't seem out of place in it.

He holds up a hand, straight-faced now.

"Just to reassure you—all the furniture's gone. No beds."

"I feel so much better. Totally at ease now, Creepy Luring Guy."

"You know, I really preferred Test Date."

Outside the mullioned window at the top of the stairs, a knife of silver sunlight slashes through the gray clouds—illuminating just enough for you to make out a tall, hunched figure in the corner of the landing. You clap your palm over your mouth, stifling a shriek.

"Don't worry." Sean steps to the side, giving you a better look. "It's just Dad."

Good God, it is a huge gold statue of Rupert Lowell.

Naked except for a fig leaf.

"Um. Wow."

"I know. There's not enough money in the world to pay for the therapy my sister and I will need for that one."

You look at that gold-plated statue, the forbidding face, eyebrows drawn together, chin lifted, as if challenging the world to deny that Rupert Lowell knows better than most people. The opposite of the boy who stands in front of you, with his open face and his honest eyes. You can't tell everything by looking at a person.

But you can tell a lot.

You just can.

"You don't look anything like your father."

"Well, I dress better." Sean flashes you a smile.

Now you're on the second-story landing. This part of the house even smells the same—pine, salt water, musty carpet—as though you've stepped back through time. This house belonged to your grandparents, your grandfather's parents before that.

But you left it all behind when you were thirteen. You never stood in this spot, with a boy watching you . . . like . . . like this. Attention paid. Intent. The corners of Sean's eyes crinkle again as his gaze meets yours, then he bows his head, kicks his Converse back and forth on the worn carpet.

"What I want to give you—is this." He drops your hand, heading purposefully to the corner room—yours.

No furniture, different wallpaper, a window where there wasn't one, the bookshelf gone—nothing familiar but the fireplace. No other girl you know grew up with a fireplace in her bedroom. Even though it had never worked. Which is why—

Down on his knees in front of the fireplace, Sean reaches up the flue. He pulls out the black-and-white composition book you'd nearly forgotten about, hands it to you. It's sooty, encircled by at least fifty multicolored rubber bands stretching vertically and horizontally—your way of keeping it safe and private—although you didn't have prying siblings, and even Jen hadn't known it existed. Sean's watching your face carefully. He has a slash of soot on his forehead, some dusting his hair.

The Book of Lost Things, the blue Sharpie writing scrawled across the cover proclaims, *by Emma Greene. Don't Touch. This Means You. No Exceptions.*

"You hid it. People don't hide things that don't matter to them. I only found it the day we moved out. I thought—well—the title—it seemed like something you'd like to have. Get back."

You start to strip off the rubber bands. It's been a few years; the elastics are fragile, dried out. They break easily.

"I didn't read it," Sean says. "Just so you know."

"You could've simply brought this to me at the diner, you know. Without the"—you wave your hand—"dramatic atmosphere."

"The bank owns the house now. They change the locks tomorrow. Since I found it when I was going through here one last time—it seemed right that you get to do the same."

He rubs the heel of his hand across his forehead. "Plus, that was a pretty ferocious warning—'No exceptions' and all that. For all I knew there was a curse on the thing, like the one on King Tut's tomb."

You're flicking through the pages now, looking at your messy eighth-grade writing. Sean shoves his hands in his pockets, walks over to the window, giving you space for whatever deep dark secrets or spells he imagines you have in here.

"I think you're overestimating the powers of a thirteen-year-old girl," you say.

"Hey, I've been a thirteen-year-old guy. Probably not."

"You didn't read it?"

"Nope."

"You weren't curious?"

"Hell, of course I was. Am."

You flip through the pages, settle on one, read aloud, overdoing the ominous voice. "'Date: January nineteenth. Place: School Cafeteria. Lost: Jake Arruda was next to me in the lunch line. He asked if I could pass the ketchup. I passed it. I didn't say *a word*. I've been trying to talk to him for *four months*. I could have told him how amazing his time was at the track meet last week. I could have asked him how his little sister was, because I know she had that eye operation. I could have told him I liked ketchup on grilled cheese too, even though that's actually disgusting. But I choked and I lost that chance. Resolution: Next time: SAY SOMETHING!!! ANYTHING!!!'"

You turn a few pages forward. "'Date: May second. Place: home. Lost: Mom asked me if I wanted to visit Gran at the hospital. I've been there every single day and her roommate freaks me out and it smells weird. But today when I didn't come, Mom says she cried for almost the whole time Mom was there. Resolution: Next time: DON'T BE SELFISH.'

"'Date: June through August. Lost: Dad signed me up for sailing at the Pettipaug Yacht club. I would literally rather spend the summer in a gulag. Result: The gulag would have been more fun. Resolution: Next time: HUNGER STRIKE.'"

You flip your hair back from your face. "Get the idea?"

"It's the book of lost opportunities," Sean says.

You nod. "I thought it would help me remember to do stuff differently—if I got the chance."

He's shaking his head, smiling a little.

"What?"

"Did it work?"

"It turns out Jake Arruda is an asshat. Or was. I haven't seen him since I was fourteen. Maybe he's made his own resolutions."

"He's on my basketball team. And no, once and always, I'm guessing."

You shut the pages of the book. "Thank you."

"Not as important as I thought it might be, I guess," Sean says.

"This is, though," you say. "Getting to see this place one last time."

"Eh. I should have gone with mini golf."

You set the book down on the floor, walk up to him. His eyes widen but he doesn't move. So you do, closer. He smells like soot, soap, salt air . . . a little bit of sweat. All this was not easy for him.

"Resolution," you say as he leans just a touch closer, looks down at your lips, then up at your eyes.

"Mmm?"

"Do this," you say and put your lips to his as he wraps his arms tight around your waist.

As first kisses go, it probably isn't the best one ever. His forehead bumps into yours. It takes a little while to find the right angle. You breathe in the soot, your eyes water, and you lose a contact lens. You're both nervous, and you hardly know each other, after all.

But you will.

— — — —

Before you and Sean leave the house for the last time, you take pictures with your phone. Of the view out your bedroom window—the sun comes full out and the bay sparkles exactly the way you remember. You take one standing on the widow's walk. One from the porch steps where your dad used to sit and read to you while you lay in the grass, half listening and half daydreaming. You take the Book of Lost Things with you, sure, if only to remember you were once idiotic enough to think that a summer of sailing camp was worse than logging time in a gulag. You take with you the sound of the waves slapping against the breakwater. The memory of sitting on the stone wall, stripping the husks off sweet corn and tossing them into the water, hoping to see that green flash that your mom swears happens when the last of the sun sinks down.

You take with you the memory of how the house smelled when you woke up in the morning—coffee, the gasoline pungency in the air as motorboats headed out—usually combined with the faint—or not so faint—tang of dead fish and seaweed that your dog, Charcoal, rolled in before bounding, licky and loving, onto your bed. You'll remember how your grandmother told you the story of all the furniture and art she and your grandfather bought for this house—for you and your children and their children . . . how they'd thought it would be there forever.

But you know now that any object you can carry out of the house could get lost or broken, sold or stolen.

What you get to keep is the friendship—and someday more—of that boy whose life unexpectedly collided with yours, who made it a resolution to right a wrong, whatever way he could.

— — — —

The next day Sean strides into the diner all alone and orders vanilla ice cream with hot fudge sauce.

You adjust your crooked name tag, smooth your sweaty hands down your apron, flip back your hair, lift an eyebrow. "What, no iced tea?"

"Resolution," he says, leaning forward with his elbows square on the table, fist cupping his chin, as though he's fighting everything that might keep you apart, "take chances."

"You mean like driving a stick shift when you have no clue how?"

"Among others."

"Deal," you say.

— — — —

Resolution: Just don't be so afraid.

You will take chances.

You will find your way.

You will lose opportunities.

You will find luck.

You will lose your heart.

He will give you his.

That? You get to keep.

THE DEPARTMENT
OF DEAD LOVE

— — — — —

NICOLA YOON

THE DEPARTMENT OF Dead Love looks nothing at all like I expected. For instance, Cupid is not hanging by his entrails out front, bow and quiver lying cracked in a pool of viscous, semisweet pink fluids. The building is not a drab and windowless gray monstrosity designed to cow you into submission the moment you enter it like so many government buildings are. The DODL is not even just one building. It's a campus of them, and they are quite beautiful, actually. The committee of architects who designed the campus believed that aesthetic beauty could stave off despair.

They were wrong.

Nevertheless, the buildings are exquisite. Unrequited Love is the color of lavender tea steeped a little too long and shaped like a cresting wave. Breakups is an orange starburst of a building, like a firecracker just exploding. Bereavement is the most sedate of the buildings—a periwinkle blue lily at dusk.

Most people agree that Young Love is the prettiest of all the buildings. It's the tentative green of a new leaf and shaped like a single blade of grass. Separated from the main campus by a wide blue lake and a wooden suspension bridge, it's only intended for anyone eighteen or younger. Before the building was commissioned there was a great debate about whether young people should be excluded from the general populace. After all, they too experienced unrequited love. They agonized through unexplained breakups. They suffered the debilitating loss of death. In the end, it was decided that the intense nature of young love warranted a building all its own.

The DODL's beauty is not limited to the buildings. It extends to the employees. HeartWorkers, as they're called, must have excellent Empathy Exam scores and complete a long apprenticeship before they're allowed to tend to the brokenhearted public. City workers though they may be, they are an attractive, generous, and joyous people, always ready with a smile and a hug and a "Time Heals."

That's the department's motto, by the way. *Time Heals.* It's inscribed on the facade of each building. It's stamped on all the stationery. It's inscribed in cursive on small golden plaques in each stall of every bathroom on every floor. I would know, as I've been in them all.

By now you're asking yourself, What brings this young man here to Young Love? More specifically, what brings him to the Office of Emotional Recovery located on the very highest floor? Even more specifically still, what brings him to the cubicle of Gabrielle Lee at the Relationship Autopsy desk?

It was a breakup.

An abrupt one.

An unexplainable one.

When relationships end, a negligible percentage of them get to have a Do Over. No one knows what the rules for getting one are, but if you are granted one, you get to have your memories reset and do your relationship over.

So. That's why I'm here. I'd very much like to do my relationship over.

———   ———   ———   ———

"I don't understand. Everything was perfect when she ended it," I say as soon as I enter the cubicle. It's what I've said to every Heart-Worker who's interviewed me so far. It takes a very long time to get referred to Relationship Autopsy. You have to make it past the Other Fish in the Sea; It's Not You, It's Him/Her; and Did You Really Love Him/Her Anyway? desks. The counselors there are excellent at helping you cope, recover, and move on so that you don't end up here.

But I don't want to cope or recover or move on. I want to understand. And then I want another chance.

The HeartWorker in the cubicle—Apprentice Gabrielle Lee, according to the nameplate—puts down the tablet she's holding and looks up at me. I'm surprised by how young she is. I'd guess she's around my age, seventeen or maybe eighteen. All the HeartWorkers I've met so far in Emotional Recovery are considerably older. Then I remember that she's an apprentice—the sole apprentice ever to have a position in Relationship Autopsy. Her Empathy Exam scores must have been perfect.

"Please have a seat," she says. Her face is a polite blank, no everything-is-going-to-be-all-right smile here. I'd heard that Autopsy workers weren't quite as cheerful, not quite as indulgent as others. Less ready with a smile and a platitude. I can understand that. It's a tough line of work, sorting through the detritus of dead relationships all day, trying to find the reason for their demise.

I sit. Unlike all the other chairs in all the other DODL offices, this chair is straight-backed and hard and uncomfortable. This is not a place to get comfortable in.

She picks up the tablet she'd been reading when I walked in and begins: "It says here that Miss Samantha Fuentes broke up with you ten months ago. Is that correct, Mr. Marks?"

"You can call me Thomas."

She just waits for me to respond.

"That's correct," I mumble, looking down at my hands. Even now, after all this time, thinking about the night we broke up makes my stomach lurch.

"And you were together for five months, four days, and twenty-one hours. Is that also correct?"

Did I imagine the arch tone in her voice? I look up and meet her eyes. They're clear brown and almost too big for her small face. I can't read any emotion in them.

"Yes," I say. "That's correct."

"So at this point you've been broken up for more than twice the length of the relationship."

Was that a question? I'm fairly certain HeartWorkers aren't supposed to judge you. It's in the Charter. Of course things might be different for Autopsy workers. No one knows much about them.

Nevertheless, I'm definitely feeling a little judged. I take a closer look at her. Her skin is pale brown, almost the same shade as mine, but with pinkish undertones. Her hair is short, with soft curls that frame her face. She reminds me of something out of a fairy tale—a pixie or a woodland sprite.

If I noticed pretty girls anymore, I think I might think she was pretty.

I scan her desk hoping to find something personal so I can get a handle on her personality, but there's nothing, not even a bowl of you'll-feel-better-soon-but-for-now-bury-your-feelings-with-candy candy. Apprentice Lee is not trying to convince me that everything is going to be okay. Maybe she realizes that if you've gotten to the Relationship Autopsy offices, you already know that. There's something kind about that honesty.

"Yes," I say. "It's been over for more time than we were together and I'm still not over it. I don't think I'll ever be over it."

Her face softens, wide eyes meeting mine. I almost expect her to say *Time heals*, and I'm glad when she doesn't.

It's not that I need to convince her to perform my Autopsy. She's going to do it anyway. But I want her to understand *why* I need to be here. That way maybe she'll agree to grant the Do Over when the time comes.

"Have you ever been on a roller coaster, Apprentice Lee?"

She nods.

"You know when you get to the top of the first drop, how the car pauses there for a few seconds to build up anticipation and then it starts to plunge and you get that sick, terrified, hollow feeling in your stomach? I mean, in your mind you might not actually be scared, but your body doesn't care about that. It only knows there's been some mistake and it's falling. That's how I feel all the time now. I need it to stop. I need to know what happened."

She doesn't say anything for a few seconds, but presses her hand flat against her chest like she's trying to keep something in. "Thomas," she says, "you can call me Gabby. Come back tomorrow and we'll get started."

— — — —

I've loved Samantha Fuentes my whole life. Well, almost my whole life. My mom says she saw the whole thing happen. I was six. We'd just moved to Sapphire City from the Plains. I'd been moping around the new house for a few days, so she took me to our neighborhood playground and insisted that I introduce myself.

"Make some new friends, for heaven's sake," she said.

Every playground has rulers, and the king and queen of this one took one look at me and decided I was not a good subject. Maybe it was obvious that I wasn't from the big city. Whatever it was, no one would talk to me, let alone play with me. For the next week, every time I went to the playground, all the other kids ignored me. On the eighth day, Samantha broke ranks and sat next to me on the swing.

My mom says I gave my heart to Sam in that moment and that she's been holding on to it ever since.

I tell this—our supercouple origin story—to Gabby pretty much as soon as I sit down in her cubicle the next day.

She leans forward in her chair, rests her face in her chin, and listens closely.

"Did you tell her how you felt?"

"No, I was six. I didn't know how I felt. I just knew I wanted to be her best friend. And we were."

"When did you realize you wanted to be more than friends?"

"Puberty."

"Did you tell her then?"

I laugh. "No way. Are you kidding?"

She frowns and a small dimple forms just between her eyebrows. "I'm not kidding," she says, confused.

"Well, probably you were a good-looking and well-adjusted thirteen-year-old, but I was not. Pimples the size of mountains. Braces. Oh, and I was awkward. Not just a little bit awkward. A lot bit awkward."

She smiles wide and it transforms her face from pretty to slightly goofy. For a second, I forget she's a HeartWorker.

"But Samantha was thirteen, too, right? Wasn't she awkward?"

"Nope. She's always been perfect."

The look on her face says I'm hopeless. "So you suffered from unrequited love for a while?"

"Yup."

She picks up her tablet and swipes for a few seconds. "I don't see a record of you visiting UnReq about it."

"No. I thought it was only a matter of time until she would love me back. I mean, we were so perfect together. And my pimples couldn't last forever."

"Pimples aren't a character flaw," she says.

I study her perfectly clear face. "Says someone who never had them."

"That's not true." She says it gently, but I can feel a pained history behind the words. Kids can be cruel to each other. To themselves.

She clears her throat and looks back down at her tablet. "Tell me about your friendship." Her voice is more official than it was a moment ago.

I tell her how we went to elementary and middle and high school together. We had long conversations about nothing. We agreed on books and movies and games and people. So many of our conversations started with "Do you remember that time . . . ?"

I love having all that history with someone. I remember her first middle school crush. I remember that red-and-blue-and-yellow-striped skirt that she loved so much that the elastic waist wore out.

We were inseparable until high school and high school boys. Sure, I was a high school boy, too, but somehow I didn't count. And she had crappy taste. The guys weren't mean. But they definitely liked themselves more than they liked her. They never noticed how she stuck her tongue in the gap in her front teeth when she was thinking. Or how she kind of walked like a duck when she was tired. Or how she scratched at her palm when she was uncomfortable and wanted to be anywhere but where she was. I was the one she complained to about them. It drove me crazy.

I look up at Gabby. "Why did she date those guys?" I ask. "How come she doesn't know she deserved better?"

"I don't know," she says. "Love is complicated. That's why we have entire departments dedicated to it."

I nod, even though that's not really an answer. "Why did you become a HeartWorker, anyway?" I ask.

"Everyone in my family is one."

"Did you always want to work in Relationship Autopsy?"

"Actually, UnRequited was my first choice, but it turns out my Empathy scores were too good. Also, I'm good at solving mysteries."

"Like why perfect relationships end?"

"Something like that," she says. It's easy to see why she's the first-ever apprentice to work in RA. She has an easy, soothing way about her.

"How come UnRequited was your first choice?"

"I'd get to tell people all day that they were worthy of being loved and give them hope for the future. It sounded like a nice way to spend a day."

"Instead you're stuck here with poor sobs like me." I smile and try to relax into my chair, but it really is the worst chair. "You must think I'm ridiculous," I say.

"I'm a HeartWorker. I don't judge. It's in the Charter."

"I'm pretty sure you were judging me yesterday when you calculated our time together versus our time apart," I say. "Admit it."

"Maybe just a little bit." Her eyes dance as she says it. "And, for the record, I was neither good-looking nor well-adjusted at thirteen years old."

"Well, you've made up for it since then," I say.

Her wide eyes get even wider and then she blushes and then she smiles.

I was right about her smile before. It's both pretty and goofy.

— — — —

The next day we meet in the Autopsy room instead of her cubicle. I take three separate elevators to get to the sub-sub-sub-basement. It doesn't escape my notice that there's still another floor down. Is that where the Do Overs are done?

A HeartWorker wearing white is waiting for me as soon as I step off the elevator.

"I have an Autopsy appointment with Apprentice Lee," I say. I don't try to hide my nervousness.

He smiles a soothing smile and checks his tablet for my appointment. "Follow me," he says.

We walk down a long hallway the color of rain clouds.

"Here we are," he says as we get to the Autopsy room door. He places a gentle hand on my shoulder. "Time heals, Mr. Marks."

Gabby is waiting just beyond the threshold. Until this moment, I've never actually seen her standing. She's taller than I thought, almost as tall as I am. She's not wearing black and white, but a muted blue-heather suit that looks vaguely like surgical scrubs, except more fitted. It looks good on her. I'd guess that most things look good on her.

"Welcome to Autopsy, Thomas," she says, interrupting my noticing of her. Her voice is deeper than normal, almost spooky. She's teasing me.

"Being a little bit dramatic, aren't we?" I ask her.

"Gotta have some fun, right?" she says, grinning.

I look past her to the platform bed sitting in the center of the room. "This isn't going to be fun?"

She doesn't say anything, but her eyes do.

Besides the bed, there's no other furniture in the room. The walls are the same gray as the hallway but more metallic. They almost seem to be pulsing.

Gabby closes the door behind me, and the room is so quiet you can hear us both breathing.

"You should sit," she says.

I hop up and sit right in the middle.

She presses a button on the frame to adjust the height so we're face-to-face.

"So, how does this work? I mean, I read the pamphlets and I've done some research, but maybe you could tell me anyway." It comes out all in one sentence.

"First you have to relax," she says, and touches my shoulder. I know it's the standard HeartWorker soothing gesture, but when Gabby does it, it doesn't feel like part of her job. Her hand is small and too warm and I can still feel it there even when she takes it away.

"Does everyone get nervous?" I ask.

"Yup. And everyone asks if everyone gets nervous, too."

"You're teasing me again," I say.

"Yup."

"Is teasing in the Charter?" I ask.

"Is it working?"

It is. I'm less nervous than I was a minute ago.

She sits on the stool in front of me. "There are three stages. Stage One, I autopsy your relationship history and determine the cause of death."

"But how will you know when you're only reading me?"

"You'd be surprised. Most times I can tell by reading just one side of the relationship. Usually the reason is buried somewhere in their memories, even if they can't see it. The cause of death is usually there from the beginning, like a dormant virus."

"I don't think that's the case with me." I'm sure that sounds as defensive as it is. "What's Stage Two?"

"If Stage One fails, then I'll have to perform the Autopsy on her. With her consent, of course. She'll have to come in. Will you be okay with that? Have you seen her since the breakup?"

"At school. From a distance. And she texts. She wants to be friends."

"But you don't want that?" she asks.

I shrug. "I already have friends."

"Well, you're honest," she says.

She gets up from the stool, but then sits back down right away. "Do you mind if ask you a question?"

"Sure," I say.

Her voice drops like we're conspiring. "What do you think the difference between wanting to be friends and wanting to be more than friends is?"

I nod fifty times and lean in. "You have no idea how much time I have spent thinking about this."

She laughs. "I had a feeling you would have thoughts."

"Why?"

"Thomas, no one makes it to Relationship Autopsy without being a deep—some might say obsessive—thinker."

"Would *you* say obsessive?" I ask.

She doesn't answer, but her eyes are definitely laughing at me.

"You really are very judgy for a HeartWorker."

She leans in, face serious. "Shhhh, don't tell anyone, but we *all* are. On lunch breaks, we sit around making fun of you guys."

"Wait. Is that true?"

"No, Thomas. Of course it isn't."

I don't know why, but this has me doubling over with laughter. When I look back up at her eyes are bright and her cheeks are a rosy brown. She liked making me laugh.

"So," she prompts when I'm done. "The difference?"

I blurt out my theory: "Some people you want to get to know and some people you want to know you. I think that's the difference."

For whatever reason, there are people that you want to tell your weird, secret thoughts to. You want to show them your pimples and tell them about your braces. You want them to love you because of those things, not in spite of them.

"Some people make you want to be known," I say.

Our eyes meet and hold and the air feels different, like the words have changed it somehow. I want to tell her more of my weird theories of the world.

"That's, um, pretty good," she says, and then stands quickly. Is she breaking some HeartWorker protocol by talking to me this intimately?

She walks over to the wall on the right and waves her hand in front of it. A hidden drawer slides open. From inside, she retrieves a pair of black gloves and puts them on. The lights in the room fade to near darkness. The gloves glow a pale pink.

"Lie back, please," she says.

I do. "What now?"

"I'm going to open you up."

"Um—"

"Not with a scalpel," she says, waving the gloves in the air. "I mean I'm going to open your heart. Metaphorically."

"Will it hurt?"

"Yes. You'll have to relive the whole relationship and then you'll have to relive the moment it ended. It's intense for most people."

Something in her voice makes me ask: "How is it for you? Does it hurt you, too?"

"No one's ever asked me that before." It's too dark to see the pain on her face, but I can hear it.

She clears her throat. "When I'm doing it, I feel all the things you feel."

I want to ask more about that, but she touches her hands to my chest. "Ready?" she asks.

"Ready," I say.

She's right. It does hurt. It hurts to see all I have lost with Samantha.

I see our first kiss. I was in her room helping her with an essay for history class. She was pouting because she hates writing almost as much she hates learning about old things. Out loud, I said, "I love that pout." I kissed her, and we began.

I see my mom's face when I told her. "Only took you twelve years," she said, laughing.

I see the first time we go to school holding hands. It's not official until your classmates see you as a couple. A few people yelled that it was about time.

I see the first time I go to her house as her boyfriend instead of her best friend. Her dad said we were no longer allowed in her room alone together. I was pissed, but happy, too. I spent the afternoon watching the Robot Games with him.

I see the sunshine-yellow daffodils I bought her for our one-month anniversary. Cotton-candy-pink tulips for our second. Ruby lilies for our third.

Gabby moves her hands across my chest and presses down a little harder. She's searching, pulling our history up to the surface. Pressure builds in chest. My overfull heart wants to burst.

Four months into our relationship, it takes Sam a little longer to text me back. Four and a half months into it, the kisses aren't the same. I mean, they're the same physically, but something's missing. She's missing. I gave her coral daisies for our five-month anniversary. She said we don't have to mark every single occasion.

We break up where we began: on the playground.

She's sitting on a swing. It's too big for her and her feet are touching the ground. Her arms hug the chains. I'm about to ask her what's wrong, but then she scratches at her palms. Why doesn't she want to be here with me?

She says: *I think we were a mistake.*

She says: *I think we were better as friends.*

I don't say anything. She scratches at her palms again. For the first time I wish I didn't know her as well as I do.

I say: *You don't have to stay here.*

And she says thanks and leaves.

I sit on the swing and I'm six again and the playground is full of kids who won't talk to me. This time, though, Sam's not coming to rescue me.

The lights bloom to life. It's hard to move, like a weight is pressing against my chest, pinning me to the bed. I open my eyes, but Gabby's hands are no longer touching me. She's at the foot of the bed now and she's crying.

"It *does* hurt you," I say, sitting up.

"Please don't tell. I'm not supposed to cry."

"I'm sorry," I say and put my hand on her shoulder the way the HeartWorkers do.

"You're kind," she says, swiping at her tears. "You're only my sixth case. I'll get used to it. Your case was supposed to be an easy one."

"But it's not?"

Her eyes fill with tears again. "None of them have been easy. People feel so much. Love is so big and it leaves behind a crater. Even when it's wrong."

At the word *wrong*, the pressure on my chest increases and I remember why I'm here. Does she know the cause of death now? Was there something wrong with my relationship with Sam?

She must guess what I'm thinking, because she straightens her shoulders and swipes at her tears firmly. She walks over to the paneled wall with its hidden drawers. When she comes back, she's gloveless and holding her tablet. All traces of her tears are gone.

"I'm sorry, Thomas, but your results are inconclusive."

"What does that mean?" I ask.

"I wasn't able to determine the cause of death."

"So now you have to autopsy Sam, right?"

She frowns her dimple frown, considering. "Did you ever think that maybe you've just had this idea of who you guys were supposed to be for so long that—"

"No," I say, cutting her off. I've been down this road with other HeartWorkers. I don't want to guess why we ended. I want to know. "Now we autopsy Samantha, right?" I say again.

She starts to say something, but decides against it. She nods. "Yes, if she agrees."

Of course. But I think she will agree if only so I can have closure and maybe we can be friends again. She says she misses being friends. I guess I do, too.

"When will you ask her?"

She waves the tablet at me. "I've already sent the results to Heart-Worker Danica. She's contacting Samantha as we speak. We should know in a few minutes."

I really haven't considered what I'll do if she doesn't say yes. I rub my hand across my chest. It still feels like Gabby's hands are on me, searching, examining, pulling.

I hop off the bed and stroll around the room, but there's nothing in it to distract me. I pace from one gray wall to the other.

"Have you ever been in love?" I call out.

"Please stop doing that," she says.

"Doing what?"

"Pacing."

I pace over to her and then stop. "Have you ever been in love?" I ask again.

She cradles the tablet to her chest. "No. I've been studying for this my whole life. I'm the very first apprentice ever to be assigned to RA. My parents are very proud."

"So, your only experience with love is living it through broken-hearted people like me?"

She nods.

I asked the question idly, just talk to distract myself, but now I really want to hear her answer. "Would you ever want to? I mean, with all the stuff you know about it now, would you even want to fall in love?"

"I'd give anything to fall in love," she says. She meets my eyes and they don't look clear brown anymore. They're a moonless black.

"Really? Even knowing how much it hurts? Even knowing how it ends in most cases?"

"Thomas," she says. "All love ends. Sometimes it's a breakup. Sometimes the other person dies."

Her voice is so quiet that I have to move closer to hear her.

"Do you know why I was crying before? It wasn't because of the pain of your heartbreak. It was because you felt so much in the first place." She takes a deep breath. "And anyway, isn't that what you're doing here? Hoping that I'll reset your memories and you can have a Do Over so you'll feel that much again?"

Her tablet dings. She checks the screen and moves away, widening the space between us. "Samantha has agreed to the autopsy," she says. "We'll do it tomorrow."

— — — —

"Hey, T," Samantha says as soon as I arrive at Gabby's cubicle. She looks the same as she always has, which surprises me for some reason. Since our breakup I've seen her, but only from a distance. I don't know why I imagined she'd look different. One of my biggest fears has been that while we're apart, she'll change so much that one day I won't recognize her at all. But no. She looks the same.

"Hey," I say, or I try to say, but no sound comes out. I clear my throat and try again. "Hey," I say again, this time too loudly.

I feel Gabby's eyes studying me, but when I look at her, she looks down at her tablet. "Did you already autopsy—" I start to ask her.

"No, Samantha wanted to wait until you arrived."

I didn't expect that.

I look back at Samantha. "Why?"

"You're my best friend, T. Who else would I ask?"

"You don't have to do this," I blurt, shocking all three of us. Why did I say that? I've been waiting for this moment since we broke up.

"It's okay, T." She looks at Gabby. "I want to know, too."

We take the elevator to the sub-sub-sub-basement level and down the long gray hallway in silence. In the autopsy room, Gabby immediately puts on her pink gloves and directs me to stand off to the side. Samantha's nervous. I know because ordinarily she'd be talking and asking lots of questions. At least she's not scratching at her palm.

Watching the autopsy is strange. The pink of the gloves reflects off Samantha's dress, washes Gabby's face in a rose light. Her eyes are closed and her face is more open than I've ever seen it. This is what it means to be a HeartWorker. You have to be open to the world, to be able to absorb the range of human emotions and make sense of them.

It is beautiful to watch.

A few minutes later Gabby pulls her hands away from Samantha: "Thomas, can you join us over here, please?" Her voice is soft.

I walk toward her, searching her face for signs of pain. "Are you okay?" I ask. I know it's her job, but I feel guilty anyway.

"I am fine, Thomas." Her face is as blank as the first day I met her. She looks past me and over to Sam.

"Are you okay, Samantha?"

I turn to see Sam staring at me. Her eyes are shining with tears. "I'd forgotten how much fun we had together," she says.

I'm not sure what I expected her to say, but that wasn't it. All at once the enormity of my selfishness hits me. I know that Sam didn't have to agree to do this, but I didn't have to ask.

"It's okay," she says, reading my face. "I missed you, T."

Does she mean that she misses our friendship or something else? She slides off the bed and stands next to me. My heart pounds and I rub my hand across my chest. For a moment it feels like Gabby's hand is still right there, pressed against it, trying to find the love I've lost.

Gabby clears her throat and we both turn toward her. "Samantha, I need your consent to disclose the results in front of Thomas."

Sam nods.

"I'm afraid your results are still inconclusive. I was not able to determine the cause of death."

"Wait, what?" I say. "But you said—"

"I know what I said. This is quite rare."

"What does it mean?" Sam asks.

Gabby looks down to her tablet. "It means that there was nothing wrong with your relationship that caused it to die. You have compatible intellects, temperaments, goals, philosophies, moralities. You are even aesthetically compatible. Samantha, I could find no evidence of you cheating or falling in love with a third party.

You weren't annoyed by Thomas's quirks. In fact, you seem to love Thomas quite a bit."

"Then what happened?" She slips her hand into mine and squeezes. Her hand is small and cool and familiar. "It's not like I wanted to break up with him. One day I just woke up feeling less."

It hurts to hear her say it. What surprises me, though, is that I can tell it hurts her to say it, too.

"I wish I had an answer for you both," Gabby says. "Think of it this way: back in the twenty-first century, when the elderly passed away in their sleep and a cause of death couldn't be determined, the doctors referred to it as dying from 'natural causes.' I think that's what happened to your relationship."

She pauses to take breath. "Sometimes loves just ends," she says.

"Can it be fixed?" Samantha asks.

"Maybe," she says.

We go back to her office and Gabby explains the mechanics of the Do Over. Samantha and I will have the memory of our relationship erased back to when I first kissed her. Since I initiated the autopsy, I'll have full knowledge—such as it is—of why we broke up. I'll also know the date of the breakup. It will be up to me to prevent it from happening again.

"Does this ever work?" I ask.

"The success rate is 9.83 percent," she says.

"That's practically a guarantee," I say, and she smiles. It's the first smile I've seen from her all day. I watch as it spreads across her face.

"One last thing. Neither of you will have any memory of this experience."

I lean forward in my chair. "You mean I won't remember the autopsy?"

"No, I mean you won't remember any of this. The last ten months of your life will be erased."

It takes me a second to realize what she's saying. "So I won't remember you?" I ask. I try to catch her eye, but she's focused on the space between Samantha and me.

"It's just the way memory pruning works. We can't cut from the middle of the tree."

"It's okay, T," Sam says. "We'll get to do it all again anyway."

I don't say anything.

Gabby stands and I understand we're being dismissed.

"Obviously you must both consent before we can proceed. If you do decide to do it, come back tomorrow morning. We'll have you happy again in no time."

— — — —

I arrive on campus early the next morning. It's an overcast spring day with the sun not quite committed to the sky yet.

A few HeartWorkers greet me as I walk across the suspension bridge toward Young Love.

"Time heals," they call out.

I smile and nod, but don't respond.

Young Love looks different in the hazy almost-light. The color is deeper, less like new grass.

What did people do before the Department of Dead Love existed? Did they just live with uncertainty, never quite knowing why love ended? What a cruel time that must have been.

I make my way past security and up the glass elevators to the Relationship Autopsy floor. When I get to Gabby's cubicle, I see an older woman leaning over her shoulder. They're both looking at something on Gabby's tablet.

"Hi," I say.

The woman straightens. Her name tag reads *HW Danica*.

"Mr. Marks," she says. "Come right in. I was just going over some last-minute instructions with Apprentice Lee. Nothing for you to worry about. You are in very capable, very talented hands."

She puts her hand on my shoulder and squeezes. I wonder if I'll miss that greeting now that my time at the DODL is coming to an end.

"Hello, Thomas," Gabby says after Danica leaves. She's using her official voice on me. "Or would you prefer me to call you T?"

I sit. "No, no. Only Samantha calls me T. Call me Thomas. Please."

She nods, and even her nod feels official. "Well, you are a few minutes early." She stands up and sits back down again. "I guess you can just wait here."

"Samantha's not coming," I say into the quiet.

"But she has to come in order for this to work." She stops talking. "Oh, no. Thomas, I'm so sorry. After yesterday, I thought for sure she'd agree to the Do Over."

"*She* didn't decide against it."

Her dimpled frown comes back.

"*I* decided against it."

She stands back up. "You did? But why?"

"Gabby, sit down. Please. You're making me nervous."

She sits. "But you've wanted this for so long."

"I know. And now I don't want it anymore."

"But why?"

"You have perfect Empathy Exam scores, Apprentice Lee. You can probably guess why, can't you?"

She shakes her head.

"I don't want to forget," I say.

"Ten months doesn't seem like such a bad trade so you can have her back."

"I don't want to forget *you*," I say, making myself clear.

She clasps her hands on top of the tablet. "I see," she says.

Oh, no. Have I made a mistake? Maybe I'd been imagining a spark, imagining that we could be at the beginning of something.

"Thomas."

"Gabby."

"I've never even been out on a date. I wouldn't know what to do. Also, you're in love with someone else."

"Was. I *was* in love with someone else."

"You're not saying that you're in love with me now? I'll have to refer you to ReBound."

"No, I'm not saying that. I'm saying that I don't want to forget you, Gabrielle Lee. I want to know you. I want to be known by you."

"You know we might end up right back here."

"The HeartWorker in need of a HeartWorker," I say.

"It could happen."

"Or not."

"All love ends," she says.

"Maybe," I say. "But it has to start somewhere."